END

ROAD WORK

A NOVEL BY

W. SCOTT JONES

OTHER BOOKS BY W. SCOTT JONES

A Storm in the Carolinas
The Treasures of A Carolina Summer
What A Crowd
The Stand-Up
The Coaches' Wives

DEDICATION

For Liz and Billy

"This one had been in my mind for many years. Thank you for always supporting my writing journey and helping me make this novel come to life."

ACKNOWLEDGMENTS

It is always so rewarding to finish a book and have it published. The time and effort to write is easy for me; however, the editing, marketing, and publishing is always tedious work. I dedicated this book to my amazing editor, Liz Simon, and her husband Billy, who have supported me since the beginning of my writing journey. Also, Liz had a good feeling about this book several years ago. None of my work would have been possible without their dedication and support.

I am also very appreciative of my wife Bridget and my two daughters who continue to support me. Thank you all for allowing me to continue to write and for always being so encouraging.

To my close friends who have followed me- I thank you. I know some of you were shocked that I would ever write one book much less six.

To my new author friends, I can't thank you enough for your guidance. Helen Bradley- you are amazing, and I thank you from the bottom of my heart for always being there for me when I needed help. Your advice and friendship is priceless.

To the ARC readers who have read my work, I sincerely thank you for your willingness to critique my books and offer suggestions.

A sincere thanks to Kaye McCoy who offers invaluable-suggestions of my work and who has been so supportive.

To the many patrons that have read my work, I sincerely thank you for your kind words and encouragement. For those of you whom I have met, you have no idea how much joy it brings to me when you offer feedback or ask questions. I enjoy interacting with you, whether face to face, or on social media. Always feel free to contact me if you have any questions.

I will continue this writing journey as long as the Good Lord allows, and as long as I inspire people through my words and stories.

Thank you all so much!

TABLE OF CONTENTS

PROLOGUE

"The most important thing in the world is family and love."
Coach John Wooden

The vibration from the bucket of a backhoe hitting an unidentifiable object that was embedded in a secluded creek bed, startled the machinery operator so much, he quickly raised the bucket arm, cut off the engine, and peered into the hole he had started digging. He wasn't sure what he was looking at, but after climbing down off the backhoe, and stepping down into the one-foot hole, he knew that the object in question was something more than the usual nemesis of rocks, tree roots, or metal pipes, he encountered every day. He was a member of a construction crew that was clearing land near an inlet cove-situated on an undeveloped section of the Tennessee River along the shoreline of Joe Wheeler State Park in Northern Alabama.

He poked around the wet clay and small rocks with a small Sycamore stick while he removed several handfuls of earth and small petrified branches from the top of what appeared to be a large metal spike protruding through the outer layers of sediment. He retrieved a small plumber's spade from the side of his backhoe and began carefully digging. His excavation eventually revealed what appeared to him as a metal spike type of wheel. Without looking any further, he concluded that he had uncovered-something he had never seen. After removing more soil and finding several other spikes that appeared to be a part of a solid piece of metal, he surmised that what he had discovered was the wheel of an old piece of machinery. He kept digging wanting to know exactly what treasure he had uncovered. The more he dug, the more he became convinced that he had found something very old.

A few minutes later, he carefully pried loose a large rock from what appeared to be the inner rim of a wheel. When he removed the clay-colored smooth rock from the soil, he almost fell backwards because he noticed the sole of a shoe. He kept digging. He then discovered that it wasn't a shoe but rather some type of boot. After he brushed away the soil and small rocks away from the top of the boot, he saw a swath of clay-stained cloth somewhat attached to the boot. He slowly reached down, and he pulled on the edge of the cloth trying not to tear it. Clay and small rocks impaired his efforts. Finally, with a forceful tug, he accidentally tore the cloth above the boot. He immediately fell backwards when a bone was revealed from the portion he tore.

That fog covered morning March 5, 1978, a team of deputies from the Dogwood County Sheriff's Department were dispatched to the scene and worked for two hours as they meticulously kept-

uncovering a portion of skeletal remains. Once they had carefully removed the soil and rock from a small portion of the upper part of the torso, they shockingly realized that they had found the remains of what appeared to be a person chained to the seat and steering wheel of a 1921 Fordson tractor. The tractor had undoubtedly been placed in a gulley and had tipped over sideways.

The Dogwood County coroner whispered to the Dogwood County sheriff, "We need to stop diggin' and let the state boys from the Alabama Law Enforcement Agency and the archaeologists from Tuscaloosa come up here and help out with this excavation and investigation. We might even need to get the FBI involved in this one. I guarantee ya, that whoever put that bag of bones on that tractor never thought there would be a dam built in this area makin' a lake that would slowly become a tourist attraction."

The sheriff lit up a Winston cigarette, inhaled a big puff of smoke, and then exhaled as he squinted his eyes, and replied, "Yep, I guess whoever did this never thought they'd be condos built along the shoreline of a lake that did not exist." He then put his cigarette in his mouth, pulled out a small notepad from his front shirt pocket before saying, "You are right about callin' the state boys and the FBI. I ain't 'bout to screw this up before it gets started. The last thing I need is for it to be determined that whoever is chained to that tractor is a Colored man, and the Colored folks round here think I'm coverin' somethin' up. No, sir, you are right. I'm gonna let the state boys, the FBI, and the historians figure this out."

The coroner replied, "That's the smart thing to do. Whoever is chained to that tractor has been a missin' for quite some time."

The sheriff asked, "How do you know he has been missin' for a long time other than him sittin' on that old tractor?"

"Unless he was wearin' his grandpappy's boots and suspenders, I'm here to tell ya that old boy had to have been killed somewhere in the 1920s or 1930s."

Two months later, the Alabama Law Enforcement Agency did identify the body that was found on that tractor in that remote area of North Alabama. I remember watching the CBS national evening news in 1978 when it was revealed that a person missing since 1927 had finally been found and identified. I was a teenager living in Florida at the time, and I normally would have never paid attention to the nightly news this particular night except for the fact that I couldn't believe they had identified a person who had been missing for over fifty years. I remember thinking that forensic science was an interesting field. I was already interested in this because I had become a big fan of the NBC television series *Quincy, M.E.* starring Jack Klugman. Every week I never missed that show which featured a Los Angeles investigator, who would solve crimes using the new tools associated with forensic science. Ten years later, I would be unexpectedly reminded of *Quincy, M.E.* along with the unresolved case of who killed Vernon

Daniels, placed his body on a tractor, and buried him in a remote section of North Alabama.

CHAPTER ONE

I was a twenty-four-year-old, first-year high school teacher and football coach working at North Tallahassee High School in Florida when a random phone call in 1988 would forever change how I perceived the world and take me to places I could have never imagined.

On an unusually frigid day in December, most everyone at North Tallahassee High School had long departed when I heard the telephone ringing in the gym's coaches' office. All of the other driver education and physical education teachers had left campus early because it was the last day of semester exams, which meant that it was the first day of Christmas vacation. I, however, had been informed by my athletic director that since I was the youngest coach on staff, I had been "elected" to be the last staff member to secure the gym doors once all of the students had left campus. This arrangement did not make me happy, but I knew that I had to pay my dues.

When I first heard the phone ringing, I was beginning to lock the outside doors of the gym. My initial inclination was to not answer it. It was the beginning of Christmas vacation I thought to myself. Whatever was so important could surely wait for another two weeks. Blaring across the school's intercom system, I heard the principal's secretary say, "Students on bus number eleven will ride today on bus number four. Have a great Christmas vacation."

Even though I was distracted, I could still hear the phone ring. I changed my mind and began running toward the coach's office. It rang one more time before I reluctantly decided that I needed to answer it in case it was my athletic director, checking in on me.

"Coaches' Office, how can I help you?"

For a couple of seconds, I did not hear anything. Finally I heard an old but vaguely familiar voice reply, "Yes, I am looking for Coach Tim Jackson."

"This is he."

"Well, hello, Tim… I wanted to let you know that I have decided to come home."

"Excuse me, but- Who is this?"

"It's your Uncle Dean. Who did you think was callin' all the way from California?"

"What in the world? It has been a really long time since I have heard your voice."

It had indeed been a long time since I heard my Great Uncle Dean's voice. He was my grandmother's only sibling, and I couldn't even recall or faintly remember when was the last time I had spoken to him. As I listened to him ramble about the weather in California and how the girls out there wore skirts that were short enough to see their private parts, I began doodling on a yellow notepad sitting on my office desk. After listening to him for a few more minutes, I concluded that he had to be suffering from dementia, as none of what he was saying was making sense.

Out of respect, I listened. I was not amused, and I wondered why he was calling me. I knew that he occasionally spoke to my mother, but I, myself, had never had an adult conversation with the man. I also remembered my mother telling me that his wife Aunt Emma Jean had recently passed away. I briefly thought he was going to tell me that Great Aunt Emma Jean had left me something of sentimental value. The more he rambled about various topics, I once again assumed that dementia was the culprit for the call.

How did he have my number to the school I wondered? He kept talking, and I kept doodling with a BIC pen that was about to become inkless. As my attention waned, I began to focus my attention on a poster in the corner of the office wall. It was a poster of legendary basketball coach John Wooden's Pyramid of Success. As I looked at the poster, I couldn't help but notice a quote from John Wooden that read: "Success is peace of mind which is a direct result of self-satisfaction in knowing you made the effort to become the best that you are capable of becoming."

Obviously, I had seen the quote many times, but on this day, it hit me differently as I was becoming bored with the rambling of my great uncle's conversation on the phone.

I then peered across the office and caught a quick glimpse of another poster which was on the wall next to the large office chalkboard. It was a 1988 State University Football Schedule with a large photo of Head Coach Robbie Brown standing next to some of his star players. This poster had sentimental value because I had graduated from State and had actually played football for Coach Brown. As I momentarily continued to daydream, I wasn't paying much attention to Uncle Dean rambling away on the phone until he suddenly caught my attention by saying, "Like I said earlier, I have decided to come home. I need you to come and help me move."

"Now hold on Unk… I have only met you one time in my life…"

He interrupted me, "I know we haven't been close, but I need your help."

"Are you planning to move back to your old home in Alabama?"

"Not exactly."

As I began to question him more extensively, Uncle Dean revealed to me that he had decided to move to my hometown of Shady Branch, Florida and live with my mother and father. I immediately asked him if my mother knew about this arrangement. He answered, "Well, I guess so- she always told me that I was more than welcome to come and stay."

"Where are you now?" I asked.

"Bell Canyon. It is not too far from Los Angeles."

"Why don't you ask one of your grandchildren in California to help you move?"

In almost a whisper he replied, "Because they all want to send me to a nursing home. They are all part of the conspiracy. I can't trust any of 'em. They are plottin' against me to take my money."

"Why are you asking me to help you move?"

"Because I know you have some time off during the holidays. I have it all planned. You can fly to Los Angeles and then drive me and my belongings back to Shady Branch."

"I'm confused… Haven't you been living in California with your son and his family for about ten years? Why do you need to move, now?"

"I know it sounds crazy, but I need to get out of this prison I call California. I know how all of this must sound to you, but once you come and pick me up we will have plenty of time to catch up."

I then asked, "Does your son know what you are planning?"

"I told all of them a few days ago. He and his wife think I am off my rocker. That is why I need you to come here the day after Christmas. I've heard them talking behind my back. If you don't come and get me they will have me locked up in a nursing home, poppin' those little pills which make you want to do nothin' but watch television all day long." He paused, cleared his throat, and continued, "You know- before long you begin to believe you are part of whatever television show you are watching. I've seen this happen many times."

He then paused again and spoke in a tone that reminded me of a sad and pouty child. He said, "It's all pretty simple. I would like to spend my last days on this earth with my sister and her family before it is too late."

He then went on to explain in great detail how he had already rented a U-Haul truck and that I would be driving it.

I asked, "I assume you will be following me in your car?"

In a tone of aggravation, he blurted out, "Hell, no… Don't you think it is askin' a lot for an eighty-two-year-old man to drive clear across the country? We will be towing my car behind the U-Haul."

At this point of the conversation, I knew without a doubt that I had neither the time nor the inclination to drive this man across the country. I had already made plans for my Christmas vacation, and there was no way that I would be a part of this family feud. Before I was able to end this conversation, Uncle Dean blurted out, "Don't you worry 'bout a thing. I have it all planned. Write down this number. You call me next Tuesday mornin' around eight, and I will give you all the details regarding your flight. With you drivin', we will be in Florida in no time."

As I wrote his telephone number on the front page of the sports section of the *Tallahassee Democrat* newspaper, I began to laugh to myself. I knew without a doubt that once my mother and my cousin in California heard about these preposterous plans there would be no trip to Los Angeles. Uncle Dean then yelled over the phone, "Get ready… This will be the trip of a lifetime."

***

Five minutes later, I was finally able to reach my mother, Sandy Jackson. She happily accepted the charges for a long-distance phone call. My mother ran a small beauty shop next to our home in a rural area of Florida, not far from Tallahassee. At the time, the tiny map dot called Shady Branch was an unincorporated town located in one of Florida's least populated counties. A good portion of the rural county of Apalachee was part of the Gulf Bay National Forest. Mainly known as a dry county where no legal liquor was sold, it is also known for its abundance of forests, swamps, and small vegetable farms. It also had more livestock than people, and some of the prettiest girls ever born in the great state of Florida. Geographically located one county away from the beaches, Apalachee County never quite developed like its neighboring counties located on the Gulf Coast. Many of its long-time inhabitants were opposed to any new development. They were not in the least bit interested in any new construction and attraction of new business for their community. New construction in their minds did not mean progress; it meant changing a way of life that allowed them to remain content.

On the outskirts of Shady Branch, it was not unusual to find a few roadside vendors selling luscious vegetables, and fresh seafood. Many of those vendors also sold oranges and grapefruit they had purchased in Central Florida for the out-of-state travelers who assumed that every place in Florida grew citrus.

If a person wanted to purchase alcohol in Shady Branch legally, their only option would be to drive one county away. Illegally, there was enough alcohol for anyone who asked. It was once said that half of the Panhandle of Florida could not drink enough on a weekend to even compare to what was being produced in the swamps near Shady Branch. Although this was a far-fetched exaggeration, there were some people who actually did venture into the rural area to find tax free, homemade, potent alcohol. Those customers traveled from outlying counties in Florida, Georgia, and Alabama to the backwoods near Shady Branch for a prohibited bargain.

My mother, Sandy, who was quite the entrepreneur, always referred to her operation as a beauty salon. However, I grew up knowing that the small trailer which housed one beauty salon chair, one shampoo sink, and three stationary beauty shop dryers, was more than a typical beauty salon. My mother sold everything from handmade candles to bottles of bee pollen pills.

She never officially sold alcohol, but she had been known to barter her services and other items for a few bottles of homemade wine. There were several occasions when she resold puppies and cats to her customers, who coincidently left thinking that they had done something good for the Lord. Local baked goods, jams, and preserves could always be found in her shop along with homegrown vegetables. She also prided herself in selling Vidalia Onions, South Georgia Pecans, and Claxton Fruit Cakes.

My mother became the best salesperson in the community through her unique gift of gab and her clever way of making ordinary people feel guilty if they left her place of business without purchasing at least one item. It was widely known that she had convinced an entire generation of women in the area that they needed to purchase a special type of shampoo called Renovation for the Next Generation. This came about once her beauty supply vendor agreed to her exclusive right to sell the overpriced shampoo in Shady Branch.

Also, long before a little blue pill was invented, my mother sold a special Asian herbal tea which produced remarkable results. When several of the teenagers of the community found out about the 'special tea', they joked and laughed whenever they saw an older man walking out of her shop carrying a brown paper sack. Crazy enough, my mother sold a junk yard bound tractor for a local farmer who couldn't sell it anywhere else. Livestock even sold better at her shop than they did at the local Farmer's Auction.

If you couldn't sell an item to the local pawn shop, everyone knew that Sandy would purchase the item and sell it for a lot more than it was worth.

The official name of her business was Styles by Sandy. The unofficial name of the place for the people in the community was simply Sandy's. Black people and White people of the community both regularly stopped in Sandy's for more than a haircut or a perm. It was a place where a neighbor could ask for a specific prayer request and a place where that same prayer request was sometimes answered when there was little hope. Although, through the years, it had become somewhat of a spiritual haven for some of the ladies of the church, it was also a place where many tall tales could be found alongside a steady stream of local gossip. Those tales and the gossip associated with them had far reaching implications for many people in my community.

Some of the biggest losers in the area found comfort from my mother, who always took time to listen to their problems in between answering the phone and giving someone a perm or a hair frosting. At the height of her career, she would have been regarded as a "life coach" in today's world.

Once I reached her on the phone I asked, "Do you have a few minutes to talk?"

She replied, "For you, I have plenty of time. Mrs. Googe is drying right now. My next appointment, Nancy Smith, just called and canceled. She said something about having to go to see her banker. Lord knows that woman can come up with some incredible excuses to cancel on me, but what am I going to do? She is my best customer. She buys something every time she comes in here. I sometimes think I could pee in a bag of crap, and she would buy it. I'm not sure if she would buy it just because she has more money than she knows what to do with or because she loves me like a sister. Lord knows, I love her…"

I yelled over the phone, "Okay, Mom, I need to talk to you. I don't have time for you to gab about Mrs. Smith. I have things to do."

She giggled before asking, "Why didn't you say that to begin with? What do you need, my Sweet Shuga?"

I replied, "You will never believe who just called me at the school."

She paused for a moment before saying, "Let me guess. Was it Johnny Carson or President Ronald Reagan?"

CHAPTER TWO

After breaking the news about Uncle Dean to my mother, I couldn't believe her reaction when she calmly replied over the phone, "If that is what Uncle Dean really wants to do, then I think it will work out."

I shot back, "I can tell that you have already made plans with him. I'm not stupid, Mom. Why in the world would you agree to have this old man come and live with you?"

My mother raised her voice, "Because he is family, and family means more than anything."

I asked, "What about Daddy? He is gonna flip out when he finds out Uncle Dean is coming to live with y'all."

My mother giggled loudly before replying, "He will get over it. Trust me when I tell you that he will be fine with this arrangement. Your Daddy is so lazy, he may not even notice if someone else is livin' in our house."

I asked her about Uncle Dean's son, Roy. I knew in my heart that Cousin Roy would not be too happy about this arrangement.

My mother did not hesitate in her warped explanation of how Roy would get over it.

She cried out, "For God's sake, he and Linda have had Uncle Dean and Aunt Emma Jean as live-in babysitters for a very long time. Aunt Emma Jean practically raised those children while Roy and Linda traveled all over the country."

My mother took a deep breath and continued speaking in a more dignified sounding dialect, "Lord knows that Cousin Roy, better known as Dr. Royce Lee, has delivered speeches to over a hundred colleges and universities- not to mention all of the- Church of Christ congregations from California to New York. That one book he published; *Quiet Prayer Time For Those Who Can't Stop Talking* or something like that, took off like a bottle rocket on the Fourth of July. The next thing I know, the popularity of that little book, which was nothing more than a pepped-up devotional, has my cousin and his wife travelin' everywhere. What amazes me is that over half of that book is nothin' more than scripture. For crying out loud, a man copies right out the Good Book, writes a few comments about what the Disciples wrote in the Bible, and the next thing you know, he and Linda move into that mansion in Bell Canyon. I'm not jealous, but give me a break. Every time I would talk to Linda on the phone, she would say, 'Jesus always smiles on those who do his work.' I'm sorry, son, but whenever she would say those words, I would want to vomit. There she was prancing around Los Angeles like Nancy Reagan or Lucille Ball.

She forgets that I know the truth about how she was a student of Roy's. She never wants to talk about the miraculous conception when she became pregnant on the night of their honeymoon. Do you know to this day that she has never said one thing about how my Aunt Emma Jean, God rest her soul, figured out their jaded math, and called them out when Ava was born? Anyway, all that is beside the point. Now that their kids are all grown, and Aunt Emma Jean has passed away, they really don't need Uncle Dean around every day. Deep down, I don't think he wants to be a burden to them."

I shook my head before asking my mother, "Don't you think Cousin Roy will be worried about his father living so far away?"

Mother began yelling over the phone, "Roy can love him right here in Florida, just as well as he can in California. Besides, Roy and Linda have plenty of money. They can afford to fly out here at least once or twice a year to visit. I think it would be good for everyone in that family if they have a break from each other."

I told my mother that I really did not have time to drive her uncle all the way back from Los Angeles. I tried to explain to her that my girlfriend Maria's family had purchased tickets for the Sugar Bowl, and they wanted me to come with them and hang out in New Orleans for a few days.

My mother screamed loud enough that I had to remove the phone receiver from my ear, "You hush up right now, Timothy David Jackson… That girlfriend of yours can wait a few days. You don't have to see her every single day of your life. I hate that you can't go to a bowl game, but this is more important. Your Great Uncle Dean has asked you to help him out, and that is what you are going to do."

Perturbed to no end I asked, "Why didn't you volunteer Daddy to drive Uncle Dean across the country?"

My mother calmly lowered her voice when she replied, "Are you kidding me? I would have had better luck asking Elvis Presley. Now, you, on the other hand, are available to make this incredible journey. There are not many people who can actually say they have driven across the entire United States. Just think of it- you will be one of the few who has ever made that trip."

The more I objected, the more my mother insisted that I assist her uncle. In less than thirty minutes it was settled. I would be flying to Los Angeles to drive my Great Uncle Dean to live with my mother and father in the rural Florida community of Shady Branch.

CHAPTER THREE

The day after Christmas, 1988, I found myself reluctantly checking a large red Samsonite suitcase at the Tallahassee Airport. I tried hard not to show it, but I have to admit that I was a little nervous. This would be only the second time in my life that I had ever flown. An elderly looking man at the Eastern Airlines luggage check-in counter could tell I was nervous when he asked, "Is this your first time flying?"

I quickly snapped back at him with a somewhat sarcastic tone, "No, it's not."

I heard the elderly man at the counter mutter under his breath, "Rookie."

"What did you say?"

He replied, "Not a thing… Have a great flight."

As I walked up to the terminal gate, I immediately noticed a young beautiful flight attendant with long blonde hair and an amazing body. There is no doubt that she could have been a model. She greeted me with a big smile along with two top buttons on her blouse left unbuttoned. I was sure she had left her blouse open on purpose. Every person who boarded that flight couldn't help but notice that she was revealing a tad bit more of herself than expected, and for many; not quite enough of herself to satisfy their curiosity.

I smiled and said, "Good mornin', ma'am."

Her pleasant demeanor quickly changed when she rolled her eyes and replied with a crisp Midwestern accent dripping with harshness, and extreme nasal interjection, "Did you call me ma'am? Do I look like an old lady to you? Gees... I've been called a lot of things before, but never a ma'am."

I stopped dead in my tracks, threw up my hands, and replied, "I didn't mean any disrespect. I've always been taught to address any lady as ma'am."

She harshly and rudely interrupted me saying, "You've said enough, Mr. Big Shot- Southern Boy… Go find your seat... Like right now, how about it. Jesus Christ… You are holding up the entire passenger line for God's sake."

I wanted to reply with something clever, but the words never came. A few minutes later, I found myself on aisle nine of the plane, trying to claim my seat next to an older gentleman. The man appeared to be in his fifties or sixties. I almost fell over on top of the man while I carefully maneuvered myself over to the seat next to the window. I plopped down like a weary traveler. I then grabbed my seatbelt and said, "I am so sorry to disturb you, Sir."

Without hesitation, the older looking man replied, "No problem, Big Guy… My name is Eston Harper. Looks like we are going to be friends for at least a few hours."

He chuckled before extending his hand toward me, while I was wrestling with my seatbelt. Once we shook hands, I said, "Nice to meet you, Mr. Harper. My name is Tim Jackson."

Eston smiled big while replying, "You can stop right now with the Mr. Harper stuff. All of my friends call me Eston." He then leaned a little closer and whispered, "If these people at Eastern Airlines don't learn how to treat their customers with a little more respect, they will soon be out of business. That cute young lady they had greeting us when we boarded needs an attitude adjustment."

I couldn't have agreed more. For the next few minutes before takeoff, I listened as Eston Harper revealed a lot more information about himself than I wanted to hear. As soon as I heard Eston talking about attending a funeral in South Georgia, I tried to tune him out. I purposely kept looking out the window before our early morning departure in hopes that Eston would quit talking. I had no intention of listening to Eston Harper. I yawned a few times to give a hint to my new travel partner that enough had already been said. Eston kept talking until the good-looking blonde flight attendant told everyone to pay attention while she thoroughly explained Eastern Airlines emergency procedures in case the plane crashed. I began trying to make eye contact with her while she belted out instructions over the plane's microphone in a voice that irritated most of the passengers. When I was finally able to make solid eye contact with her, I slowly and deliberately winked at her three times. I knew she saw me because she paused for a few seconds and gave me the evil eye before continuing her crusade to prepare the passengers of Flight 677 from Tallahassee to Los Angeles for a possible emergency exit.

Once takeoff occurred and the No Smoking Signs were turned off, I looked out of the window and saw the Tallahassee area landscape clearly. I had no idea that so many people had-swimming pools in their backyards. I thought that our-conversation had ended when Eston decided to pick up where he had left off. I was in no mood for small talk, but I occasionally nodded out of respect. My attitude quickly changed when I heard Eston say, "Toxoplasmosis is what killed her."

I turned toward Eston and asked, "Killed who?"

Eston adjusted his seatbelt before replying, "My Aunt Julia. I told you that I attended a funeral in South Georgia. My mother's sister, Julia, passed away. Toxoplasmosis is what killed her. It is a parasitic disease. Toxoplasmosis is the medical term, but I have always called it the cat disease."

I wasn't sure if Eston was kidding or being serious when I said, "I have never heard that word before."

"What word?"

"Toxoplasmosis." I replied.

Eston laughed before educating me, "Yeah, it's not all that common. I call it the cat disease, but most of the time, it is spread by eating poorly cooked food. In my Aunt Julia's case, I'm afraid her cats did her in. She was an eccentric lady, who lived by herself, seldom left her house, and had twenty-five cats she called her babies. Toxoplasmosis in some cases can also be contracted from cat feces. After I entered her home, I couldn't believe the mess those cats had made. God bless her soul. Poor Aunt Julia was at the point in her life where she could barely take care of herself, much less a hoard of cats."

Five minutes later, I thought to myself that Eston would never shut up about his Aunt Julia and her toxoplasmosis. I yawned two more times. Eston kept talking. Finally, Eston asked me, "So what do you do for a living?"

I turned toward him and replied, "I am a high school football coach and teacher."

Eston seemed really interested when he replied, "Is that right? Now that is an honorable occupation. Good for you, young man. It looks like you may have played some ball yourself."

I reluctantly replied, "I did. I played or should I say, I was on the team at State."

Eston listened carefully as I then began explaining some of the details about my college football career. I tried to be brief, but Eston kept asking me more questions about football; later revealing that he was a huge college football fan. Tired of talking about myself, I finally asked, "What is that you do for a living, Eston?"

He replied, "Boring and tedious work is what I do. I am sure you wouldn't want to hear about what I do."

I inquired with anticipation, "Well, don't leave me hanging, Eston. What is it that you do that is so boring?"

Eston slowly and reluctantly replied, "It's called Forensic Science. I investigate homicides. Most of my work is done in a lab in Los Angeles."

Before responding, I thought to myself that Eston's dialect was dripping with the roots of South Georgia delivered in a tone and speed that had California written all over it. I then asked, "Do you actually work on dead people?"

Eston leaned forward in his seat before saying, "We do it every day. I am employed by the Los Angeles Coroner's Office." He then paused before continuing, "It seems like all we do is perform autopsies."

He definitely piqued my interest. I said, "That is so cool. There was a TV series that I loved to watch a few years ago about a forensic pathologist who solved crimes. I think it was called…"

Eston interrupted me saying, "*Quincy*. The name of the show was called *Quincy* M.E. Jack Klugman played the main character."

I immediately became more interested in the conversation. I replied, "That's right. I hated when they canceled that show." I briefly paused waiting on his reply and then asked jokingly, "Do you know Jack Klugman?"

Eston couldn't wait to reply. He said, "It's funny you ask. I actually did get to meet him once when he visited with us to get a feel for what we do. Unbeknown to us at the time, his appearance was intended to be a Hollywood publicity stunt. He was a nice guy, but he only stayed about thirty minutes. He took one look at an autopsy of a grotesque burn victim, and that was all she wrote. Jack turned a little pale and politely thanked us before he left the room very quickly. I could tell that he was not mentally prepared to witness such a gruesome autopsy. One of the lab techs later told us that he saw poor Jack in the restroom holding on to a toilet for dear life."

I asked with ambivalence, "Do you really have to dissect dead people to find out how they die?"

Eston laughed before replying, "We slice 'em and dice 'em every day."

I asked, "What has been your biggest case that you have worked on or solved?"

Without hesitation, Eston leaned back in his seat while replying, "We don't always solve them, but the biggest case I have worked on in my career would have to be the Ted Bundy case."

I immediately sat up in my seat and became even more interested when I asked, "Ted Bundy? I know all about that case.

I grew up not too far from Tallahassee and… Wait a minute. I thought you said you worked in Los Angeles."

Eston responded, "I do work in Los Angeles, but ten years ago, we were one of a handful of offices in the United States that employed all the new techniques of forensic science to investigate crimes. The Florida Law Enforcement Division requested our help through the FBI. The next thing I know, they sent me to Florida. Off and on, I spent about two months in Tallahassee assisting their investigation."

I unintentionally interrupted him, "Tallahassee is nice. I can tell you that to this day, most everyone in the city is fully aware of what happened when Bundy brutalized those girls."

Eston took out a handkerchief from his front shirt pocket and wiped his forehead before altering the conversation by saying, "I wouldn't know much about Tallahassee. When I was growing up, the biggest city we ever visited was Valdosta, Georgia. Once when I was a teenager, we took a trip to Jacksonville Beach. When I went off to college at Georgia Tech, I thought Atlanta was… Anyway, back to Tallahassee… I worked so much on the Bundy case, I barely had time to see the city. I do remember driving by that sorority house where Bundy killed those girls. Funny thing about that case that a lot of people don't remember."

I asked, "What's that?"

Eston, with a prideful look on his face replied, "Bundy bit one of those girls during his killing spree. It was the bite marks that ended up matching his teeth. I was there the day they forced him to take a mold of his teeth. He squirmed and fought the officers and dental workers like a mad man. He knew that once that mold was compared to those bite marks, he was a dead man walking."

I asked, "I can't believe you met Ted Bundy. Did you get to talk to him?"

Eston rolled his eyes while saying, "No, I did not. But after I went through all of the evidence- I did not want to talk to that psychopath."

I wasn't sure how to reply before saying, "I certainly don't know all the particulars like you, but I do know that everyone in my community back home wants Ted Bundy to fry. I have never seen so many people angered by what he did to those girls."

Eston nodded in affirmation while saying, "Tell me about it. I grew up in a small rural area of South Georgia. It's about a three-hour drive from the Florida State Prison. I have relatives who intend to be present there next month when they finally electrocute that scoundrel."

I leaned up in my seat while saying, "You told me you had a boring job. I think what you do is so cool."

Eston rubbed his hands together while replying, "It sounds glamorous, but there are literally days when all we do is lab work. With the new developments in the research of Deoxyribonucleic Acid over the past couple of years, we spend a good bit of our time trying to learn all the new techniques."

"What is D… uh, whatever you said?"

Eston began opening a packet of Eastern Airlines peanuts while replying, "I'm sorry. I meant to say DNA. Deoxyribonucleic Acid is the technical name for DNA." After pausing he then continued by saying, "The Bundy Case obviously was the biggest in my career, but I have a buddy who works with the FBI, who is currently working a case that might be even more interesting."

I asked, "What is it?"

He replied, "It is an unsolved murder case regarding a victim who had been missing for over fifty years. My friend, FBI agent Drew Geddings, spends all of his free time trying to find out who killed a man that was chained to a tractor and buried in a rural section of Alabama."

I enthusiastically responded, "I remember seeing a news clip about that case years ago. It has always been in the back of my mind."

Eston chewed and swallowed a couple of peanuts before saying, "Drew has done everything humanly possible to figure out what happened to a man identified as Vernon Daniels. He thinks he has a hunch about who killed him, but his problem is time."

I asked, "What do you mean?"

"Most of the people who know anything about Mr. Daniels have already departed this world. The only thing Drew and I are both sure of through the help of modern science is that Vernon Daniels was shot in the back of the head with a shotgun before he was put on the seat of that tractor, chained, and buried in a place where he was never supposed to be found."

I asked, "You said your friend had a hunch about who killed him. Who exactly was this guy, Vernon Daniels? Was he an important person in Alabama?"

He replied, "From what Drew has found out, Vernon Daniels was evidently quite a character. He was forty-four years old, 6 feet tall, blond hair, strong as an ox, and a large landowner. He evidently had his hands in a lot of different enterprises. According to Drew, he was involved in a few shady business dealings as well. He and his tractor went missing in the 1920s and at the time, it created quite a media buzz in the local papers. However, after a few years, the case went cold and was never mentioned again. Drew has looked at every known record of his disappearance and has stumbled onto a few leads. Unfortunately for Drew, the list of people who wanted Vernon Daniels dead has led Drew down a rabbit hole. Like I said earlier, so much time has passed, I'm pretty sure that my friend will never solve this case."

I changed the subject by saying, "You must have a wonderful feeling of satisfaction when you are able to help solve a big case. I can imagine that it is pretty exciting."

Eston leaned in a little closer and whispered, "You are right, it is pretty satisfying, and it does create a sense of comradery amongst the team. As a matter of fact, we have a large orange sign in our Los Angeles office hanging on the wall. You know, it's one of those orange Department of Transportation signs that reads, 'End Construction'. Every time we are able to solve a case, we all slap that sign. This group act symbolizes that the case is closed, and our 'construction work' is done. In my line of work, you need these bonding rituals to keep the team sane and centered."

That morning, we only stopped talking to each other one time when Eston had to go to the restroom. Eston spoke about how he ended up in Los Angeles after graduating from Georgia Tech, and I talked about how I was able to land a job teaching and coaching at a local Tallahassee high school. We also briefly mentioned our families, religion, and politics.

By the time we finished sharing our opinions about education, UFOs, and the state of the economy, we were preparing to land in Los Angeles. We shook hands like we were old friends, and then exchanged phone numbers and addresses, promising to stay in touch with each other. As we exited the doorway of the plane, I stopped in front of the good-looking flight attendant and said, "Have a nice day... Ma'am."

She growled back at me, "Welcome to Clown Town, Bozo."

CHAPTER FOUR

I stepped into the LAX terminal and could not believe its enormity. As I looked at a large clock mounted on the wall of the terminal, the time change threw me for a loop. I looked twice at the clock, before remembering the time zone differences. I thought it was cool that I had left Tallahassee in the morning, and it was still morning when I arrived in Los Angeles.

I then asked an Eastern Airlines attendant where I was supposed to go to pick up my suitcase. Before the attendant could reply, I distinctly heard the voice of a woman call out my name. I quickly looked up and noticed that my new friend, Eston Harper, had disappeared through the crowd. I then scanned across the terminal and could see my two cousins, Ava and Randy. Never having met them before in person, I immediately recognized them from Christmas cards, and photos that were sent to my grandmother through the years. As my cousins both walked toward me, Ava cried out in the crowded terminal, "Cousin Tim, welcome to California."

After a brief exchange and a few hugs, we walked to the luggage area to retrieve my Samsonite hardcase suitcase. While we waited for my suitcase to arrive, Randy, a tall, skinny twenty-something college student at Pepperdine University said, "We have heard a lot about you over the years. It is finally good to meet the football coach in the family. I hope you had a good flight."

I continued to scan the revolving luggage belt looking for my suitcase while I replied, "The flight was fine. I actually met a very interesting gentleman who helped me pass the time." While I was talking, I noticed that my cousin Ava was laughing. I smiled at my twenty-five-year-old graduate student cousin from UC Berkeley and asked, "What seems to be so funny?"

She ran her fingers through her blonde hair while replying, "That Southern accent. Man, these Cali girls are going to love you."

We walked through a maze of parking lots and finally made our way to Ava's car. I was impressed by her new red Ford Mustang convertible. After putting my suitcase into the trunk, we began making our way to Bell Canyon.

Top down, with music blaring, I was excited to be with my newly acquainted family members. As Ava drove, I was in the back seat trying desperately to hear what my cousins were saying. With the speakers of the Mustang pumping out the hit song, "Wild, Wild, West" by the Escape Club, I thought how appropriate that particular song was playing on the radio. Randy turned around and looked at me before screaming, "You are going to love LA."

I motioned with both of my hands toward my ears while screaming that I couldn't hear a word that Randy was saying.

Randy turned off the radio, once again yelling, "I said, you are going to love LA." He then turned toward his sister before looking back at me and continuing by saying, "We know you only have one day here, but we have decided to give you a tour of LA after we eat lunch. Too bad you can't stay longer."

Ava looked up in the rear-view mirror and shouted, "You will find out that GP is very opinionated, even when his opinions are not wanted."

I asked, "Who is the GP?"

Ava replied, "We call our grandparents Gigi and GP."

"About that… Are your parents ok with your grandfather, I mean your GP wanting to move to Florida with my parents?"

Randy laughed before replying, "My father has tried for a week to talk him out of it, but the old coot has his mind made up. We can't begin to tell you how many Alabama stories we have heard over the years. He seems to think that he is about to die. He goes on and on about dying in the South. When we laugh at him or dismiss his crazy talk, you can tell it angers him. What is so funny to all of us is that he has a burial plot next to Gigi right here in Bell Canyon. He might die in Florida, but he will be coming back to California to be buried. All that nonsense about dying in the

South seems pretty backwards to all of us, but Dad says that if that is what he wants, he will not stand in his way."

I was shielding the bright California sunshine from my eyes when I replied, "I see. You do know that he thinks y'all are tryin' to put him in a nursing home?"

They both laughed before Ava replied, "We've been hearing that since we were old enough to understand the concept of a nursing home. He is obsessed with the subject. Don't get me wrong, we love GP, but he is a pill. The man has an opinion on everything. He has embarrassed all of us at one time or another with his obnoxious political or religious opinions in the most inopportune times. The man does not possess one ounce of social grace or etiquette. Stubborn as a mule, and ornery as an old cowboy, he is one unique character, but we love him."

Randy chimed in, "Yeah, GP can say the craziest things sometimes. One time when one of my friends from high school came over, we went swimming in our pool. GP embarrassed the crap out of me. My friend, Sam, who is Jewish, was stepping out of the pool when GP told him that he did not know that Jews liked the water. GP thought he was being funny, but you can imagine how we all felt after he said it."

Ava changed lanes before saying, "We all know about his Alabama roots, but I can honestly say that he has talked about Alabama so much, I'm not sure I ever want to go back there. He acts like the place is so much better than California. She then pointed out the window before saying, "I'm pretty sure they don't have any Jack in the Box fast food restaurants in the backwoods of Alabama."

I really didn't know how to reply and to tell the truth, I was somewhat offended. I finally said, "I hope y'all know that I tried to talk him out of moving to Florida. I did not want any part in this, but my mother threatened to disown me if I didn't come out here and help him move."

In unison, both of them replied, "We know." Ava then yelled, "GP has been talking about this ever since our grandmother passed away. I have to give him credit. Whenever he puts his mind to something, he never quits. He has been working on this plan to move to Florida for several weeks. He first tried to figure out how he could move back to Alabama, but the only people he really knew there were dead or already in a nursing home. That is why he has latched on to your mother. We are glad he will be going with you and not trying to make the trip to Florida by himself; something he was threatening to do."

While I sat in the back seat, I was enjoying the California sunshine as Ava sped around a delivery truck before taking the entrance ramp onto the 405 Interstate. Immediately, I noticed the multi-lane freeway, something I had never seen. I was enamored by the beauty of the surrounding vegetation, the majesty of the palm trees, and the warm humid-free weather. Back in Shady

Branch, I remembered that my mother always referred to the hot, humid climate of Florida as the "air you can wear".

What appeared to be an infinite number of vehicles on the freeway was thrilling. The height of the cloverleaf freeway connectors in Westfield gave me a sensation of being on a roller coaster. Five minutes away from the Los Angeles International Airport, I fell in love with the beauty of California.

CHAPTER FIVE

By the time we reached Bell Canyon, a little more than one hour's journey, I was feeling sentimental as I was really thinking about how I had missed out by not growing up near my distant relatives. To me, Randy and Ava appeared to be top notch; cousins I could relate to; they seemed more refined and educated than me and my side of the family.

I quickly realized they thought my Southern accent was country sounding. They didn't say it to me, but I could tell by their reaction to my dialect, they perceived me as being a little backward. They weren't disrespectful, but I noticed that they laughed every time I said 'y'all or ain't'. I had experienced similar feelings about my Southern roots during a psychology class at State University, where my professor from Upstate New York tried very hard to embarrass any student he encountered who had even the slightest Southern accent. The time spent in that class made me realize for the first time in my life that I spoke in a dialect that was completely different from the rest of the world.

As we continued to drive, I never mentioned it to my cousins, but it painfully bothered me that I never had the opportunity to get to know them. I suddenly felt cheated out of knowing that there was another side of my family that I had never been around. I wondered quietly why my grandmother and her own brother seldom visited each other in their later years. They lived one state away from each other most of their adult lives. How could it be possible that a brother and sister never visited with each other during that time period in their lives?

I had grown up in Florida hearing all the tales about Uncle Dean from my mother, but only one time in my life had I ever met the man of high esteem. I remembered when my mother and I visited with my great aunt and uncle on their farm near Cool Shoals, Alabama. I was nine years old when I first met my quick-witted Uncle Dean. On that day, he was dressed in overalls, drenched in perspiration from a hard day's work, and saddled with a smile that would have welcomed a long-lost friend.

During those three days on the farm, I became acquainted with a man, who appeared relentless in his quest to work harder than any of his neighbors, and yet sensitive enough for a small baby chick to eat from his strong hands. At that time in my life, he seemed to be the most intelligent and hardworking man I had ever met.

While on the farm, I watched Uncle Dean feed the animals, gather eggs, and round up cattle near the most beautiful pond I had ever seen. Uncle Dean even allowed me to drive around the 110-acre farm in an old US Army issued WWII model Jeep after he taught me how to change the gears of the manual transmission and properly release the clutch.

I ate food that had been grown on the farm-- every bit of it except for the sugar, flour, Crisco, and the salt that was used for preparation. I experienced the aroma of fresh sausage, country ham, eggs, and homemade biscuits which were cooked by Great Aunt Emma Jean early in the morning. The sweetness of fresh blackberry cobbler topped off with hand-churned homemade vanilla ice cream would be a memory I would always cherish. I experienced the culinary genius behind fried chicken, which was so crispy outside, yet tender enough to cut with a plastic fork on the inside. I was taught by Aunt Emma Jean an old secret handed down several generations. She taught me to fry the chicken slowly, fry it two times on both sides, and to use a batter that included cornstarch, honey, and fresh buttermilk.

After I learned about what Uncle Dean called "farm-time", I never appreciated going to bed before ten o'clock each night. I remembered sleeping under the coolness of a window fan in a house that had no air conditioning; however, I distinctly remembered staying cool from the shade of two large oaks, and one of the oldest magnolia trees in the great state of Alabama.

The recollection of the early morning wake-up calls where darkness prevailed, along with the soaked grass from the morning dew, made me realize that farming was not for the faint of heart. I vividly remembered swimming in a pond after working in the heat of an Alabama summer day. That pond water was so clear I remembered being able to watch the fish swim by my toes on the bottom.

During those three days, I was fascinated by a man, whose formal education was cut short by the circumstances of life. Uncle Dean was forced to drop out of the eighth grade because his father died during the Influenza Pandemic of 1918 at the end of World War I. Uncle Dean's father tried to assist other neighbors, who had been infected. He came home one cold, rainy night, went to bed coughing, and died three days later.

Soon after his father's death, Dean Lee began working full-time to help his mother and younger sister survive. Their family was already devastated because Dean's grandfather had been tragically killed only two months before Dean's father died. Dean's grandfather, Tanner Lee, lived with the family until he passed away. His influence on young Dean and his father was seldom mentioned by other family members because Tanner was a bad alcoholic who had embarrassed the family. He died walking from a local tavern when he was caught in a thunderstorm. During that mini flash flood, Tanner was swept away and drowned in a three-foot-deep Alabama red clay ditch, drunker than the law allowed.

After losing his father and grandfather a few months apart, fourteen-year-old Dean Lee found himself working ten to fourteen hours a day in a sharecropping deal that had his mother and little sister always living one meal away from starvation. His hard work not only allowed the family to survive; he eventually thrived. He perfected the craft of welding by the time he was eighteen years old. He also farmed and began reading books that would eventually qualify him to take the Alabama Bar Exam. After being married and starting his own family, Dean was twenty-five-years-old when he completed a mail-in correspondence course preparing him to take the Alabama Bar Exam. To everyone's surprise he not only passed the final exam, but he also aced it. A few months later, he officially became a part-time attorney for a law firm in Florence, Alabama.

During the Great Depression, he worked hours that were ungodly. A couple of years later, he opened up his one-man law firm. He operated his law practice out of his home and worked on the cheap. Dean became popular in his community as the farm attorney who would help the poor and downtrodden. When the Tennessee Valley Authority decided to build a dam near his community, to generate hydroelectric power to the Muscle Shoals region of North Alabama, Dean ended up representing many rural families, who were being legally forced to leave their homes through eminent domain. His ability to persuade the Federal Government Land Agents to give his clients top dollar on the purchase of their property was pretty impressive. However, it was not quite as impressive as his ability to convince his clients to sell properties that had been owned and worked by several generations of cash poor people. His negotiations with the Federal agents led to unexpected deals where he would secure work on the dam for many of his clients. Those clients were willing to sell only if they could help build the dam. He himself became a part-time pipefitter during the construction of Wheeler Dam in 1933, all the while continuing his duties as an attorney, a husband, a father of two boys, and the operator of his small independent farm.

His success as a negotiator for workers seeking unionization propelled his career further as he became a sought-after labor negotiator all over the Southeast. He never allowed any success to diminish his work ethic, and everyone knew he was tight when it came to money. Dean only wore two sets of overalls that Emma Jean would wash daily. He owned only one church suit for many years.

Dean and Emma Jean grew their own food and saved money in mason jars buried at various locations of the farm. They saved enough money to send both of their boys to the University of Alabama. Their boys were the first in their immediate and extended family to obtain a college education. His oldest son, Tom (Thomas), not only graduated with honors, but he also became a neurosurgeon, who had a successful practice in Dallas,

Texas. His youngest son, Roy, (Royce), also graduated with honors from the University of Alabama, securing a Doctorate in Theology, then teaching at Pepperdine University.

When I began to compare my side of the family to my great uncle's, the differences were polarizing. Hearing my cousins refer to their grandparents as Gigi and GP, stood out to me. I thought it added a touch of metropolitan class and sophistication that I had not been privileged to as a child. My immediate family in Florida was in my mind, only a few notches above being called "poor white trash". My parents always struggled financially. When my mother found out that she was pregnant with me, she was forced to drop out of high school during her senior year. She worked with her mother at a local truck stop, during her teenage years. At the truck stop, my mother met and fell in love with my father who drove a pulpwood truck for a living.

My father, Hank, had been a ball player during high school, but couldn't keep up academically. When it appeared he would not graduate from high school, he left town and joined the United States Army. He served a tour of duty in Berlin during the 1958 Berlin Crisis. While he was stationed in Germany, he was dishonorably discharged two years after he arrived for punching out a First Sergeant who called him a worthless hick. My father ended up back in Shady Branch and began driving pulpwood trucks for a living.

I knew that my parents worked grueling hours over the years to make sure I would have the chance to be successful. Unfortunately, my father was now sidelined from working very often because of a bad back and because of mechanical failures related to his diesel trucks. In the eyes of many people in the Shady Branch community, he was considered worthless. Their assumptions came about because my father's inability to work never interfered with his ability to drink cold beer and occasionally wander away from his family for a few days.

On the other hand, my mother was always busting her tail- 24-7, doing things to make money. It always bothered me that she worked so hard and that my father did not seem to care. What bothered me the most was that when I was younger, he was a hard worker. My father, who once worked me like a mule while I was growing up, now appeared to be giving up on life itself, giving up the ghost; lying down in the road; checking out long before his time. His lack of ambition deeply annoyed me because he was not the man that I knew as a child. I desperately wanted a better life for him, my mother, and myself; something I wasn't sure Shady Branch, Florida could offer when I was able to leave home to attend college.

CHAPTER SIX

As we entered the Bell Canyon subdivision, known as Bell Towers, I noticed the winding streets which in essence, circled two large hills; hills that were not quite large enough to be called mountains. The homes in the subdivision were large and expensive. I was told by my cousins that some of the residents had connections with the Hollywood film industry. The other residents were professionals who held positions of power in various industries or in the state government of California. The yards in Bell Towers were manicured with various natural rocks, native vegetation including cactus, and very little grass. I was amazed by the stunning views as we wound our way up to the home of Dr. and Mrs. Royce Lee.

We pulled into the driveway at a much faster speed than I was used to driving. While Ava was braking, I could see two brand new Mercedes, a sleek garnet 1987 Oldsmobile Ninety-Eight Broughman, and an old beaten-up Chevrolet farm truck. Randy laughed while opening his door. He said, "That old truck is GP's pride and joy. He is leaving it here. He told us to sell it."

Ava shouted, "We just need to take the thing to the junkyard. I would be embarrassed if someone came here to buy that pile of junk."

Once we were all out of the car, the garage door of the home began opening. My cousin, Dr. Royce Lee appeared. When the garage door was completely opened, Royce, better known as Roy, walked briskly over to me, shook my hand, and gave me a slight hug. He said, "Tim, I am so glad to see you. You don't remember meeting me, but my wife, Linda, and I came by to visit with you and your family when you were just a toddler. I always told my parents that you were going to be a big one."

I was relieved that Cousin Roy didn't initially seem to harbor any ill will toward me. I took a deep breath and replied, "I have heard so much about you. I am so glad to finally meet you and this side of the family. I truly hate that we had to meet under these circumstances."

Roy patted me on the back while replying, "Well, once you have the chance to know my Daddy, you will understand that when he makes up his mind- there is no turning back. Please come into our home. Daddy is waiting to see you. Linda has prepared a light lunch for everyone."

We entered the garage up through an architecturally unique set of steps into a modern-looking kitchen. I was greeted warmly by Roy's wife Linda. Through the years, my grandmother and mother had only a few positive comments to say about this woman. Not knowing what to expect, I was pleasantly surprised by her conservative appearance along with her warm greeting. Her words were crisp, precise, and as pristine as her family's state of Washington heritage - a heritage which included a long line of fundamentalist Christian pastors and missionaries. My mother once told me Linda's family was part of some kind of cult. This stuck in my mind.

Linda slightly kissed me on the cheek with a business-like touch of class while leaving behind a smudge of lipstick. She then said loudly, "Since this is your first visit to California, we want you to be able to see as much of LA as you can in one day. She then gently patted me on my shoulder before saying, "As good looking as you are, I have no doubt that the girls in Florida love you." She then looked at her children and said, "Ava and Randy are going to be your tour guides today. If they don't do a good job of showing you around Los Angeles, you let me know." She then laughed a controlled sounding giggle almost seemingly fake, and then said, "Follow me. Granddaddy Lee is patiently waiting in the den for your arrival."

She led us through a large dining room with elegant place settings and silverware already displayed on the table. I then saw the man I had met once as a child. As with my previous visit with him, Uncle Dean was dressed in a pair of overalls, a flannel looking shirt, and work boots. He was sitting in a rocking chair, smoking a pipe, while he read the most recent edition of *Newsweek* magazine. The aroma of cherry tobacco filled the room with a sweet scent. The aroma was so appealing I wanted to sit down and smoke a pipe with him. Uncle Dean's magnetic smile, I remembered as a child, had not changed. However, I immediately noticed that the once strong-bodied farmer had aged considerably. With his hair grayer and thinner, I almost did not recognize him. Uncle Dean now appeared in front of me with leather looking skin, harsh age lines, and a small pot belly. His aging body had radically changed his appearance from the vibrant, youthful one that I remembered. Before Uncle Dean tried to stand up, I walked over to him and tried to shake his hand. He stayed seated and quickly put down his pipe. He then reached for me, grabbed my hand, and pulled me close. His grip was stronger than I expected.

He whispered, "You have no idea how glad I am that you are here."

I knelt down beside his chair and said, "It has been a long time."

While the entire family looked on, Uncle Dean, with a big smile on his face, began talking to me as if we were old friends. He said, "Gosh almighty! You are so big now! I would have never recognized you on the street."

I replied, "You haven't changed a bit."

Uncle Dean laughed before saying, "Now I know you are a good liar."

For a few more minutes, Uncle Dean talked while everyone stood around him and listened. He rambled about reading a news article about trains before saying, "Did you know that most people only see about five hundred trains in their lifetime? That is a fact. The older you get, the more you appreciate those iron horses when they pass by you. I remember being stopped by a train in Chattanooga back during the Great Depression. It had to be the longest train ever. I quit counting cars after..."

Linda interrupted him in mid-sentence and said, "GP, I think we need to go ahead and allow our special guest to dine with us for lunch."

Uncle Dean looked at me, held up his right hand, and slowly stood up from his rocking chair. He asked me, "Did you eat on the plane, or are you ready for some dinner or should I say lunch? These California people call dinner- lunch, and they call supper-dinner. I'll never get used to that."

After I told him that I had not eaten on my flight, Uncle Dean put down his pipe while saying, "Come on into Linda's cafeteria. You can taste some of my fresh garden vegetables." He then pointed out toward the back, glassed-in porch, where I was able to peek at one of the most elaborately designed vegetable gardens I had ever seen.

Before we all walked into the dining room, Cousin Roy, a nationally known theologian, prayed a long blessing. I wished I had recorded it. It sounded more like a mini sermon than a blessing. To this day I have never heard anyone return thanks so formally. When Roy eloquently intertwined the Israelites fleeing Egypt into the blessing, I understood why Dr. Royce Lee was such a sought-after speaker across the country.

A few minutes after we began our formal "lunch", I noticed that Uncle Dean tried to dominate the conversation. He rambled on and said something about cattle. He said, "Tim, if you have never seen the birth of a baby calf, then you have missed out on one glorious miracle that God allows people to witness."

I also noticed that my cousins had a hired Latino lady who came from the kitchen and began pouring water into the glasses on the table. After pouring Uncle Dean's water she said, "Mrs. Linda, whenever you are ready, please let me know when you would like me to serve the pasta primavera."

Uncle Dean shouted, "Bring it on. I am starving." He then continued to ramble on about topics that ranged from the medicinal value of turnips to how air conditioning had made our nation soft. The more he talked, I began to think Uncle Dean was definitely showing signs of old age. Everyone at the table politely allowed him to speak; however, when they tried to speak, Uncle Dean was not as gracious. Twice, he was reminded by his daughter-in-law, Linda, that someone else was talking. She calmly spoke to him as if he were a small child. Each time she corrected Uncle Dean, she would slowly glance at everyone at the table and smile. I could tell that her words aggravated Uncle Dean. I felt uneasy about how the conversation was unfolding.

Another thing that stuck out to me was the formality of the lunch as we ate from fine china, and the most expensive silverware I had ever seen. We drank from imported crystal goblets. The thick, elaborately embroidered linen napkins were so elegant that I was hesitant to use mine to wipe my mouth. As the conversation began to wind down, Uncle Dean looked at me before saying, "Go have your fun here in Los Angeles, but you make sure you are ready to leave with me bright and early tomorrow morning."

Unexpectedly, Cousin Roy then threw his napkin on his plate and said in a stern voice, "Daddy, I still can't believe that you are moving to Florida." He paused for a few seconds and then continued by saying, "Excuse me, Tim, but we are baffled as to why my father wants to leave our home. No disrespect to you, but we all know that your mother is in no financial position to look after my father. She has her own mother to take care of. Taking care of another person can't be good for her or your family."

I did not know how to respond. The last thing I wanted to be involved in was this highly sensitive family discussion. Before I could find the right words to respond, Uncle Dean yelled, "You listen here, Roy. Nobody needs to take care of me. I don't understand what is so wrong with me wantin' to spend some time with my sister and her family in Florida. I'm going to Florida to help Sandy look after my sister."

Cousin Roy leaned over on the table with one arm supporting his chin while saying, "Daddy, you are making a huge mistake. Aunt Claire is in a nursing home. Cousin Sandy has told me there are days when Aunt Claire doesn't know a cat from a dog. I predict that you will be begging to come back home in less than a month."

I immediately insisted that I needed to unpack my suitcase and rest for a few minutes. I interrupted the conversation to excuse myself from a familial discussion that was becoming rather heated. While I was shown my room upstairs by Randy, we could still hear my cousin Roy and Uncle Dean debating a questionable move to Florida. Randy looked at me while saying, "We are sick of hearing this every day. Both of them say the same thing, and nothing changes. I guess with you finally arriving, reality has set in for my father. He feels totally betrayed by GP."

Once Randy left the room, I noticed a telephone sitting on the nightstand. I leaned over and called my girlfriend in Tallahassee. Maria, a business major from Pensacola, was about to begin her final semester at State University. Once she accepted my collect call, she asked, "I take it that you made it to LA. How is it out there?"

I whispered, "LA is nice, but this family is not cool with my great uncle moving to Florida. I feel like I am in the middle of a family feud."

Maria, in a sarcastic tone replied, "I told you before you left that this was a bad idea. Your mother is absolutely crazy to think otherwise. It doesn't take a family counselor to figure out that this is going to cause a lot of hard feelings."

"You are absolutely right. Anyhow, I wanted you to know that we will be leaving here early in the morning."

In a peppy sounding voice, Maria said, "Well, if your great uncle is not going to allow you to spend a few days touring the sights of LA, maybe you can talk him into meeting us in New Orleans for the Sugar Bowl. I'm sure Daddy can find him a ticket to the game."

I sat down on the four-poster bed before saying, "I don't know about that. Uncle Dean seems bent on making it to Florida as fast as he can. I'm not even sure I want you or your family to meet him. He seems a little senile to me. When are y'all flying to the Big Easy?"

She replied, "Daddy wants us to be there on Wednesday when the team, the cheerleaders, and the band arrive. He and my mother love New Orleans. I'm not sure what they have planned, but we all know that at some point, we will be eating breakfast at Mother's Restaurant and having dinner at Galatoire's. They love the food at those places. It is no secret that my parents are big fans of boudin, jambalaya, and gumbo yaya. I wish you could go out with us on Bourbon Street and to the game. You know that I am really sad that we will not be together on New Year's Eve. When I told my Daddy that you wouldn't be able to make it, I could tell he was disappointed. Sometimes I think he likes talking football with you more than being around all of us. If truth be told, he would rather go to the game with you than anybody else. You know my Uncle William went to Auburn. I swear if Auburn wins this game, I think Daddy will be one miserable human."

Our conversation came to an end when I said, "Don't get too many beads, and please be careful on Bourbon Street. I love you… And bring me back a t-shirt from the game if we win."

Five minutes later, Randy walked back into my room. He said, "Whenever you get dressed, we are ready to show you around Los Angeles." He briefly yawned before saying, "While we are out, we will grab some dinner, and then we are going to take you to a couple of LA night clubs." He paused and then continued, "Make sure you have your dancing shoes on because this will be a night you never forget."

I put up my hand and said, "Randy, I really appreciate you and Ava going out of your way to show me around town, but the truth of the matter is that I do not have a lot of money with me. I hope all of this will not be expensive. I didn't come here prepared to party."

Randy shook his head while stating, "Our treat. Don't worry about anything. Mom has instructed us to make sure you have a good time. Although it is a Monday, the clubs in Hollywood will still be busy because of all the college students being on Christmas vacation. Relax. You are our guest, and we will take good care of you."

I stood up from the bed while saying, "Please, I do not want to saddle you two down…"

He pointed at me while saying, "Change your clothes, Coach. We are going to have a good time. Who knows we might even bump into Meg Tilly or Burt Reynolds while we are in Hollywood. We always see famous people."

After making me change my hideous looking, stained, ¾ sleeve t-shirt to a more fashionable tight-fitting buttoned-down shirt given to me by Randy, Ava gave me another look before saying, "Those jeans you are wearing will be fine, although they are about three years out of style."

Ava could immediately tell that she had hit a nerve as I shook my head, evidently giving off a negative vibe. She said, "Don't get upset with me, big boy. I tell Randy all the time what he should or shouldn't wear. I guess that's why they call me the fashion expert of this family."

CHAPTER SEVEN

va allowed me to sit in the front passenger seat of Randy's light blue 1987 Mercedez-Benz 560SL so I would be able to take in all the sights. Less than one block away, Randy stopped in front of one of the large homes in the subdivision. He pointed at the home and said, "That is where Jamie Farr lives."

I asked, "Who is Jamie Farr?"

Ava looked at me like I was crazy while she replied, "You know, he played Klinger on the TV series, *M.A.S.H.* He was the guy who always dressed up like a woman so they would think he was crazy and kick him out of the military."

"I do remember."

Randy said, "He lives right here. He and GP are good friends."

I replied, "That is pretty cool."

Ava leaned up toward the front seat and said, "GP grows and sells vegetables to all of the people who live around here. He has been selling Jamie fresh tomatoes, garlic, kale, and sweet potatoes for years. Jamie always sends GP a box of Tony Packo's Hot Dogs every Christmas. Jamie's wife, Mrs. Joy Ann, told us that Jamie thinks those famous hot dogs from Toledo are not only the best tasting; he swears they have medicinal qualities as well. GP freezes them and eats them once a month for his health. Believe me, you will hear all about this on your drive back to Florida."

Winding our way down Bell Canyon Road, I loved the scenery which reminded me of pictures I had seen of the Rocky Mountains.

Ava said, "Living here is beautiful, but we do have an occasional mudslide or forest fire. Everyone, especially GP, is always worried about the fires. Santa Ana winds can turn an entire neighborhood into a ghost town in a matter of hours."

Randy cried out, "Good grief, Ava. Enough of the negative talk. It is time to show Tim what Los Angeles is all about."

Less than an hour later, tour guide Ava gave me a play-by-play rundown on every important site as we rode through Los Angeles County. We drove through Culver City while Ava pointed out all of the big Hollywood studio offices and many homes of movie stars. As we traveled further into Los Angeles, our first official stop was at the Los Angeles Coliseum. Ava thought that since I was a football coach, I would enjoy seeing the stadium. While we were parking, I told them that I had always wanted to see or play a football game there.

We found an unlocked gate and were able to walk into the empty stadium. I marveled at the famous structure which had been a part of the Los Angeles landscape since 1923. We began walking across the stadium field when a worker in the far end zone yelled at us to leave. We quickly exited the field and walked back to Randy's car.

Randy drove us through a rough part of South Los Angeles. He then turned north and headed for Hollywood. Before we reached Wilshire Avenue, Randy drove us by the iconic Hollywood sign on Mt. Lee. Randy slowed down and said, "When Ava and I were little kids, our father used to tell us that they named Mt. Lee after our family. We were in high school before we learned that he had been kidding us."

The more we toured, the more I could not believe the display of gaudy wealth along with the beauty of Beverly Hills. It was the first time in my life that I ever saw a Rolls Royce and stretch limousine. As we rode down streets surrounded by enormous palm trees, I imagined that roads in Heaven must look similar.

We rode by the Hollywood Bowl, and we stopped at the famous Capitol Records Building. While we rode further, I was surprised by the number of Cali girls, who walked down a portion of the Sunset Strip on a Monday afternoon. They were dressed in a way that was far more revealing than anything I had ever seen in public. We stopped at a busy intersection because of traffic. An older looking prostitute approached our car and propositioned me for a good time. I had no idea what she was talking about. When the traffic light changed, and we began driving away, Ava laughed at me, explained what had occurred, and said, "I told you these Cali girls would love you."

After riding all over Hollywood, Randy found a parking space behind the notable Hollywood Roosevelt Hotel. Ava and Randy led me through the lobby like they were taking me to an amusement park. I barely had enough time to take in all of the grandeur as my cousins proceeded to walk out the front entrance to Hollywood Boulevard. I kept asking where they were going, when Ava laughed and said, "You will be surprised."

A few minutes later, they led me down the street to view the historic Hollywood Walk of Fame. After walking up and down the legendary sidewalk, and looking at the names of thousands of Hollywood's most honored stars, Randy looked at me and asked, "Isn't this the coolest place ever?"

I nodded, smiled, and replied, "Yes, it is," while I continued to read the name of Morton Downey, The Irish Nightingale. I had never heard of the popular singer from the 1920s. As we continued to walk, reading more names of people I did not know, I had seen enough. I never said it to my cousins, but it was not what I had imagined. To tell the truth, I was a little underwhelmed. Not fully appreciating the Hollywood history that I was witnessing, I felt the area looked a little rundown and somewhat trashy. When a couple of homeless people approached us for money with more than usual persistence, I felt the area was a little unsafe.

Later, after walking, and again driving through Hollywood, Ava insisted that we eat at Barney's Beanery located on Santa Monica Boulevard. I knew nothing about the place which had been around since 1927. I could tell that my cousins were very excited about showing me one of Hollywood's most iconic hangouts. While we were parking, Ava told me, "This place has the best chili and hamburgers you will ever eat. The best thing about this joint is that every time we come here, we always see somebody famous."

Randy chimed in, "That's right. The last time we came here, Tommy Lasorda, the manager of the LA Dodgers, was eating right across from us."

I could not believe that the place which looked rundown on the outside was packed with so many people on the inside. It was loud. It was busy. It was one of the coolest places that I had ever seen. More bar than restaurant, I immediately noticed two men holding hands while they waited in line for a drink at the bar. I asked Randy, "Is this some kind of a gay bar?"

Randy, dressed like a cross between Miami Vice and Hawaii Five-O, laughed and replied, "It is whatever you want it to be. You will see all kinds of people here."

I hastily scanned the place. Some people were dressed as conservative as corporate CEOs, while others were dressed as wild as Cyndi Lauper or Madonna. I witnessed numerous hair styles, different races and ethnic groups, along with some people dressed up like the opposite sex. I tried hard not to judge, but being from Shady Branch, Florida, I was definitely not mentally prepared for what I was seeing. Before we were able to be seated, Ava punched me in my ribs and whispered, "Oh, my God! Don't look now, but sitting right behind us is Mel Gibson."

I quickly turned to see one of my favorite Hollywood actors eating with a very large man sitting across the table from him. The huge man had muscles dripping on top of muscles. He looked like he could bench press a Volkswagen. I wanted Mel's autograph, but Ava politely told me that would not be cool.

A few minutes later, we were approached by a very hot looking waitress, who told us she had landed a non-speaking role in a television sitcom. I was somewhat shocked when Randy ordered a round of tequila shots for everyone. I knew my cousins grew up under the umbrella of the Church of Christ. I was pretty sure the church did not condone the use of alcohol. I said nothing and went along with their request. I had never been a big drinker during my college experience, but truth be told, I was not immune from drinking a few cold beers.

By the time we ordered our food, and a second round of tequila shots, I was stunned when I noticed my morning flying partner, Eston Harper, sitting with a few older looking men at the bar. I politely excused myself from my tequila guzzling cousins, walked up behind Eston, and tapped him on the shoulder. Eston quickly turned around and said, "Coach Jackson… What in the world are you doing here?"

I pointed across the bar while saying, "My cousins sitting over there have been giving me a tour of Hollywood before I head back to Florida."

Eston wiped his mouth with a napkin before saying, "I see. Well, they have brought you to one of Hollywood's most acclaimed places to eat and drink."

I said, "My cousins have been pretty cool so far. I can tell all they want to do is to show me a good time."

Eston, who had been eating a bowl of Barney's signature chili, stood up and shook my hand. Once he stood, I was able to clearly see down to the other end of the bar. I saw Head Coach Pat Riley, superstar players Magic Johnson and James Worthy of the Los Angeles Lakers sitting beside each other eating and drinking. They were deep in conversation. I glanced back at Eston, who then said, "Your ears must be burning, Coach. I was telling my friend, Don Frost, about meeting you on our flight today. It just so happens that Don is a regional Vice-President for a little company called Carnation. I'm sure you have heard of them. Don is a Ft. Lauderdale legend, who spends most of his time in Los Angeles when he is not gambling in Las Vegas doing what he loves best. We have known each other for what seems like a hundred years. Whenever he is in town, he stays at a condo right across the street from where I live. I guess you could say we are part-time neighbors. Don travels everywhere." Eston then introduced me to his friend.

Completely bald, the jovial looking Don shook my hand before saying, "That's right, Tim. My old friend Eston shared with me that he had met this amazing young man on his flight from Tallahassee. I'm not quite sure why he felt the need to tell me about you, but I am glad he did. It happens that our company, which has offices all over the world, is currently looking for a few good men like you to join our sales management team. For the past three years we have been going through a transition as we are now owned by the Nestle Corporation. We have a sales management trainee program which is second to none. Eston told me that you played football at State University, and that you are now a high school teacher and a football coach."

I nodded in agreement before answering, "Yes, sir. This is my first year as a full-time teacher and coach. I graduated a year ago from State."

Don took a quick sip of his drink before replying, "Well, I won't hold that against you since I am a Miami man. He then took another sip of his drink before saying, "We, at the Carnation Division, like coaches, teachers, or former athletes. We have found out through the years that people with backgrounds similar to yours become our most successful heavy hitters. How would you like to schedule a formal interview with us?"

Caught off guard, I replied, "Well, I appreciate that, but I hate to sound ignorant. I have no idea how to sell powdered milk. On top of that, there is no way that I will have time for an interview before I leave to go back to Florida."

He replied, "I completely understand. Let me explain that this is a management position. Once you completed the year-long training program, you would never be out on the ground selling milk products. In this particular job, you would be training, coaching, and managing a team of sales reps on how to deal with vendors from all over the world. We, at Carnation, do not sell milk products door to door. We need young men like you who know how to motivate others. If it is all right with you, we can arrange to meet with you in Tallahassee in a few weeks. I'd like to interview you right here, but I have an associate who lives in Virginia. He would need to be involved in the interview process. Bill Kelso is his name, and he heads our new sales management recruitment program. Let me conclude this business talk by saying that I think you will be surprised at how much money you could make with us. I am positive it would be a lot more than what the school system is paying you in Tallahassee."

There was no doubt that I was flattered; however, I had no intention of going through with the interview. After talking a few more minutes, I politely took Don Frost's business card and promised him that I would give him a call once I made it back to

Florida. I then leaned over and whispered to Eston Harper, "I don't know about this. I feel like I was born to coach football."

After I thanked both Don and Eston, I left them and walked back over to my cousins where I had to explain how I knew someone in California. After my explanation, Randy said, "How unusual is that? You meet some dude on your flight out here and now somebody here in LA wants to offer you a job. That is so cool."

I then pointed to the LA Laker crowd sitting at the end of the bar and said, "Speaking of cool."

CHAPTER EIGHT

I sat alone, nursing a cold beer while I watched Ava and Randy tear up the dance floor. Twice, Ava tried to make me join them and the rest of the dancing crowd. I politely declined. I was not into group dancing. As I sat alone, I wished I could hear the large television on the wall behind the bar. I was interested in an ESPN sports segment about Coach Lou Holtz and Notre Dame's quest to win a national football championship in a few days.

About twenty minutes later, Randy came back over to the table and said, "After this last song, we are going to take you to the best nightclub in Hollywood."

I was not much into the club scene and did not want to go. I replied, "Randy, I really do appreciate all this, but please don't feel like y'all have to take me out. I promise- I am good. Besides, I have to leave with your granddaddy bright and early in the morning."

Randy laughed before saying in a very slow, and intentional, country sounding accent, "Well, Y'all ain't worried about YOU.

Y'all wants to have a good time, so don't be a party pooper for Y'all. You get my drift, Coach?"

Less than thirty minutes later we were standing in line at Hollywood's newest and hottest night spot, the Spice Club. While we were waiting in line, I could tell that Ava was already showing signs of being intoxicated. She stumbled on the Hollywood Boulevard sidewalk, almost falling into oncoming traffic. Randy was not much better as he became a little mouthy with the bouncer of the Spice Club, who was checking identification. I quickly interceded and smoothed things over with the big bouncer. Once we were inside of the club, the end of Bon Jovi's hit song, "Bad Medicine" was blaring at a deafening level. I was amazed at the wild scene on a Monday night. This place was crazier than what I had seen or experienced at Barney's Beanery. Some of the most gorgeous girls I had ever seen seemed to outnumber the guys by a long shot. Right as we were making our way toward the bar, the place erupted when the song, "Wild, Wild, West" by The Escape Club was played by the DJ. People who weren't even on the dance floor began singing the words to the song as if they were participating along with a college fight song. It appeared to me that this was the theme song for Hollywood. It was so loud that it was difficult to hear the person standing next to you.

Within five minutes, Ava and Randy disappeared into the crowd. There were so many people jammed up against each other,

I knew a fire marshal would not be happy. I tried in vain to find my cousins. Before I knew it, I was hauled onto the dance floor by a wild, Pat Benatar looking woman dressed in all black. She would not let go of my arm. I reluctantly obliged her request to dance. We danced fast, and we danced furiously. She grabbed my rear end several times. She even tried to lick my eyebrows. I knew without a doubt that she wanted more of me than being a dance partner. I thought about my girlfriend back in Tallahassee before I pulled away from that wild woman who seemed possessed, determined, and willing to do anything to latch onto me. When she asked me if I wanted to do some cocaine, I ended the conversation and abruptly walked away.

After searching the place for quite some time, I finally found Randy passed out in the lap of a young woman with a Valley Girl accent. Her bloodshot eyes perfectly matched her tight fitting red mini skirt. She was so high that she looked to be insane. She spoke with such a high pitch; it sounded like she was speaking a foreign language. She kept saying phrases which all began with the word "like". She kept saying, "Like, what a party dude! Like, you're so hot, man! Like, this is totally awesome, man!"

I was barely able to interpret her scattered speech pattern. Finally, I was able to understand that she wanted to take Randy home with her, when she said, "Like, totally. Like Randio can go home-io with me-o."

After reviving my cousin enough for him to be able to walk, I literally began dragging Randy away from a Valley girl who called herself Tish the Wish. As I pulled Randy through the Sodom and Gomorrah known as the Spice Club, I saw Ava all the way across the dance floor. She was dancing with an Asian guy, who looked almost old enough to be her father. By the time I made my way over to her, I could tell that she was out of her mind. As I kept Randy propped up next to me, I yelled at Ava to come with us. Her Asian dance partner kept smiling, and dancing slowly in one spot. He repeatedly yelled at me, "She is hot, man…She is hot."

I kept trying to make her leave with us. He kept pulling on her arm saying, "She mine. She mine."

The situation almost became ugly when I pushed him away and yelled, "Hey, look here, Pops… If you don't let her go with me, I will kick your ass."

Ava was so out of it, she didn't have enough sense to know if she was coming or going. The walk to Randy's car, which was parked two blocks away, was the tale of a man from Shady Branch, Florida, trying his best to tame two wild cousins on Hollywood Boulevard. They wanted to go back into the Spice Club. Ava yelled at me, "The hell with you, redneck boy. You can't tell us what to do." She then suddenly tried to hug me and apologize. I shoved her back so forcefully I was afraid I had injured her. Several F- bombs were dropped. She and her brother were in a pathetic state of mind. I avoided several physical altercations with both of them. Ten minutes later, I was finally able to find Randy's car. Before throwing my cousins into the Mercedes, it took me at least five minutes to retrieve the car keys from Randy.

During our journey to their home, I was forced to stop twice to wake them up for directions to Bell Canyon. I pulled over once for Ava so she could puke on the side of the road. Randy later begged me to pull over at a 7-Eleven convenience store so he could use the restroom. By the time we had taken several wrong turns in Reseda, I had seen enough of the greater Los Angeles metropolitan area.

Around 2:30 a.m., I finally pulled into their driveway. I woke up my impaired cousins and helped them out of the Mercedes. I shushed them several times as Randy and Ava giggled and spoke loudly enough to wake the neighbors. Once we entered the back door through a large glassed-in porch, my stumbling college-aged cousins were met in the den by their disapproving parents. They sobered up momentarily while their mother whispered loudly, "You all should be ashamed of yourselves. This is not what we do in this house."

The esteemed Doctor of Theology, Dr. Royce Lee, then whispered, "Keep your voices down. You will wake up GP."

From behind him a voice cried out, "You can forget that, Son. The G and the P are wide awake."

While Uncle Dean entered the den, Randy yelled, "I know this looks bad, but Tim is the one who made us take him to all of the bars in Hollywood. I swear on Gigi's grave that we did not want to party. He…"

The oldest person in the house then interrupted Randy by saying, "Don't be swearin' on my wife's grave, you little punk. I don't care who is at fault- I'm leavin' for Florida in three hours, so I suggest that Tim gets a little shut eye before we depart."

CHAPTER NINE

Three hours later, I was abruptly poked in the side of my ribs by Uncle Dean. My grandmother's only sibling yelled, "You have fifteen minutes to shave, shower, crap, and whatever else you need to do before we head to Florida."

There was no fanfare or long goodbyes when Uncle Dean and I began our cross-country trip to Shady Branch, Florida. All of my cousins were still asleep at 5:15 a.m. I tried to make Uncle Dean wake up the rest of the family to tell them goodbye; Dean Lee refused. He said, "No time for another fight with them."

Dressed as if he were heading out for a safari, the eighty-two-year-old retired attorney, welder, and farmer from Alabama-climbed into the twenty-four-foot orange U-Haul cab. He was carrying an army issued knapsack filled with various items including crackers, fresh fruit, a WWII era canteen, and a Rand

McNally Atlas. I couldn't help but laugh before asking him, "Are you sure you didn't leave anything behind?"

Uncle Dean snapped back at me, "I had this dang U-Haul packed and ready two days ago. No thanks to anyone who lives here."

Before I put the U-Haul in gear, I read the bright orange warning sticker on the cab's console: WHEN TOWING- DO NOT EXCEED 45 miles per hour. I then began to wonder if we would ever make such a long drive traveling so slow. I took the time to adjust the side mirrors because I had never hauled a car behind a truck.

Uncle Dean yelled, "Hurry up, Tim. We need to be on the road before we hit big traffic."

It was still dark outside when I began a slow departure from Bell Canyon. On the freeway, Uncle Dean cried out, "The hell with that 45 mile per hour bullcrap. Put the pedal to it, or I may be dead before we make it to Florida."

I laughed before asking, "You don't want me to get a speeding ticket, do you?"

In a somewhat defiant tone, he replied, "I'll take my chances. If you get pulled over, I will pay for the ticket. For Pete's sake, at least try to hit seventy miles per hour."

As soon as I began to speed up, he gave me the thumbs up sign before saying, "For your information, I wanted you to know that Roy and Linda didn't believe a word that came out of Randy's mouth when y'all stumbled in last night. That is not the first time my grandchildren have come in late, smellin' like they had been swimmin' in a barrel of whiskey. Both of them are spoiled rotten. I blame Linda for that. She would never make them do any real work. My sweet Emma Jean worried herself to death over those grandchildren."

He then pulled out his Rand McNally Atlas and an empty plastic milk jug from his knapsack. He took a quick look at a map of California before saying, "Once we make it past Pasadena, it will be clear sailing all the way to New Mexico."

"What's with the empty milk container?" I asked.

He replied, "If we had to pull over every time I had to take a leak, it would take us a month to make it to Florida. Ever since my prostate started acting up, I have to go all the time."

A few minutes later, we rode by the largest cemetery I had ever seen. Uncle Dean laughed and said, "People are dyin' today that have never died before." He paused and continued, "My grandfather used to say that every time we rode by a graveyard. It always cracked me up."

I certainly did not think he was funny. Out of respect, I listened as he described his impoverished upbringing in Alabama. He explained about how corn pone and fresh ground grits were a staple of his diet as a young man. I almost gagged when he said, "There were many mornings on that farm where I would run into the chicken coop and find a fresh 'egg on the go'." He laughed for no apparent reason before stating, "Yes, siree, bobcat tail... You haven't lived until you suck the yoke of a raw egg right out of the shell and then go plow with a mule for three hours before you take a break."

Almost bragging, he spoke about being so thirsty he would sometimes suck the leather reins of his plow mule as he broke ground in fields where his only contact with life were the birds who flew in the sky. His description of cotton boll weevils as the worst enemy he had to fight when he was fifteen years old brought a smile to my face. His explanation of how a rat bit him on his big toe one night while sleeping on a pallet on the floor of their small home was hilarious.

He then began sharing a plethora of random thoughts, by saying, "Through the years, I have noticed several things. Whenever you think you have solved all of life's problems; trust me, you have not. Even the best man on earth faced trials and tribulations. Always remember, the redemption of one person has the power to redeem many others who will cross that person's path in life. The best food can sometimes be found in places where you would feel more comfortable changing your oil or a flat tire. When people die, their earthly possessions can cause more heartache than anyone could ever predict. One jealous family member wanting Grandma's jewelry or antique armoire can cause family members to never speak again. Trust me on this one! A good lap dog is the best investment you can ever purchase. That lap dog will always love you and never judge you. And the best advice I can ever give you is- Making laps around a Chinese Buffet is the best exercise known to man." He then paused and continued by saying, "You are too young to understand this now, but the older you become, you will build up a resistance to bullcrap. You will feel empowered to say whatever is on your mind without worrying what people think. There will come a time in your life when you will have no problem looking someone in the eye and telling them that they are full of crap." He smiled before saying prophetically, "Our society is headed for a rude awakening. When ball players and entertainers make more money than the President of the United States; our priorities are definitely misplaced and out of whack."

He kept talking about various subjects. For the most part, I ignored what he had to say, thinking to myself that the old man was losing his mind. He then reached over and pushed me on my shoulder while saying, "You better always remember this- A person who chooses not to read is a person who chooses not to succeed. For me, the Bible ranks at the top of my list. After the Bible, I enjoy reading articles from *Reader's Digest* and *Newsweek*. I can honestly say that I still enjoy reading novels by Mark Twain, William Faulkner, Ernest Hemmingway, and Harper Lee in no particular order. Although, I don't believe everything the *Old Farmer's Almanac* says about planting and harvesting; I have to say that publication still ranks as one of my top choices for obvious reasons." He paused for a moment and then continued, "At least once a year, I make myself re-read portions of the autobiographies of Ben Franklin, Frederick Douglass, Abraham Lincoln, Anne Frank, and George Patton."

I interrupted him asking, "Since you like to read about Patton, did you ever serve in the military?"

"No, I did not. But I would have if I could of."

He then explained to me that he was too young for World War I. He was too blind in one eye and hobbled on one knee from a bucking mule kicking him when he was sixteen, which made him ineligible to serve in World War II. By the time the Korean Conflict and Vietnam rolled around he was too old. He told me that on the Tuesday after Pearl Harbor was bombed, he drove over to Florence, Alabama and tried to enlist. After going through the army physical, some fast talking army doctor from New Jersey marked a big 4-F in red letters on his chart. Uncle Dean had no idea what that meant. The army doctor patted him on the back and told him to go check out with a pencil-pushing corporal sitting next to the door. The corporal looked at his chart and thanked Uncle Dean for his willingness to serve. Uncle Dean asked him where he needed to report, and the corporal told him to hit the road.

Uncle Dean argued with the corporal for a few minutes before a major came over and explained that he was not fit to serve because of his teen injuries. Uncle Dean tried to tell the major that although he was legally blind in one eye, he was the best shot in his community. The major didn't seem to care that Uncle Dean had a freezer full of squirrels, doves, quail, and wild turkeys from a successful hunting season. Uncle Dean told him that if he could shoot a dove or a quail with his bad eye, then by God, he could certainly shoot a Jap or a German with a high-powered rifle. Uncle Dean went back twice more, and each time he was marked 4-F.

He said, "To this day, my rejection to serve in World War II still burns me up."

I asked, "I'm a little surprised that you read about Frederick Douglass. Why do you read about him?"

With a serious look on his face he replied, "When I read his autobiography in 1947, it changed my life."

"Get out of here. How did that book change your life?"

He replied, "I can tell you have never read it because when you do, you begin to understand the pain and suffering that our Black brothers and sisters endured during slavery. Before I read the Frederick Douglass story, I had no real understanding of how brutal the whole slavery experience was for those who came to this country. Trust me. When you read it, your life will be changed."

I replied, "I don't know about that."

Uncle Dean calmly responded, "What happened here in this country is unthinkable. As a young man growing up in the South, I did not think much about race relations until I read that book.

Then when the Civil Rights Movement began, particularly in Birmingham, it made me sick to watch what was happening in my own state. The only way that race relations will ever improve in this nation is if people will talk about it with an open heart and mind. Those who refuse to listen to the plight of their neighbors will never fully receive the blessings that God has in store for them."

I did not know how to respond and kept driving. After changing lanes to allow an eighteen-wheeler to enter the interstate off the entrance ramp, I glanced over at Uncle Dean. I saw him unbuckling his seat belt. He then began to slide his body up toward the roof of the truck's cabin, before he began to unzip his pants.

I screamed, "Whoa, Unk... What in the hell are you doin'?"

He yelled back at me, "When a man has to go- a man has to go."

I yelled, "Stop it right now. I will pull over."

He shouted back, "We don't have time for that. You just keep drivin', and don't look over here."

He then proceeded to urinate into the empty milk container while motorists in both adjacent lanes passed by the U-Haul. When one car blew their horn at us, I knew that Uncle Dean had been exposing himself to a handful of horrified drivers.

After he zipped up, and slid back down in his seat, I did not know what to say or think. I felt awkward. I was certain that he was not in his right mind. Several minutes later, I asked, "So tell me again why you and Aunt Emma Jean decided to move to Los Angeles. Didn't it have somethin' to with her health?"

At first, he did not reply while he pulled out his pipe from his shirt pocket and began filling it with tobacco. Once he lit a match, and was able to fire up his pipe, he proceeded by explaining to me that his wife, Emma Jean was a very sick woman. She was suffering from a bad case of asthma. Her physician in Alabama informed them that the only thing that would help her would be if she lived in a warm, dry climate. Once Uncle Dean made it home from the doctor's office, he called his son Roy. He-explained the situation and talked to his son about the possibility of them moving to California and living with them. A month later, Uncle Dean sold the farm and started driving the love of his life to California. Once they arrived in West Texas and spent a few days there, Uncle Dean began to notice a change in Emma Jean's breathing. The change in climate helped her tremendously. It was like she had found the fountain of youth. By the time they made it to California a week later, her condition was remarkably better. Emma Jean quickly fell in love with California. The weather along with being around her grandchildren brought her more joy and happiness than any drug a doctor could have prescribed.

While changing lanes, I asked, "I take it that you did not like California?"

Before he could answer, I interrupted him, "So that is the famous Rose Bowl. I wish we had time to take a tour. When I was a small kid, I dreamed about playing in that stadium on New Year's Day."

He did not reply so I decided to stay the course and keep driving. I then asked, "Hey Unk, did you ever like anything about California after living here all these years?"

He paused before replying, "I don't regret moving here for Emma Jean, but honestly, I always felt like I was cooped up in a place that was as foreign to me as Shanghai. There are a hundred things I could tell you, but the simple answer is that me and California didn't hit it off. Of course, the weather is fabulous, the girls are pretty, and the soil is good for gardens, but other than that, I could care less if I ever see this place again."

I said, "You know that your grandchildren told me that you wanted to die in the South. I hope you don't mind if I ask you why that is so important to you."

He replied, "I did tell them that I wanted to die in the South. What I should have said to them was that I wanted to live my last days in the South. After I spent a year in California, I became homesick. Sure, I met some really nice folks in California, but most of the people I encountered were always in a rush. Roy and his family are no different. They are all too busy trying to advance in their careers or their social standing."

He further explained that from what he remembered, things moved much slower in the South. He missed the little nuances about the South that many people took for granted. He spoke about people in the rural sections of the South doing things like waving at each other when they passed someone on a highway or bringing a neighbor something to eat when there was sickness or death. In his nostalgic view of the old days, he told me that people in the South seemed to place a bigger emphasis on family, friends, and manners. The manners part of his explanation seemed to be something that really bothered him.

He said, "One of the first things that I had to get used to when I moved to California was the number of people who used the F word as a common part of their vocabulary. I've known sailors who talk better in public than some of the checkout clerks I have encountered in Los Angeles."

He explained that he did not remember hearing that kind of vulgar talk in public places throughout the South. I didn't want to upset him, but I already knew that particular part of the Southern culture was changing.

Uncle Dean then explained that he noticed how the young people he encountered in Los Angeles talked back to their parents in a disrespectful way. He had witnessed small children in stores cuss out their parents without the threat of retribution. This seemed to weigh heavy on his mind.

Then as he further explained his love for the South, he wanted me to know he had missed the simple kind of interaction with family and friends you sometimes find in small Southern towns. He pridefully reminded me that a person can go to any small town in the South and find some kind of historical themed festival or celebration where the whole town comes together. His explanation of Southern towns centering celebrations around food like barbeque, boiled peanuts, grits, sweet potatoes, watermelon, fried chicken or fried fish had not changed. He also wanted me to understand that the celebrations were not so much about the food; they were about community involvement. He noted several times that he desperately missed the feeling of being a part of a big extended family he once remembered.

He finally explained to me that only in the South will you find people who are willing to tell their family history along with their secrets to anyone that will take the time to listen. He said, "Trust me. You will never find any of that type of social interaction in Los Angeles."

I laughed at him and tried to change the subject. Uncle Dean beat me to the punch when he began talking about his gardening operation in Bell Canyon, which he claimed annually produced in the neighborhood of twenty thousand dollars a year. I believed he was exaggerating and full of crap. I thought to myself that there was no way a backyard garden could produce so much income.

An hour later while I was listening to a predicted explanation about how Uncle Dean became friends with Jamie Farr, traffic slowed down to a snail's pace near the city of Loma Linda, California. Road construction crews were repaving a long section of the interstate as traffic was being diverted into three lanes which soon turned into one. Several times we came to a complete stop. Each time we would stop, I would sarcastically say, "It's not too late for me to turn around and take you back to Bell Canyon."

He would reply, "I'd hate to shoot my own grandnephew."

CHAPTER TEN

Time was ticking away, and the road construction was hindering Uncle Dean's original goal of making it through the middle of New Mexico by the end of the day. An hour later when traffic began to move more than five miles per hour, I realized that we were way behind his schedule. Once we were in the clear near Calimesa, California, Uncle Dean began laughing.

I asked, "What's so funny?"

He snickered a second more before saying, "That orange highway sign back there that read: End Construction. Whoever came up with that must have been drinkin' or tryin' to save money."

"Why do you say that?" I asked.

He slowly cracked his window before saying, "Because that sign makes no sense. Technically the sign should read-

Construction Ended or End of Construction, or better yet-Leaving Construction Zone. One could interpret the present sign to mean that we should end all construction. The way it reads now is definitely confusing." He laughed again and said, "I bet you a hundred dolla's that there have been some good ole boys who have wondered what fool put out those signs. They were probably scratchin' their heads tryin' to figure out who it was that was actually tryin' to end all construction work. I am sure that some poor soul has wondered if their construction job was in jeopardy."

I then tried to explain the story I had been told by Eston Harper concerning that same warning sign. I could tell Uncle Dean was not interested as he kept talking about how the government had some strange ideas when it came to highway safety. He continued to ramble.

I paid him no attention as we were nearing Palm Springs and the exit toward Joshua Tree National Park. We stopped at an upscale Exxon gas station convenience store a few miles outside of Palm Springs. While I was climbing out of the truck, I noticed him pulling a .38 caliber revolver out of his knapsack. I shouted, "Why do you have a gun?"

"You don't think I'm going into that place without some protection?" he replied without hesitation.

"Unk… I'm not sure that is a good idea. That gun might go off. You might accidentally shoot yourself."

Perplexed by my statement, he yelled at me, "Hell, boy, I've been handlin' guns longer than you have been alive." He then hopped out of the cab of the U-Haul, gently slid the pistol into his pocket, and began walking to the front door of the convenience store. While I filled up the U-Haul truck with gas, I began pondering more about his sanity. In all reality, I did not really know this man at all. He may have been family, but for all I knew, he could be insane. Urinating in front of God and Country was my first clue that he may have some mental issues. Taking a gun into a convenience store was the second clue that my great uncle was not operating on all cylinders. Then suddenly, the worst thought came to my mind- What if? Oh, my God. What if… What if he was committing an armed robbery? I quickly screwed on the gas cap to the U-Haul and ran into the Exxon convenience store.

Once inside the store, I was relieved to see that he was talking and laughing with the store clerk. The store clerk was a slightly overweight, short, middle-aged, Native American lady. From behind the counter, she laughed before saying to Uncle Dean, "I can tell you broke some hearts when you were younger."

He laughed back at her before saying, "You are more than welcome to leave this palace and move with me to Florida, my queen."

The Native American lady handed him back his credit card, laughing at him before saying, "I certainly would leave right this minute, but who in their right mind would leave this paradise of a place where I work; the Exxon station?"

I then thought to myself that my mother would love it if we showed up in Shady Branch with another house guest. Relieved there was no armed robbery taking place, I walked into the restroom. As I washed my hands, I looked into the soap splattered restroom mirror. Although I could barely see myself in the mirror, I could tell I needed a shave. I then began to worry about the possibility of spending a few nights in the same motel room with a man, who was carrying a gun. I wondered what I had gotten myself into on this journey.

***

We were back on the interstate when I decided to ask Uncle Dean a loaded question that weighed heavy on my mind. I asked, "Before we make it back to Florida, I would like to know why you have never visited with my grandmother or why she has never visited you. She has lived a hard life, and I don't understand why you two never made time to visit each other when I was growing up."

He replied, "I tried several times, but she is the one who never wanted me to come and visit."

I was puzzled because I had always been told by my family that Uncle Dean was the one who didn't have time to visit. I kept pressing by saying, "Now that doesn't make any sense. My entire life, my mother made you out to be the one who was always busy with important work. She made you out to be a saint. I know for a fact…" I then paused and realized that it was indeed my mother who spoke so highly of her uncle. I couldn't remember a time when my grandmother had anything really nice to say about her own brother. My grandmother spoke more about the other side of my extended family than she did about her own brother.

Before I could continue, Uncle Dean said, "We had a fallin' out which I regret more than ever. That is one of the reasons I want to move to Florida. I figure I can spend time with my sister and help your mother out. Your grandmother is quite a lady. She and I need this time to make up for lost time." He then looked at me and said, "I have been prayin' that she will forgive me. I am hopin' to spend our last days together like brothers and sisters are supposed to do."

I asked, "What is the big secret? What did you do to make her so upset with you?"

He replied, "I will tell you later. Before I forget, you need to know that there is a big brown folder case in the trunk of my car. Inside that case is a record of everything I own. It contains my checkbook, my savings account information, the title to my car, all of my life insurance policies, and my last will and testament. You need to make sure that you don't forget about it if something were to happen to me on the way to Florida."

While he was talking, we passed the Arizona Welcomes You sign. I noticed the cactus and the vast amount of open desert land

and another roadside sign which caught my attention. It read: Caution: High Winds May Tip Trailer Trucks. I could care less about all the fuss Uncle Dean made over the End Construction signs. This particular highway warning sign made perfect sense to me. I then began to worry about the U-Haul truck tipping over if we encountered heavy winds. A few minutes later, I then tried again to find out the family secret concerning the relationship of my grandmother and her only sibling.

Uncle Dean avoided the subject by asking, "Tell me about your football days at State. That Coach Brown must be the real deal. I bet you loved playing for him."

Intentionally sidetracked, I obliged and began talking about playing at State. I said, "You may not remember this, but I was on the scout team my first two years. I never saw the field. Finally, during my junior year, I dressed out in the home opener against Memphis State. I played a total of two snaps as a tight end in the first two offensive series of the game. I can honestly say that when I looked up and saw the crowd in that big stadium, it was one of the most fantastic feelings I have ever experienced. In the second quarter, my football career came to a screeching halt when I went down to cover a punt. Out of nowhere, I was blindsided by a linebacker from Memphis State. That hit destroyed everything in my right knee. At first, the team doctors said I would be able to play again by the end of the season; however, after two surgeries, and countless hours of rehab, the doctors finally met with me and told me that it was never going to happen. Coach Brown was gracious. He allowed me to hang around my senior year to assist the coaches without losing my football scholarship money. That is how I ended up in the coaching profession."

Uncle Dean asked, "Did you ever consider coachin' in the college ranks?"

I replied, "That is a good question. I talked to one of the assistant coaches named Mike Morris. He told me that if I wanted to be living out of a suitcase, spending most of my time away from home, and willing to gamble that I might be fired any day, then I should consider it. He then pointed at a graduate assistant named Matt Wright. Coach Morris reminded me that they had Matt running around Tallahassee like a chicken with his head cut off in hopes that he would one day be a full-time assistant coach. I talked to Matt a long time about it and at the time, he wasn't even sure if he was going to continue down that career path himself. After talking with him several more times, I decided that the high school ranks would suit me better. Coach Brown made one phone call to North Tallahassee High School before I graduated. I hate to admit this, but I know I was hired before I actually interviewed for the job. Coach Brown's referral was good enough for them. I will never be able to thank Coach Brown enough for what he has done for me on and off the field."

Uncle Dean quipped, "It sounds like you have it all figured out in a roundabout way."

"Not exactly. I don't know… There are days when I can't wait to be a head coach. Then there are other days when I think I will never be ready to be in charge of an entire program. I also sometimes think that I should be doing something else for a livin'."

He asked, "What else would you want to do?"

I paused and thought for a few seconds before saying, "I'm not sure, but I met a man last night in Hollywood, who wants to interview me for a sales job with Carnation Milk."

As the Arizona desert winds became a little stronger, I found myself worrying about the U-Haul tipping over while conversing with a man a few hours before I wasn't sure had all of his marbles. Uncle Dean's advice about career choices was a breath of fresh air when he told me, "Money is a wonderful thing. Prestige and power drive some people to do great things, but the most important thing to remember is that you, Tim Jackson, have to love what you do. Look at me. I worked three jobs during my career. Everyone assumed I did it because I was forced to do it for financial reasons. The truth of the matter is that I enjoyed being a welder. I was challenged beyond my wildest dreams as an attorney, but I absolutely loved farming more than you will ever know. To this day, the most inspirational thing I have experienced in my career was when I would go out on the farm on a cold frosty mornin' and look at a calf walkin' with its mother. Watching a Hereford eat hay from your hand can only be described as a spiritual awakening. For me, walking through a row of freshly sprouted corn stalks near sundown and smelling the scent of honeysuckles in the spring is as close to God as a man could ever be. I absolutely loved everything about the farm. For you, however, there is nothin' wrong with you tryin' out somethin' new. You already know you like coaching. If you decide to take a sales job, and things don't work out, you can always go back to the coaching profession. If you wake up each day and miss coaching so much it hurts, you will know that coaching is in your blood. Who knows, you may fall in love with being a salesman. I say you have nothing to lose by at least goin' on an interview."

As we kept talking, mainly about my life, I realized that Uncle Dean was making a lot of sense. By the time we decided to stop and eat at a small diner near the Arizona town of Buckeye, I was convinced that Uncle Dean was as sane as anyone I knew. As we made our way out of the U-Haul cab, I politely asked Uncle Dean to leave his pistol in the truck.

He replied loudly, "I'm sorry, Son, but Mr. .38 Special travels with me wherever I go."

Once we were finally seated in the diner, we were waiting on our drinks when we overheard a woman sitting behind us, asking her husband, "Did you see that sign they have up near Fork Ridge Road? It said- End Construction. Can you believe that?"

Her husband replied, "Yeah, it didn't surprise me. Those communists want to end all the construction jobs around here."

We began laughing. Uncle Dean then leaned close to me and whispered, "I told you those signs are confusin'."

After we walked through the lunch buffet line and sat back down at our table, we heard a man two tables away start cussing at a young waitress. The man said, "I don't give a …. what you thought. You can kiss my…"

Everyone in the place became quiet. To my surprise, Uncle Dean slowly rose from his chair and yelled at the man who appeared to be a biker. Uncle Dean cried out, "That is no way to talk up in here. There are ladies and small children present for Pete's sake."

I slowly turned around in my chair. I could see the Hispanic biker sitting with several rough looking friends. I just knew we were about to fight. The biker, who was sporting a long beard and several large silver chains around his neck, stood up from his chair and yelled, "What did you say, Old Man?"

Uncle Dean stood up straighter, and calmly replied, "You heard me. Now clean up that ugly talk or be on your way. There is never any need for a man to talk like that around women and small children."

I couldn't believe Uncle Dean had decided to challenge the tough looking man. I felt that at any moment a gun battle was about to take place inside the diner. The biker then took a few steps toward an eighty-two-year-old man, who I knew was carrying a gun. Uncle Dean steadily warned, "Now hold on, partner. You take one more step, and I will blow you to kingdom come." Uncle Dean then slowly began to pull out his trusty .38 Special.

The biker stopped walking. He slowly held up his hands and said, "Sir, I apologize for what I said. You are right. Please forgive me. I am having a bad day. We will be on our way."

As soon as the biker and his friends left the diner, everyone inside stood up and gave Uncle Dean a standing ovation. The manager of the diner insisted that we eat our meals for free.

I was on an emotional rollercoaster ride. I honestly did not know what to think. On one hand, I was proud that Uncle Dean had stood up to the abrasive talking man. On the other hand, I wasn't sure if Uncle Dean was a genius or plain off his rocker. After finishing our free meals, I looked hard around the parking lot to make sure the biker, and his friends did not have a change of heart. Once we were back inside of the U-Haul truck, Uncle Dean laughed before saying, "I can't get over that couple talkin' about the End Construction sign."

I yelled, "You can't get over them talking about a road sign? What about you almost gettin' us killed in that place? You pullin' out a pistol in public is not cool."

He calmly replied, "You are right, Tim. I should have loaded my gun before we went inside. I promise the next time we stop somewhere I will not forget to put in the bullets."

"You mean to tell me that you pulled a gun on that man, and you didn't have it loaded?"

He replied, "Trust me, Tim, when I tell you that Mr. 38 Special doesn't need a bullet to make a lasting impression."

I was not happy. I said nothing as we drove past Phoenix. To avoid any conversation with the man that I thought put my life in jeopardy, I found Phoenix's largest rock station, KSLX on the U-Haul's radio. After the hit song, "Every Rose Has Its Thorn" by Poison finished playing, Uncle Dean said, "Now that is a pretty good song. I could actually understand the words to that one."

I did not reply. I kept driving. The DJ from KSLX then said, "It's a slightly breezy afternoon and 51 degrees in downtown Phoenix." He then cried out, "Now it's time for the segment we call Stupid Facts You Will Never Forget." Then a loud deep voice accompanied with silly sounding music and an echo sound effect came blaring over the radio, "Stupid Facts You Will… Never Forget… Never Forget…Never Forget.".

I tuned out the voice of the DJ momentarily until the DJ closed the show by saying, "Did you know that adult cats do not meow at other adult cats? Scientists say that cats only meow at each other when a mother cat meows at her baby cats. Bottom line- adult cats do not communicate verbally with each other."

Uncle Dean laughed and said, "Now that is somethin' I will never forget."

I did not respond to him about the stupid radio segment. The DJ on KSLX then said, "In national news today, December 27, 1988, the headliner is that Governor Bob Martinez of Florida says that he will not block the execution of convicted serial killer, Ted Bundy; scheduled to be electrocuted next month."

Uncle Dean interrupted the rest of the news broadcast when he said," Now that is a shame. God alone needs to be the judge of that man."

I turned off the radio and angrily replied, "I know you don't believe what just came out of your mouth. A man that carries a gun with him surely doesn't believe that Ted Bundy shouldn't be put to death."

He replied, "I might carry a gun with me, but I have never fired it at anyone. Hell, I can't remember the last time I had it loaded."

I was not amused when I replied, "You know you could have caused us to be killed back there at that diner. Pulling that stunt with your pistol was insane."

He responded in a soft voice, "I know you're a little upset with me right now, but hopefully you will see that my intentions were good."

I was very aggravated and couldn't let it go when I asked, "Do you really believe that Ted Bundy should be allowed to live?"

He paused momentarily before responding, "The church does not think we should be the ones who carry out executions."

I asked, "What church?"

He replied, "The only church that will get you into Heaven."

"What church is that?" I asked.

"The Church of Christ," he replied.

I raised my voice asking, "You mean to tell me that you really think that the only way to Heaven is to be a member of the Church of Christ?"

"Yes, sir. It's the only way."

I became even more aggravated when I said, "Well, I hate to break the news to you, but everyone in my family, who actually attends church, is a member of the Methodist denomination. That would include your sister. She has been a member of the Methodist…"

Uncle Dean interrupted me, "I know. I know. That is one of the reasons why we haven't talked much over the years."

I lit into him, "Let me get this straight. You believe that if your sister does not convert to the Church of Christ, then she is eternally doomed?"

Uncle Dean nodded in affirmation before saying, "I hope not, but that is the way I have been taught, and that is my belief."

In total disbelief I asked, "A self-educated man like yourself, who knows about the law, reads books, and studies history can actually look me in the eye, and tell me that my grandmother is headed to Hell if she doesn't go through some archaic formality of joining your church?"

He replied, "I'm not movin' to Florida to judge you or your family, Tim; however, I do pray that all of you will see the light before it is too late." He then paused before saying, "The scripture says- Judge not lest ye be judged."

The religious debate continued for several more minutes as darkness began to prevail over the Arizona landscape while we passed Tucson. I finally gave up arguing with a man I wasn't sure had all of his marbles. In my mind, I knew Ted Bundy was going to fry whether Uncle Dean believed he should or not. I also knew that my grandmother was going to be all right on Judgment Day.

Turning up the volume of the radio, I couldn't help but laugh when that song was being played again. I thought to myself, "I can't escape this crazy song, 'Wild, Wild, West'." I knew then that it was the theme song for my cross-country adventure with an eighty-two-year-old man.

CHAPTER ELEVEN

Although I was weary from a very long drive and a late night in Hollywood, I would have kept driving a few more hours if Uncle Dean hadn't insisted that we stop once we crossed the New Mexico state line. He pointed out a motel off the interstate. After I pulled into the parking lot of the small 1940s era motel outside of Lordsburg, I noticed the catchy name of the place, which was simply, MOTEL. I was not impressed by the sign next to the front door of the office which read: Free- Color TV and Free- Swimming Pool.

I stood beside the U-Haul while Uncle Dean walked to check in at the motel's office. I then spotted a streetlamp shining on a phone booth at the back of the property. It was located next to a large cactus plant growing right beside a rusted barbed wire fence. I hustled over to the phone booth, noticing that the 'free' pool was covered in algae and thick green slime. Inside the phone booth, I made a collect call to my mother in Shady Branch. While I was waiting for her to accept the charges, I noticed a large desert rat poking his head up against the bottom of the phone booth's retractable door. I yelled, "Get away from here you crazy rat."

My mother on the other end of the line yelled, "Tim, who are you talking to?"

"I'm sorry, Mom."

I then explained myself to her before quickly changing the subject. I said, "I can't talk long, but I can tell you that your uncle is one crazy dude. Whenever we arrive at Shady Branch, you need to have him committed or put in a nursing home."

She replied, "Wow, Tim. That is a pretty harsh analysis of my only uncle, but you are not telling me anything I didn't already know. He may be a little eccentric, but you would have to admit that he is harmless."

I yelled, "Are you kidding me? Did you know he carries a gun with him?"

My mother yelled back, "So what! I know plenty of people in Shady Branch who carry a gun with them. That doesn't make them certifiable."

I looked up and noticed that Uncle Dean was walking toward the U-Haul. I told my mother that I had to hang up. I then quickly made my way back to the U-Haul where Uncle Dean was already opening the trunk of his car. He looked at me and asked, "What were you doin' over there? I bet you were callin' your mother and telling' her that I was a crazy old fool."

I felt myself begin to blush before replying, "No, sir. I was just letting her know that we had made it to New Mexico."

He grumbled something I could not hear before saying clearly, "Let's go eat. We can't drive across the country on empty stomachs."

After eating at a small meat and three across the street where he talked to the waitress and the manager like he had known them for years, we walked back to our motel room. While I waited for him to take a shower, I walked back across the parking lot to the payphone to call my girlfriend, Maria.

Ten minutes of meaningless conversation went by faster than expected. Maria politely interrupted me and said, "You know I love you, too, but I'm going to hate myself when my MCI phone bill comes in next month. I sure will hate myself if I have to pay for a big phone bill for both of us saying that we love each other over and over again. Good night, Tim."

I then walked back to the room and showered. When I entered the room after my shower, I noticed Uncle Dean laying on one of the squeakiest beds in the great state of New Mexico. Whenever he moved, it sounded like he was trying to start up a chain saw. My bed was worse when I flopped down on it. A few minutes later, I jumped out of my bed and tried to turn on an ancient looking television set with no success. Uncle Dean walked over to the antique television, turned a few knobs on the back of the set, and adjusted the rabbit ears enough so we could receive decent reception from a CBS affiliate station out of Tucson. We watched a fuzzy commercial advertising for an ambulance chasing, local lawyer, who called his law firm the Accident Patrol. Uncle Dean laughed when the lawyer on the commercial said, "Call the Accident Patrol if you need a roll of fresh green cash!"

Uncle Dean sat down on his squeaking bed before saying, "I saw one of those types of commercials in Los Angeles last week. I can't believe anyone would ever hire one of those sleazy guys. I guarantee you those commercials won't air long because those lawyers will never be able to keep clients."

I did not reply.

After watching about ten minutes of a late night "Star Trek" episode rerun, Uncle Dean slid out of the bed and turned off the television. He fumbled around his nightstand, set his personal alarm clock, and turned off the lamp next to his bed. He then said, "Good night, Tim. I hope that you and I can patch up our relationship before we make it to Florida."

I mumbled, "Good night." I then thought how much I was hating that I ever agreed to come on this godforsaken trip.

***

The next morning, I woke up to the sound of an old-fashioned, Baby Ben alarm clock at 5:30 a.m. I rolled over and asked, "Do we really need to leave so early?"

He replied, "It's time to get a move on, Tim. The weather in these parts can be so unpredictable. If we are lucky, we can avoid any major winter storms. The last thing we need is to be caught in a blizzard or an ice storm. We need to push on through Texas as far as we can drive. You know it is almost impossible to drive across Texas in a day."

On the outskirts of town, we stopped at a gas station which was located next to a McDonald's. While Uncle Dean filled up the U-Haul, I ran over to McDonald's and bought a couple of Egg McMuffins and some coffee. Back on the interstate, Uncle Dean could tell that I was still not very talkative. To break the ice, he began to pry into my personal life by asking, "So your mother tells me that you are pretty serious with that girl from Pensacola. Is she the one you intend to marry?"

"I think so," I replied.

"You think so? What is her name again?"

I reluctantly responded, "Her name is Maria. Maria Lewis. She was Miss Teen Pensacola when she was in high school. Two years ago, she was the second runner-up in the Miss Florida Pageant. After that pageant, she decided to focus on her studies and is no longer participating in the pageant world."

Uncle Dean asked, "Besides her obvious good looks, what else attracts you to your beauty queen?"

I paused momentarily as I thought about all the things which made me so attracted to Maria. I unintentionally began to smile before saying, "That girl is a bundle of joy and energy. Daddy calls her a 'firecracker'. I can honestly say that I have never met anyone like her. She is one of the most caring people I have had the honor of knowing. She always goes out of her way to make others feel special."

Uncle Dean blurted out, "That's nice. So, is she or is she not the one for you?"

I slowly responded, "I think so, but sometimes I think she wants more out of life than being the wife of a high school football coach."

He asked, "Why do you say that?"

I glanced over at him while saying, "I don't know. Her family is a lot more sophisticated than mine. Her father, Tom Lewis, is an orthodontist with a very successful practice. Her mother Denise is an anesthesiologist, who comes from a very rich family in Rome."

He cried out, "Those Italian women can be a handful."

"She is from Rome, Georgia, not Rome, Italy."

We both laughed. I then said, "Her mother's family owns the largest bank and real estate company in Rome. I know they have reluctantly accepted me because of Maria, but I can't imagine them ever wanting to be around my family in Shady Branch."

Uncle Dean inquired further, "How did you two meet each other since you seem to come from such different backgrounds?"

I put both hands on the steering wheel, gripping it a little tighter before explaining to Uncle Dean that Maria sat in front of me in an econ class at the university.

"Is that it?" he asked.

I then said, "The first time I heard her speak in class, I knew that I wanted to know more about her. As soon as our class met again, I mustered up the courage to introduce myself. I was so nervous. After falling all over my words like a complete idiot and thinking I lost any chance of her paying any attention to me, she stopped in the hallway, pulled out a piece of paper, and wrote down her phone number and gave it to me. She walked away without saying a word. That evening, we talked on the phone for almost three hours. We talked so long, my ear felt like it was going to fall off from holding the phone receiver next to it. On our first official date at a sandwich shop near campus, Maria immediately told me that I had passed the telephone portion of my dating interview. By the time I walked her back to her dorm, she kissed me goodnight and whispered that I had passed the first date interview with flying colors as well. After a few more dates, we made our relationship official and have been together ever since."

Uncle Dean said, "Fallin' in love is a special time in a person's life. Your story sounds similar to mine. I don't mind tellin' you that the first time I saw my Emma Jean, I somehow knew she would be the one."

I asked, "Where did you meet her?"

He replied, "I met her at school when we were in the fourth grade."

I almost swerved into the other lane before I asked, "The fourth grade? Get out of here. How did you know when you were in the fourth grade that she was the one for you?"

I could tell that he liked talking about this subject as he briefly laughed before he explained to me that he had no words to describe it, but he somehow knew she was the one. Unfortunately, for Uncle Dean, Emma Jean didn't initially share these same sentiments. They didn't become a couple until they were eighteen years old. Before that, she wouldn't give him the time of day. He further explained that he could relate to my story about being nervous. When he finally asked Emma Jean's father if he could court her, he felt like he was about to be shot while he stood with her father on the front porch holding a handful of wild lilies.

I asked, "You had to ask her father if you two could go on a date?"

"Times were a lot different back then. To properly date someone in those days, you had to get their family's permission."

I shook my head and said, "That had to suck."

"Tell me about it. No person should ever have to stand on a front porch and ask a man holding a shotgun if he could date his daughter. When I think about it right now, my legs feel like they are about to turn into jelly. I don't mind tellin' you that I was scared to death of her father."

I asked, "Did her family approve of you when y'all were married?"

Uncle Dean pulled on his seatbelt before replying, "Not at first. I know for a fact they were disappointed that she was endin' up with a common farm boy. Although her family wasn't much better off than mine financially, they had big dreams for Emma Jean. I never let their displeasure of me stand in the way of my happiness. But later, when I had my own children, I tried to think how I would have felt if I were in her parents' shoes. Trust me. Whenever you become a parent, you want nothing but the very best for your children. No matter your situation in life- that never changes."

I somewhat changed the subject by saying, "Tell me about your children. I know about Roy, but I don't know much about your other son, Tom, who died some years back."

Not immediately replying back to me, I looked over and saw Uncle Dean remove his glasses before wiping a few tears from his eyes. I immediately said, "I didn't mean to upset you."

Uncle Dean coughed before saying, "You didn't. It's been over twenty years since we lost Tom. There is not a day that goes by that I don't think about him."

He then described in great detail about how Tom grew up a daddy's boy. Uncle Dean talked about how he and his oldest son loved hunting and fishing together. He talked about how proud he was as a father of a young man who excelled in most everything he tried to accomplish. His description of how he cried at both of his sons' baptisms and weddings was moving. However, when he began to talk about how his oldest son died, it was emotionally heart wrenching for me.

He explained that Tom was a neurosurgeon living in Texas when he was diagnosed with a rare form of brain cancer. Ironically, by the time Tom was diagnosed, he had become one of the best brain surgeons in the Southwestern part of the United States. He was married and had two children. When he called Uncle Dean and told him about his terminal prognosis, Uncle Dean did everything he could to stay strong for Tom and his family.

He then paused before crying out with great emotion, "I just didn't pray to God. I begged, pleaded, and made promises to God which were unfathomable! Let me tell you, losing a child is the worst nightmare a person can ever experience! Watching your own child die is as close to hell as I have ever come! Even up to the very last day, when there was no hope, I prayed with all of my heart that God would somehow spare Tom and take me. He was three days shy of turning forty when God decided he needed our first-born baby boy more than we did."

I sheepishly said, "That had to be an awful experience."

Uncle Dean wiped a tear away from his cheek before saying, "It was. I remember sittin' at Tom's house when people started to bring food and offer their condolences. I was so mad with God. I was mad at the entire world. Innocent, good intentioned people would come up to me and say that Tom was in a better place or say that God has better plans for him. Their words were of no comfort to me. I literally wanted to die! The pain in the deepest part of my soul is something that I would never wish on my worst enemy. There are no words to describe that first month after he passed away. A cloud of sadness consumed Emma Jean and me beyond any mortal comprehension."

I tried to change the painful subject, but he kept explaining that he and Aunt Emma Jean would sometimes sit in their living room, looking at one another, and cry for hours without saying a word to each other.

Then he paused and looked at me and said, "I remember waking up one morning at three o'clock and going into Tom's old bedroom. I thought about the times he would call out my name in the middle of the night when he was a toddler. He would say, 'Hold hair. Hold hair'. I would pick him up from his crib. He would grab my hair, pull it, and then laugh. That memory and a thousand others overwhelmed me in a flood of emotional insanity. Every day, I would replay all our conversations, all the important life events, just trying to hold on to any memory of my son. To this day, not a day goes by where I don't think about the memory of him lying in that hospital bed the day he died. I remember holding an old photograph of him so much the first month after his death, that the sweat of my grip rubbed off the ink until the picture was unrecognizable."

Uncle Dean then further explained that a few months after Tom's death, he and Emma Jean drove to visit their grandchildren in Texas. When they arrived there, Uncle Dean said that Tom's wife, Carly, was rude, but they brushed it off because of what she and the children had been through. They were all hurting, but Uncle Dean and Emma Jean had decided that they would spend as much time with their grandchildren despite her reception of them. The next morning, before breakfast, Carly told them that they were no longer welcome to come and visit with her and the children. She said something about how she was trying to move on with her life and that having them around made it difficult. They tried several times to keep the grandchildren, but Carly would not go for it. Only a few months after Tom died, Carly remarried another surgeon. She never allowed Uncle Dean and Aunt Emma Jean to see their grandchildren again.

I became emotional, and he became emotional. I could feel his pain with every word he uttered. I wanted to pull over, but I knew it would upset him.

I tried again to change the subject before he wiped tears away from his eyes and continued by saying, "Back home in Alabama, I felt like I was losing my mind. On some days, I spent hours looking through dresser drawers, books, and boxes in the attic. I searched for anything Tom had written or made while he was a child. As I read old school papers or looked at newspaper clippings, I would sit and stare at one single item, sometimes for hours. On one particular day, that item which stood out to me was a Mother's Day card Tom made for Emma Jean in grade school. Every time I looked at the homemade construction paper card, I could almost hear Tom's sweet voice when he gave this card to his mother. The more I looked through his memorabilia, hundreds of regrets about things I wished I had said or done flooded my mind. I certainly wished I had spent more time with him and Roy when they were children. I remember the days when guilt would come over me like a tidal wave. On those days, I would find myself wondering if God was somehow punishing me for my sins and shortcomings."

He began to breathe heavier as he continued, "At the time, as I wallowed in my self-pity, I did not realize how selfish it was for me to think that way. Tom was the one who died. Why would God allow Tom to die because of my sins? Logically that thought process didn't make any sense, but it took me a long time to come to terms with my own misconceptions. The most pressing issue on my mind then began to besiege me. I wondered why God had allowed my son to be removed from this earth after thirty-nine years. What was the purpose or Grand Plan?"

I could feel the pain in his quivering voice as he continued, "In some of my worst moments, especially when we were not allowed to see our grandchildren, I wondered why God had allowed him to live at all? It seemed to me that his life, his memory, and his achievements were all but forgotten. That bitterness alone almost physically killed me. One morning about six months after he passed away, I ended up lying face down on his bedroom floor, crying like a baby. Before Emma Jean woke up, I reluctantly picked myself off the floor and walked into our kitchen."

He pulled out a handkerchief and blew his nose before he further stated, "As I entered the kitchen, I noticed a newspaper clipping that was sitting on the kitchen table. I assumed that Emma Jean had cut the article out of the local paper and was saving it. The article was an obituary for a Marine named Aaron Lynch. He was from a nearby town. Having been a POW in the Vietnam War for two years, Aaron helped several of his fellow soldiers escape from a prison camp in Cambodia. That same night right before he was about to be rescued, he was killed. He was twenty-one years old and his parents' only child. After reading the obituary, I quit feeling so sorry for myself. Quietly, I sat in our kitchen and grieved for a family that I had never met and did not know."

I noticed his left hand shaking as he continued, "Later that morning, I asked Emma Jean if she had cut out the article from the paper for me to read. To this day, we have no idea how that particular newspaper clipping made its way into our home. The miraculous obituary, which we taped on the side of our refrigerator, helped both of us to understand that we were not the only ones in this vast universe going through the pain and suffering of tragedies that offered no explanation."

I interrupted Uncle Dean by pointing ahead. Traffic almost came to a standstill as we were nearing El Paso at the Texas state line. We both could see busy work crews installing some type of piping under the highway.

He then resumed his story by saying, "Until we read that article, Emma Jean and I cried so much daily, we were becoming physically sick. However, about two months after Tom's funeral, we both were able to wake up each day without crying. Even though our grief process was getting better, holidays were a challenge, especially the first one without Tom. We tried to hold it together for each other, but the sadness was still too overwhelming. The memories and emotions centered around each holiday or birthday would consume and overtake us. I painfully watched Emma Jean experience her first Mother's Day without her son. I tried to be strong for her on that occasion; however, when the first Father's Day approached a few weeks later, it was excruciating for me. I cried privately for three days. Almost a year later, we both understood that we would always have to live with this emotional pain. Eventually, we slowly stopped blaming God, questioning God's judgment, and most importantly, avoiding God altogether. We realized that God still loved us, and he alone would help us on this lifetime grief journey."

Uncle Dean then wiped a tear away from his cheek and said, "One of our friends gave us a wind chime after Tom died. I didn't think much of it, until one day I sat on the front porch, staring at it. It may all be in my head, but on that day a sunbeam bounced off the chime in a peculiar way. The reflection of the sun's rays appeared to be floating all around me as the chime rang out a soft, but soothing sound. For some strange reason, I connected with that chime. I believe somehow my son visits me through it. To this day, I believe he is telling me to let my light shine for others."

Pausing momentarily, Uncle Dean then continued by saying, "I now look back on those dark days, and I am still surprised about how some of our friends and our distant family members reacted to Tom's death. Some of the most unlikely people that we knew stepped up and showered us with love and support. If it hadn't been for some of those people, we would have never made it. Others, who we considered close friends or family members, barely acknowledged our loss. A few people avoided us altogether. To this day, one of my dearest friends, so I thought, still avoids me."

At that point I could not help but to interrupt him by saying, "Look, Uncle Dean, there is your favorite road sign again."

We passed an End Construction road sign. Uncle Dean laughed before saying, "Tom was the one who pointed out that silly sign to me one afternoon when we were riding together from Alabama to Texas. I did not know it at the time, but that trip was the last one that he and I would travel together. I also remember on that particular trip, he told me that he was going to be married. He was so excited to share this news with me. Now every time that I see this sign, it is a constant reminder of one of the best times I ever had with my son."

He paused again, laughed and then said, "End Construction could mean- we all have to face that day when our construction on this earth has ended."

Later on we had to stop for gas on the other side of El Paso. I was deep in thought and honored that Uncle Dean had chosen to share with me such personal and private details of his life. I began to see this trip as an opportunity to pick his brain and find out as much as I could about the side of my family that I knew so little about.

CHAPTER TWELVE

A few miles later on I-10, I noticed a road sign which read, "Left Lane for Passing Only". I laughed to myself and wished that I could take that sign back to Tallahassee and give it to Coach Brown at State. I knew my college coach, who was an innovator of the modern football passing game, would get a kick out of that sign.

Uncle Dean then pointed across the interstate and said, "Look over there. How would you like to have one of those oil wells in your backyard in Shady Branch? Your money worries would be over."

I quickly changed the subject and asked Uncle Dean, "Do you mind me askin' about your marriage to Aunt Emma Jean?"

He replied, "Not at all. What do you want to know?"

I said, "You two were married for a very long time. I can't begin to imagine being married to the same person for so long."

Uncle Dean grinned and replied, "Sixty-two years is a long time, but I wouldn't trade it for the world. Now, don't get me wrong, we had our ups and downs, but overall, I highly recommend that you find that special someone, latch on, and enjoy your time together."

I changed lanes before saying, "I don't know. It seems so old-fashioned to me. It seems unnatural. You know, married to the same person… never again looking at somebody else."

He replied, "Who said you can't look? It's no different than being on a diet. You can look at the dessert bar all you want, knowin' that the cake and pie are off limits."

I laughed and then to my surprise, Uncle Dean began to unravel a personal secret which I did not expect to hear.

He said, "I am ashamed of what I am about to tell you, but I think it is important that you know the truth about my marriage…"

Before he could continue, we both heard what sounded like an explosion. The U-Haul began to swerve into the other lane. I barely escaped a catastrophe from the blowout of the front passenger side tire. I was somehow able to avoid driving into a shallow rocky ravine after gaining control of the vehicle and maneuvering it off the side of the road onto the shoulder. Shredded rubber from the blown-out tire littered the roadway behind us. The distinct aroma of burnt rubber made us both exit the U-Haul truck hoping for the best.

With no spare tire or tire tools on the truck, Uncle Dean and I were stranded on a stretch of I-10 which appeared to be in between nowhere and somewhere. We both realized we were in a part of Southwest Texas that looked forgotten and abandoned. I became a little nervous when I realized that the last exit we had passed was about ten miles away. I could not remember seeing the first house or place of business near that exit. Once we looked at the McNally Atlas, we both determined that it was about the same distance to the next exit in the opposite direction.

Uncle Dean, said, "Decisions. Decisions."

Ten minutes later, a flatbed truck and two cars passed without giving us a second look. I tried to wave them down. After they passed by us, I began to ponder which exit would be my best bet to find a telephone.

Standing outside of the U-Haul, next to the shredded tire, Uncle Dean said, "I think you need to wait a little longer before you begin such a long walk. Somebody will eventually stop."

I was becoming impatient and about to leave on foot to find help when a roar, which sounded like thunder, caught our attention. Standing near the rear of the truck we could see a swarm of motorcycles pulling up behind us. As the motorcycles approached closer, I immediately recognized that the leader of the pack was the Hispanic biker we had encountered in the diner the day before. Before we knew it, ten Harleys surrounded the U-Haul. With no time to fetch the .38 Special from the cab of the truck, Uncle Dean and I stood next to a desolate stretch of the interstate, both powerless to protect ourselves from possible danger and totally outnumbered. I immediately thought we were going to be robbed, killed, or both by what appeared to be the Mexican Mafia. I then looked at my eighty-two-year-old great uncle and thought to myself that no one would ever find our bodies in such a remote place. Uncle Dean looked at me and stated calmly, "Ain't this gonna be a happy reunion?"

The leader of the biker gang slowly slid off his Harley and walked up to us flanked by his motorcycle friends. He smiled and said, "Well, look here everyone. This is the old man who pulled a pistol on me and told me to clean up my language." He then spoke in Spanish saying, "Este viejo tiene pelotas grande! (This old man has big balls.)"

His friends began laughing. Uncle Dean, not knowing what he had said in Spanish, spoke up and said, "My advice to you was probably some of the best advice you have been given in quite some time."

The leader of the bikers smiled and replied, "That it was, sir. That it was." He then looked at the flat tire of the truck and said, "The best advice I could give you today is- Be careful who you talk to when you are traveling in the middle of nowhere."

I was scared when I said, "We don't…"

Before I could finish saying what was on my mind, the leader of the bikers interrupted me and asked, "Who are you, people?"

I nervously replied, "My name is Tim Jackson. This is my great uncle, Dean Lee. I am helping him move from California to Florida."

The leader of the bikers said, "Well, Tim, it looks to me that your great uncle is someone you should hope to be like one day. My name is Teddy Flores. I want to apologize again to both of you for the outburst I had in that diner yesterday in Arizona. Normally, you would have never heard me talk like that. As your uncle so eloquently pointed out, there is no excuse for the bad language I was using. I guess I need to explain that the waitress I was talking to is my son's ex-wife. Let's say that I harbor a lot of resentment over her not allowing my grandchild to visit with us as much as I would like."

I could not believe what I was hearing. Teddy Flores began to explain that he and his friends lived near the area. He told us they had been notified by a trucker that a U-Haul truck had a flat tire on the Interstate. Teddy and his friends were part of a local Harley club which volunteered to assist local law enforcement with roadside emergencies. He went on to say, "Our county is so spread out the authorities count on us to help them out. You could say that we are like volunteer firemen." He then took off his gloves before saying, "The closest U-Haul dealership from here is in the town of McCamey near where most of us live. We have already called, and the U-Haul dealer said it would be at least an hour before they can make it out here to change your tire."

I was obviously relieved when I said, "Thank you, sir, for doing that. How much money do we owe you?"

Teddy replied, "Not one penny."

Uncle Dean said, "God bless you all. We'll hop back in the truck and wait for the service people to arrive."

Teddy shook his head and said, "I don't think that would be a good idea, my friend. We are not going to leave you two out here by yourselves. At times this area has been known to be a dangerous stretch of road. I insist that you let us take you guys to our shop where you can hang out until they change your tire."

I looked at Uncle Dean who immediately said, "We sure do hate to put y'all out, but if it's not too much trouble we would love to go."

I couldn't believe that Uncle Dean was agreeing to ride with these people that we did not know. I started thinking about the movie, *Texas Chainsaw Massacre*. I was still not convinced that it was a good idea for us to ride off with strangers. I asked Uncle Dean, "Are you sure you will be able to ride on a motorcycle?"

He looked at me with a strange look on his face, and then laughed before saying, "Hell if I know. I'm eighty-two years old, and I have never been on one of those things. But I can honestly say that I have always dreamed about ridin' on one."

Teddy laughed at Uncle Dean and said, "Well, Dean, today is your lucky day. Hop on the back of this bad boy."

After I helped Uncle Dean climb onto the back of Teddy's Harley, I walked over and climbed on the back of the bike of a younger looking man named Frank Jovenelly. I asked him, "What kind of work do y'all do out here?

Frank replied, "All of us are into oil well leasing. However, most of us in this group are also into wind farming."

"Wind farmin'?"

He replied, "Yep, when we exit the interstate, you will see windmills everywhere. We own a good many of the ones we will pass on the way to our shop. When you see how large those suckers are, you will understand that it takes a crew of people to manage them. Some people are starting to call this area the Windmill Capital of Texas."

***

A few minutes later, when we arrived at the shop, Uncle Dean and I were treated to a tour by Teddy. The shop was a huge warehouse. Uncle Dean was amazed as he exclaimed, "This is truly the biggest shop I have ever seen. They always say everything is bigger in Texas."

As we continued the tour of the "shop", Teddy gave us a complete explanation of how electricity was generated from wind power in a facility which housed wind turbines and all of the parts that were associated with windmills, including panels, electrical boxes, and propellers. He explained this was a family business as most of the employees were related. They were descendants from some of the first Spanish settlers in West Texas well before Texas became its own nation. He said, "Technically our ancestors came here from Europe. This land was a part of Mexico before the Mexican-American War; therefore, our ancestors were also considered Mexicans. Then, of course, this land was annexed into Texas. Most people who are not from here call us Mexicans. Ironically, we find this to be hilarious, as all of us were born right here in the USA."

Teddy then walked us back to the main shop area where a television was playing. Several of the men and a few women were sitting on various couches, a few bean bags, and a cluster of picnic tables. They had flags of the United States, Mexico, Spain, Texas, and the Dallas Cowboys hanging on a wall next to the lounge area. After Teddy introduced us to everyone, he pointed to a big black Labrador Retriever named Cowboy before saying, "Cowboy over there is our official mascot. He loves the Dallas Cowboys."

Uncle Dean said, "Teddy, this looks like an expensive operation you have here."

Teddy walked a little closer to us before saying, "It is, but it is quite a profitable one." He continued by explaining in more detail that almost everyone who worked there was a part of his family. He said, "Our grandparents sat on very profitable land as oil was discovered here years ago. Let's just say that none of us really have to work if we don't want to." He laughed and said, "The money we are making from this venture is going to good use. We are focused on helping people in West Texas by providing job training skills, English classes, and shelters for the homeless. We manage several sister corporations that share this mission as well and help us accomplish these projects."

As we kept talking, Teddy noticed that I was wearing a State sweatshirt and asked me if I went to State. The conversation then went from windmills to football fields. Before I knew it, I became a celebrity to a group of people on the outskirts of a West Texas town that I had never heard of before. They all laughed when I tried to imitate how Coach Brown would say 'dadgum" whenever he became irritated during a practice or game. When Teddy mentioned that his nephew was the placekicker for the University of South Carolina, the football conversation became even more interesting.

Uncle Dean then became the center of attention when they found out he was a retired farmer and attorney. Uncle Dean had the whole group intrigued when he said, "I bet you didn't know that adult cats don't meow or talk to other adult cats?"

Teddy interrupted him, "You heard that on that radio show out of Phoenix. I listen to that station all the time. Those stupid facts tend to stay with you. Another one I heard a few weeks ago, was that buzzards can be found on every continent except Australia and Antarctica. That is one fact I will never forget. It sticks in your mind."

The more we talked, I was amazed that the average person would never have known that most of the people in that shop were absolutely loaded. I found them to be some of the nicest people I had ever met.

About an hour later, Uncle Dean and I were treated to some of the best beef empanadas, beans, rice, and coleslaw in the state of Texas. After pulling all of the picnic tables together in the shop, the entire crew went through a massive buffet line at the other end of the wind farm's warehouse. Before he said a blessing and everyone began to eat, Teddy introduced us to his 34-year-old cousin, named Kaylee Garcia. She had walked into the shop from her office to join in on the meal. Teddy said, "Kaylee is the brains behind our operation. She has an electrical engineering degree from the University of Texas. Kaylee is the boss. We would have never been successful without her brain power and expertise."

Uncle Dean laughed before saying, "It sure don't hurt that she is a whole lot better lookin' than some of those Beverly Hill models I've seen in California."

Kaylee smiled at Uncle Dean. She then noticed my sweatshirt. She looked at me and said, "You know what we say when we visit Florida?" Before I could reply she laughed and said, "Hook 'em, Horns."

After we all laughed, Kaylee began explaining how Teddy talked her and her husband into moving back to the area to start the windmill division of their business. She said, "At first, we thought Teddy was crazy, but when we studied his plan, we quickly understood the possibilities were unlimited. Once we started wind farming, many others followed. We are now in the beginning process of harvesting solar power." She took a bite of her food, before saying, "Teddy has a big heart. In the beginning, he wanted to give the electricity away until we convinced him that we could use the profits to help others in so many different ways."

When a teenage boy answered the phone in a nearby office, he yelled across the warehouse that the tire on the U-Haul truck had been changed. After finishing our meal, Teddy asked us to take a few Polaroid pictures with them. They took many pictures including one of Uncle Dean sitting on a Harley. Teddy handed Uncle Dean several of the pictures and said, "I hope you had a good time on your first motorcycle ride today. Keep these pictures to remember us out here in Texas, and please keep our operation in your prayers."

Teddy then escorted us to his large farm truck and drove us back to our U-Haul parked on the side of the interstate. Before we climbed out of the farm truck, I shook hands with the man I earlier assumed was going to rob or kill us. I said, "Teddy, we can't thank you enough. Your generous hospitality has 'blown' us away." We then laughed before I said, "Good luck in the windmill farmin' business. If you ever come to Florida, please give us a call."

CHAPTER THIRTEEN

U ncle Dean and I decided that we would drive as far as we could to make up for lost time. I drove faster heading toward San Antonio as we talked about our unbelievable afternoon experience at the windmill farm. I looked at Uncle Dean and said, "I really thought we were dead men when they showed up."

He cracked his window and pulled out his pipe before saying, "That is the great thing about life. When we least expect it, somebody shows up at the right time."

"Speaking of life," I said, "I had no idea that so much of Texas was so desolate. It doesn't look much different than Arizona or New Mexico."

***

Later, mainly out of boredom, I took the opportunity to delve back into Uncle Dean's past by asking, "What is it that you were going to tell me before we had the flat tire?"

He shook his head and replied, "I guess now is as good a time as any." He then mumbled a few words under his breath before he said, "I want you to know what I am about to tell you- I have never shared this with anyone else."

I could see the strain on his face. I could tell that whatever he was about to share would be painful. I could also sense that it would be a long story. I then interrupted him and said, "Hold that thought, Unk. We need to take this exit. That food we ate at Teddy's was excellent, but it needs to find a new home if you know what I mean."

He cried out, "I sure do. I was sittin' here about to crap in my pants."

I was speeding down a service road next to the interstate before I pulled into a busy Sunoco gas station near the city of Sonora, Texas. I had to wait a few minutes to be able to park the U-Haul next to the first available gas pump. Uncle Dean, however, could not wait. He scooted out of the cab of the truck and headed to the restroom. Once I was finally able to park, I tried to turn on the gas pump before I noticed a small sign taped to it which read, "You MUST Pay Inside Before PUMPING".

Having stomach issues of my own, I went straight to the men's restroom which was located on the side of the building. The door was locked. I yelled through the door, "Hey Unk, are you about through in there?"

He yelled, "I'm havin' some issues that haven't been resolved yet."

"What did you say?"

Uncle Dean yelled, "I said that I'm not through crappin'. I'm having an attack."

I was becoming so desperate I was about to enter the women's room when suddenly the door of the men's room flew open. Uncle Dean walked out and said, "You may need to give that crapper a little time to air out."

"No time for that."

Uncle Dean then walked into the old gas station which was in the renovation process of becoming a convenience store. The back half which appeared to be the old mechanic's bays was roped off from customers while the renovation was being completed. He could tell that at one time the station had been a full-service gas station and garage. While he stood in line to pay for a cup of coffee, Uncle Dean thought about how many of the full-service stations were going out of business.

Right before he was about to pay for his coffee, I walked up behind him and said, "Tell them I'm gonna fill it up so I can start pumping." I then walked outside to self-service gas pump number 2 and started to fill up the U-Haul.

Uncle Dean stood behind a rather large lady who was carrying a handful of candy and a large diet soda. He stepped closer to the store owner and told him to allow me to begin filling up the U-Haul. Uncle Dean then stepped back in line and became a little aggravated as he listened to the hit rap song, "Black Steel in the

Hour of Chaos" by Public Enemy. It was playing on a small boom box sitting next to the store owner.

"Hello, my friend," the owner of the store said to the large lady.

She looked at him and said nothing. After throwing her items on the counter, she muttered, "It's hot up in here."

As the owner began to ring her up, a man wearing a ski mask, and a full-length trench coat entered the store holding a handgun. He pushed the lady aside and waved his gun at the owner and the rest of the customers in the store. The lady screamed. The masked man pushed her and then yelled, "Everyone get down on the floor. Nobody is going to get hurt unless you do something crazy." He then yelled again saying to the owner, "Hurry up and empty that register before I start shooting."

I had no idea that a robbery was taking place while I was daydreaming and pumping gas. It wasn't until I looked up that I noticed what was going down. I immediately ran over to the passenger side of the U-Haul, opened the door and looked in Uncle Dean's knapsack. No gun was found.

Inside the store, everyone had already abided by the robber's demands as they were all down on the floor; everyone except Uncle Dean and the store owner. The robber looked back at Uncle Dean, pointed his gun at him and said, "Get the F... down old man before I..."

He was then interrupted by the owner of the store who yelled, "Get down… Get down... You crazy man. Do what he says… No need to get hurt…No need to get hurt."

Uncle Dean slowly placed one knee on the floor. The robber momentarily turned away. As he turned back toward Uncle Dean, it was too late. I came bursting through the door. Before I was able to actually engage with the robber, a shot was fired. For a few seconds time stood still. I noticed that the robber dropped his gun. He was the one who had been hit. Uncle Dean had unloaded Mr. 38 Special into the back of the robber's leg right in the middle of his calf.

The chaos that ensued was never captured by any video. It was a wild scene that could have been a part of a Hollywood script. As I wrestled the robber to the ground, the owner of the store leaped over the counter and smashed the robber in the back of the head with a small sized aluminum baseball bat. He knocked the man unconscious.

The owner then yelled, "Someone please call 911."

By the time the police arrived a few minutes later, we had already hog-tied and patched up the suspect with some electrical tape. As soon as the police walked in the store, they had to deal with the large lady who had begun hyperventilating. A call for EMS not only brought an ambulance, but it also brought the entire town's fire department with sirens blaring. For the next few minutes, there was a room full of confusion as the police had a difficult time understanding the broken English of the station owner who was originally from Pakistan.

When another elderly man in the back of the store, who had partially witnessed the ordeal spoke up, the police became even more confused. He pointed at Uncle Dean and said, "Arrest that man. He is the one."

For the next twenty minutes Uncle Dean and I were questioned by a very young member of the police department. He appeared to be only a few days out of high school. Uncle Dean said, "Now don't be upset with me. That fella was about to kill my favorite grandnephew."

The officer didn't immediately reply as he scribbled something in a notepad. He then asked, "Do you have a permit to carry that gun legally?"

Uncle Dean cried out, "I sure do."

The officer asked, "Please let me see it."

Uncle Dean shouted, "Tim, my permit is in the brown folder case in the trunk of my car. It is in the first folder that you open."

Once I unlocked the trunk, I saw the accordion style leather folder case which was much larger than I had imagined. When I opened it, I could tell that a lifetime of papers had been systematically placed into many different folders. While I looked for the gun permit, I noticed the various multi-colored tabs of the folders which had small handwritten cards placed in them. I noticed one that read Insurance and another one that read Taxes.

Once I found the gun permit, one of the tabs stood out to me. It read, "Florida Payments".

As I began to walk into the station, I noticed that the gun permit had been issued in Alabama, some thirty years prior. I slowly and reluctantly handed it over to the officer expecting that the officer would find some problem with such an old permit. After giving it only a brief glance, the officer said, "You two may have to come back here and testify at the trial."

Uncle Dean laughed and said, "The only testifiyin' I'll be doin' will be in the Florida Panhandle. Y'all are more than welcome to come and talk to me down there."

Before the officer could reply, I told him, "No problem, sir. We will do whatever we need to do." I then asked, "Do you know this guy who tried to rob the store?"

The officer replied, "Yeah, we know him. His name is Vincent Pike." The young officer went on to explain that Vince had grown up in a world that had not been very kind to him. When he was eight years old, Vince watched his father shoot and kill his mother. His father then began shooting the rest of his family. Vince, who was shot several times, survived. His two little brothers and one baby sister did not. In the final seconds of this tragic event, Vince's father killed himself. Having lost his entire family in a matter of minutes, Vince recovered in the hospital to find out that he would be living with his mother's parents, his only remaining family. Almost to the day a year later, his grandparents were killed in an automobile accident. Nine-year-old Vince, then became a ward of the state. The officer went on to say, "By the time he was seventeen, poor Vince had been in and out of a dozen foster homes." The officer continued to say, "He had always engaged in some petty shoplifting, but nothing to this level today. We all know his situation and hate it for him, but after today I don't see any hope for Vince."

While we waited to sign the official statements, the owner of the gas station walked up to Uncle Dean and me and thanked us. He then introduced himself by saying, "My name is Rehmat Chaudhary. Please, friends… Respond to me and say your name."

I did my best to communicate until Rehmat's oldest, teenage son named Ali walked up to us and introduced himself. Ali, a very handsome young man with an athletic build and thick eyebrows, spoke perfect English. Ali had been outside at the back of the store throwing away boxes when the robbery occurred. After properly introducing himself, he explained to us that his father brought their family to the United States via New York eighteen years ago only to find himself driving a taxi in Las Vegas two years later. He then explained that his father and a cousin took a big chance a few years ago moving to Texas to renovate a dilapidated full-service gas station which had been put on the auction block.

Ali said, "My father brought us here for a better life. I am so thankful that you were here to assist him in this terrible tragedy. We will never be able to thank you enough."

After we talked a few more minutes, Ali further explained that he dreamed of becoming a neurosurgeon one day. Uncle Dean, particularly, was moved by Ali's enthusiasm and drive when Ali spoke about entering the medical profession; the same profession Uncle Dean's eldest son had excelled.

As we said our goodbyes, Rehmat smiled before saying, "American Dream, Baby… American Dream. We love it here. You know, being in Big Texas."

***

After the local police allowed us to leave, we climbed into the cab of the U-Haul. It was late, and we were exhausted. Uncle Dean said, "Tim, it's all up to you. We can find a place around here or keep driving. Whatever you decide is fine with me."

I looked over at Uncle Dean and said, "Thank you for saving my life."

He replied matter of factly, "You don't need to thank me. You better thank the Good Lord, because I was aimin' at that back of that joker's rear end when I pulled the trigger. I can't believe I missed so badly."

A few blocks away when I drove onto the entrance ramp of the interstate, I looked over and could see that Uncle Dean had begun snoring. It was well past midnight. I was determined to make it to San Antonio. I cracked my window so that I would not fall asleep. I tried desperately to find a radio station that was static free. I hit pay dirt when I found a station out of Dallas that was a sports talk show. I kept driving. I laughed to myself when the host of the show predicted that State would beat Auburn in the upcoming Sugar Bowl in New Orleans.

Listening to the host describe how State University had rattled off ten straight wins since losing the opening game to Miami made me proud. When the host talked about one of college football's most famous plays called the Puntrooskie, I began laughing out loud.

The host of the radio show said, "When Coach Brown called that trick play a few weeks ago, his team was backed up on their own 20-yard line. It was fourth down, and he pulled that fake punt out of his bag of tricks. What guts! That fake punt will go down in college football history as one of the best ever."

I continued to laugh because I remembered the day at practice a few years before, when Coach Brown installed that fake punt and named it Puntrooskie. I also remembered hearing a player whisper that he didn't believe Coach Brown's Puntrooskie would ever work. I knew I had been blessed to play for a man who never cared if other players or coaches were laughing at him because he was different. Coach Brown laughed back at them because in his mind, they were all the same; unwilling to take calculated risks and limiting their own creativity.

I continued to listen to the radio about the upcoming bowl games. I was fighting hard not to fall asleep at the wheel. Finally, after finding a nice-looking Econo Lodge motel on the outskirts of San Antonio, I woke up Uncle Dean as we parked the U-Haul for the night.

CHAPTER FOURTEEN

The next morning, I woke up smelling coffee and bacon. After rubbing my eyes, I could barely see Uncle Dean sitting in the corner of the room reading a copy of *USA Today*. He peered over his newspaper and said, "I don't know how you did it last night, but by God, you drove us all the way to San Antonio. I knew that you needed a little rest. So, I decided to let you sleep in."

I asked, "Where did you get that breakfast?"

Enthusiastically, he replied, "Look here, Tim. They have a free breakfast right there in the lobby of this place. They have bacon, eggs, muffins, and cereal. I couldn't believe it. For the life of me I don't know how these people can afford to give away such a nice breakfast."

I yawned before asking, "What time is it?"

He swallowed a gulp of coffee before replying, "A quarter past ten- Texas time."

I jumped out of the bed and said, "I better hit the shower so we can head to Shady Branch."

***

After filling up the U-Haul at a Shell station next to the interstate, and looking over the Rand McNally Atlas, I had my sights on New Orleans. Uncle Dean said, "New Orleans would be good, but that traffic around Houston ain't gonna be a picnic."

I started up the engine of the U-Haul and began laughing when I heard the song, "On the Road Again" by Willie Nelson playing on the radio. Uncle Dean looked at me and asked, "What is so funny?"

"Oh, nothing."

A few minutes later, we both understood that the traffic around San Antonio was no joke. After passing the Six Flags Over Texas amusement park, Uncle Dean said, "You know if we had time, I would love to ride that big roller coaster."

I replied, "You would crap in your pants, old man."

As we passed the Alamo, I could tell Uncle Dean wanted to stop nearly as much as I did. When I asked him if he wanted to take the next exit to visit the historic site, Uncle Dean told me to keep driving. I then asked, "Tell me why you are in such a big hurry to make it to Florida."

He replied, "Because I need to see my sister before it is too late."

I kept driving, and while keeping my eyes on the road, I asked, "Too late for what?"

He squirmed in his seat before answering, "Well, if you haven't noticed, my time on this planet is limited. This old boy ain't gonna be around here too much longer."

"So, what... Why do you need to see my grandmother so badly?"

He paused for a few seconds before replying, "I need her to forgive me."

I was a bit aggravated when I asked, "Forgive you for what?"

He snarled back, "That is between us."

I hit the brakes hard enough to give him a good jolt. I then cried out, "Now look here, old man. I'm goin' to pull over on the side of the road if you don't tell me what's the big secret."

Uncle Dean did not respond. I then put on the turn signal and slowly began to pull off on the shoulder of the interstate. He yelled, "Don't stop. I'll tell you what you want to know."

I pulled the U-Haul back over into the right lane and began to listen to a story I had never heard. Uncle Dean explained that when he married Emma Jean, she moved into his family's small house on the property where he was sharecropping. His sister, Claire, and his mother both accepted Emma Jean; however, Emma Jean was not excited about the arrangement. Claire was two years younger than Uncle Dean and still going to school. Their poor mother was in bad health. She was a diabetic who was almost bedridden. At first, Emma Jean seemed to be happy, but a few months into the marriage, three women living in one small house took a toll on their relationship. Uncle Dean would come home and find out that his mother or his sister had hurt Emma Jean's feelings. It was simple things like them rewashing the dishes that Emma Jean washed or telling her that they would be ashamed to serve some of the food she cooked. Uncle Dean did not know what to do. Every time he would leave the women alone, they would be in some type of conflict. He knew Emma Jean was unhappy. Later that year, their mother died in her sleep. Uncle Dean thought that most of the problem for Emma Jean had been resolved.

He was wrong. As it turned out, Claire was the main culprit. Uncle Dean never saw it for himself, but when he came home, he had to hear about their ongoing battles every night. Claire and Emma Jean were like oil and water. Emma Jean was conservative. She thought a woman's place was in the home, doing what her husband told her to do. Claire, on the other hand, was an independent soul, who never believed a man should tell a woman what to do. When Claire was ten years old, she was one of a handful of girls in their church who supported the Women's Suffrage Movement. Uncle Dean said that he would never forget how proud Claire was in 1920 when women were finally able to vote.

Then he explained to me that the worst thing happened. He paused and began to pull out his pipe.

I asked, "What happened?"

Uncle Dean continued explaining in great detail that when Claire was seventeen, she began working part-time downtown at a women's dress shop. Sending her off to college was financially out of the question at the time even though that was her dream. Because she was an independent minded spirit, she worked at the dress shop in hopes of saving enough money for college tuition.

On her very first day of work, she became acquainted with a thirteen-year-old Black teenager named Little Cyrus McCloud. His father, Big Cyrus, was a jack of all trades. All of the downtown businesses used Big Cyrus to deliver their cooking wood, do any small carpentry, and help out with any odd job that may arise. Big Cyrus also became known as the one person in town who people could count on to deliver any goods throughout the local area. Little Cyrus was not like his father. Although he worked hard, he had dreams about higher education during a time when Black people were limited in opportunities. Like Claire, he dreamed about obtaining a college education.

Whenever Little Cyrus would work in or near the dress shop, Claire would speak to him out of kindness. By law, they were forbidden to establish any type of relationship outside of general conversation about work or details concerning the business. They could talk to each other in passing, only if Claire initiated the conversation. For several weeks, Claire befriended this young man. They talked about politics, they shared their thoughts about classical literature, and so forth. Claire even helped him at times with his schoolwork. She wanted the best for him.

It was all innocent until the sheriff came to their house to speak to Uncle Dean. It was 1927 and the laws in Alabama were tough for Blacks. The sheriff told Uncle Dean that he had to answer a complaint that was filed in his office. He explained to Uncle Dean that the complaint specified that Little Cyrus and Claire were engaged in an illegal relationship.

Uncle Dean laughed it off. The sheriff laughed with him before explaining that by law, he was bound to make a charge. He further explained that if Claire testified that Little Cyrus had been talking to her, Little Cyrus would be arrested. If Claire denied the charge, according to the law, Claire could be charged with violating the Segregation Laws of the state of Alabama. The sheriff basically explained that they were in a legal pickle.

The sheriff also told Uncle Dean that some of the people in town were accusing Claire and Little Cyrus of having a sexual relationship. A witness reported seeing them holding hands. The sheriff did not want to arrest anyone, but he was under the gun as some of his most important constituents were demanding justice. As an elected official of the county, the sheriff knew that he had to do something, or he would be out of a job. He and Uncle Dean both knew that the people who were behind this did not like

Claire. Those people didn't like her because she was so outspoken about social issues of the time. Some of her opinions about race relations or women's rights were not welcomed. Uncle Dean also knew that a trial, even if she were found not guilty, would ruin her reputation.

The sheriff and Uncle Dean talked for about two hours trying to find a reasonable solution. Uncle Dean suggested that if Claire left the county then the problem would be solved. The sheriff quickly agreed. He then gave Uncle Dean a week to find a suitable place for Claire to move. It happened that Uncle Dean knew a friend who worked at the Ben M. Jacobs & Brothers Furniture Store in downtown Birmingham. Uncle Dean sent his friend a telegram asking him to call him. A day later, his friend called him on the Barry Brown, and Uncle Dean explained his dilemma.

I interrupted Uncle Dean and asked, "What is a Barry Brown?"

Uncle Dean laughed before saying, "Barry Brown, the owner of the Landing General Store, was the first person in our community to own a telephone. We called a telephone a Barry Brown for many years."

Uncle Dean then continued the story by further explaining to me that the next day his friend at the Ben M. Jacobs & Brothers Furniture Store had worked it out so that Claire would be employed at the store as a clerk. Business was booming during the roaring twenties, and they needed help. That evening, Uncle Dean sat down with Claire and explained the legal predicament that she was in and the solution to the problem.

Claire was stunned. Her heart was broken. She couldn't believe that people in her hometown would do such a thing. To her, Little Cyrus was more like the little brother she never had. At first Claire cried. Then she began yelling. She admitted holding Little Cyrus' hand. She was holding his hand because he had a big splinter stuck in it. She dug the splinter out like anyone else would do. Claire wanted to know who had complained. She said she would go to prison if she could look those hateful people in their eyes. She had no intention of leaving town. For two days Uncle Dean and Emma Jean did their best to convince Claire that moving to Birmingham was the best thing for everyone.

The next day, Uncle Dean went and talked with the sheriff about how they could convince Claire to move away. They came up with a plan. That next Friday, the sheriff drove to their house and formally arrested Claire. She did not resist. In fact, she wanted to be arrested so she could find out who had made the complaint. She kept asking the sheriff to tell her who had made these accusations against her. Once Emma Jean handed the sheriff a suitcase, Claire knew something was up. Placed in handcuffs, she was led out of the house to the sheriff's car. Uncle Dean and the sheriff drove Claire to a small rental house in Birmingham about four hours away. She pleaded with Uncle Dean to take her back home and to let her go to jail. Once they arrived at the rental house, the sheriff told her that if she came back home, he would make sure that Little Cyrus would be the one who went to prison.

I kept looking straight ahead as I drove. I said, "I can't believe you betrayed her like that. How could you do that to her?"

Uncle Dean replied, "I did not want to send her away, but at the time, I thought it was the only way to keep her and Little Cyrus from going to jail."

I quickly asked, "What happened to my grandmother when you left her in Birmingham?"

He looked over at me and replied, "At first, she did good. The people at the furniture store loved her. Everything changed a year and half later when Wall Street crashed, and the Great Depression swept across the country. Even the Heaviest Corner on Earth could not withstand the effects of the Wall Street Collapse."

I asked, "What did you say about the corners of the earth?"

He replied, "I'm sorry. That is what everyone used to called the four largest skyscrapers in downtown Birmingham. All of them were built on or near the same city block, so everyone in Alabama called the financial district, The Heaviest Corner on Earth."

I asked, "What about my grandmother?"

Uncle Dean slowly explained to me that my grandmother lost her good job at the furniture store. She took whatever work she could find. She later worked as a waitress in a downtown diner in the morning and took up tickets at the movie theater at night. A year later she called Uncle Dean to let him know that she was getting married. It was the first time she and Uncle Dean talked since he sent her away.

Their conversation was long and satisfying. Claire told him that it took her a long time to understand that Uncle Dean was only trying to keep her and Little Cyrus out of trouble. She said that she had met an iron worker at the diner where she worked. When she told Uncle Dean that her new boyfriend was thirty-eight years old, Uncle Dean became angry with her. She was nineteen at the time. All he could think about was that she was throwing her life away on a man twice her age. However, a few weeks later, he and Emma Jean drove to Birmingham and watched Claire say her vows in a small room in the back of the courthouse.

I stopped Uncle Dean right there and asked, "I assume that you are talking about my grandfather?"

He immediately replied, "Yes, that is right. I hate to tell you this, but when I met your grandfather before the wedding ceremony, I was not impressed. He was originally from West Georgia. He told me that he had been all over Alabama workin' odd jobs. I thought it was strange that a thirty-eight-year-old man had never married and was now in love with my sister. To me, he was nothing more than another poor cracker from Georgia. At that time in my life, I did not trust anyone who wasn't from Alabama. When I asked him what he would do if he ever lost his job, he laughed and told me that he was like the wind."

As I kept driving, I did not know how to respond to Uncle Dean. I was somewhat stunned because I had never heard anything negative about my grandfather. My mother and grandmother had always portrayed the man as saintly.

Uncle Dean picked up where he left off by explaining that my grandfather said he would always be able to find good work somewhere. Uncle Dean perceived him as cocky and very arrogant. I could tell that Uncle Dean did not like him.

For the next few years, my grandfather took my grandmother with him to all the places where he found work. Uncle Dean would finally receive a postcard from her. The postcard was from Louisiana. By the time he wrote her back, his letter was sent to her new address in Meridian, Mississippi. Then he found out later that they had moved to Arkansas where they stayed less than a year. According to Uncle Dean, my grandfather would not or could not keep a good job.

On several occasions, my grandmother would write to Uncle Dean and ask him for money. At first, Uncle Dean helped her out, then one time when she wrote him they needed money for a move to Midland City, Alabama, he refused. He wrote her back and basically told her that if she had not married this man, she would not be in this position, and he was done helping them out. Uncle Dean let her know that he thought my grandfather was not stable.

Uncle Dean said, "I know my rebuke of her husband caused even more harsh feelin's. I'm pretty sure the word I used that stuck with her was 'gypsy'. I told her that she was livin' with a man who was a gypsy. I'm sorry, Tim, but that is how I felt at the time."

He continued to explain that after the gypsy conversation, his sister did not speak with him for almost two years. During the Second World War, they moved to Bainbridge, Georgia where my grandfather took over a service station. Uncle Dean couldn't believe that my grandfather had his sister working, changing oil, and greasing cars. Uncle Dean went there on a visit when Claire called him and told him she was pregnant with my mother. It pained him to watch his sister service a car with her belly poking out like a ripe watermelon. He and Emma Jean went back down there for a few days when my mother was born. While they were there, my grandmother told Uncle Dean that they were selling the service station and moving to South Alabama to join some of her husband's family in a large tobacco farming operation. Again, Uncle Dean felt like my grandfather was a fool when it came to business. He said, "Your grandfather knew as much about farmin' as I did about buildin' a nuclear bomb."

Uncle Dean continued to explain that several years later the tobacco venture went bust after the worst drought in years. They ended up in the small South Georgia town of Attapulgus. My grandparents took over a shop owned by a friend of a friend. They turned it into a cafe.

Attapulgus is located near the Florida state line. Before the interstates were built, people had to drive through it on their way to the Florida Gulf Coast. By the time the Second World War had long been over, the economy was much better, and people were traveling more. The cafe was located in a prime spot long before there were any fast-food joints. Many Yankees from Indiana and Ohio would stop at the cafe for a quick hamburger and my grandmother's famous peach cobbler and sweet iced tea.

Uncle Dean then became quiet as he pulled out the milk container from the floorboard of the U-Haul. I cracked his window and said, "I still don't know why you won't let me pull over. You peein' in a milk jug is disgustin'."

As we were passing the Texas town of Flatonia, Uncle Dean was zipped up and ready to keep talking. I looked at him and said, "I didn't even notice that the landscape had changed. I was so busy listening to you, I can't remember when we started seeing trees and green grass instead of cactus, sand, and rock."

He shot back, "That was a long way back near San Antonio."

My curiosity about my grandmother would not allow Uncle Dean to change the subject. I immediately said, "I understand why my grandmother was mad with you at times, but I don't understand what you have done to keep her from talking to you the past twenty years. Did something else happen?"

He glanced over at me and said, "Believe me when I tell you that it's complicated. I feel bad about all of it, but it happened."

"What happened?" I yelled.

He then went into great detail and explained that my grandfather became very sick. It seemed like overnight; he lost his mind. My grandmother found her husband on the front porch of their house one morning, sitting in a rocking chair naked as a jaybird. When she tried to make him go back inside, he took off running down the street. The town's only police officer found my grandfather in a neighbor's azalea bushes. He had covered himself up in pine straw and was acting like a wild dog. They sent him to two different hospitals. For a week, they took x-rays and performed all kinds of tests. They eventually sent him to the state's mental hospital in Milledgeville, but they couldn't find anything medically wrong with him. There was not one doctor in the State Mental Hospital of Georgia that could figure out his diagnosis.

During my grandfather's illness, my grandmother ran the cafe during the week and then traveled halfway across Georgia on the weekends to be with him. Two months later, a doctor told my grandmother that he thought my grandfather may have been suffering from the effects of a mild stroke, but he was not sure. He said it was his opinion that my grandfather needed to be as stress free as possible. He also told my grandmother that whenever she visited with my grandfather, she needed to go along with whatever was on his mind.

Against the advice of other doctors, and Uncle Dean, my grandmother made the decision to take my grandfather back home. Although my grandfather appeared to be doing better in the hospital, as soon as he arrived home, he began to make outrageous requests and demands. He wanted my grandmother to have their house repainted along with buying him a completely new wardrobe. The next day, when she took him to the cafe, the first thing he wanted was for her to repaint the dining area. That wasn't all. He wanted the curtains replaced, the tablecloths replaced, and he wanted her to replace all the dining room chairs. No expense was spared, and no demands were denied, even when he wanted the menu changed.

A few weeks later, he wanted her to purchase a new car and new furniture for their house. My grandmother borrowed and hit her credit limit trying to fulfill his every wish. Uncle Dean told my grandmother that she was out of her mind. He felt like she needed to send my grandfather back to Milledgeville to the State Mental Hospital before they went bankrupt.

Evidently, my grandmother did everything physically possible to keep the cafe open all while taking care of her husband. As hard as she tried, my grandfather became worse, and the business steadily declined. Five months after my grandfather returned home, my mother, Sandy, found her father one morning flopped over on the side of the toilet. He died from a massive stroke. To make matters worse, a few days after they buried him, my grandmother suffered an unexpected heart attack.

Uncle Dean cried out, "That is when your mother came to live with us."

"I did not know she lived with you."

Uncle Dean peered over his glasses and replied, "Yes, it was the summer of 1957. She ended up staying with us for the entire summer. Once your grandmother was back on her feet, she soon realized the cafe was a lost cause. A few weeks later she sold the cafe. She and Sandy then moved to Shady Branch."

I asked, "Why did she pack up and move to Shady Branch?"

Uncle Dean slightly raised his voice, saying, "We begged her to stay with us, but she still resented the people in her hometown. Also, your grandfather's cousin Dwayne and his family lived in Shady Branch. He convinced your grandmother that she could live off the sale of the cafe. He also persuaded her to take a part-time job as a manager at Toby's Truckstop Grill."

I looked at Uncle Dean and said, "That does not explain why you two have not been talking all these years."

CHAPTER FIFTEEN

A few minutes later, we pulled into Big Jack's Petro Stopping Center on the outskirts of Houston. Uncle Dean said, "This place is a lot larger than old Toby's Truckstop which used to be in Shady Branch." He then laughed at himself like a little kid.

Once we walked inside, we were both amazed by the unique gift shop. It had fresh baked pizza, clean restrooms, self-pay showers, a trucker's laundromat, a mini-movie theater, and an assortment of clothing and grocery items in a section called the General Store. After being enticed to purchase a couple of footlong sausage dogs from a do-it-yourself rotisserie, we sat down at a modern looking table in the dining area. As soon as we sat down, lights and sirens went off inside the Stopping Center. A few seconds later, the song, "Eye of the Tiger" from the *Rocky III* motion picture began playing on the loudspeakers while three men and one woman dressed in business suits approached us. They were followed by a film crew, a photographer, and three workers carrying several different items. One of the nicely dressed men was middle aged. He was wearing a Texas Tech University baseball cap. He stepped closer to our table and said, "Congratulations. Today is your lucky day." He paused for a second before looking at Uncle Dean and said, "Because you have been such a long-time, loyal customer at our Houston area Stopping Center, you have won some incredible prizes. Congratulations."

Uncle Dean stood up and said, "Sir, I think you have the wrong person. I am not a loyal customer."

The businessman smiled, shook Uncle Dean's hand, pulled him close, and whispered, "It don't matter, Hoss. Just smile for the camera and act like you are surprised."

Turning toward the film crew and photographer, the man pulled a microphone out of his coat pocket and placed it in front of his mouth before saying, "I'm Jack Cardwell, owner of the Petro Stopping Centers. Today we are giving away some big prizes to one of our most loyal customers." He then looked at Uncle Dean before asking, "So how old are you, old-timer?"

Uncle Dean smiled and pridefully replied, "Eighty-two. I'll be eighty-three in April."

Jack Cardwell patted Uncle Dean on the back while saying, "That's fantastic. Now tell everyone your name."

"Dean Lee."

Mr. Cardwell stepped back from Uncle Dean and positioned himself closer to the camera before he asked, "Well, Dean, what do you think about the service at Big Jack's Petro Stopping Center?

Uncle Dean looked into the camera and yelled out, "It has been fantastic."

In a loud and enthusiastic voice, Mr. Cardwell looked into the camera and yelled, "Did you hear that, ladies and gentlemen? Our eighty-two-year-old loyal customer said the service here was fantastic. What about the food, Dean?"

Uncle Dean smiled for the camera and replied, "Top notch."

Mr. Cardwell stepped closer to the camera gently saying, "He said it was top notch. Did you hear that ladies and gentlemen? Now that is what we like to hear." He then looked at Uncle Dean and said, "Good sir, because we value our long-standing relationship with you, we want you to have a few gifts."

Mr. Cardwell then handed Uncle Dean a poster sized gift card. Posing for the cameras next to Uncle Dean, he said, "This certificate says that you have won 500 gallons of pure Petro Stopping Center gasoline or diesel fuel." After a few photos, he then handed Uncle Dean another certificate. He said, "We would also like for you to have a lifetime of free oil changes. Did you hear that? You heard right, Dean. It is a lifetime of free oil changes."

Uncle Dean smiled for the cameras and did not reply.

Mr. Cardwell then handed Uncle Dean a basket filled with two Petro truckers' hats, a sweatshirt, several t-shirts, and a dozen pairs of Petro logo socks. Jack Cardwell thanked Uncle Dean for his loyalty. Once the cameras were turned off, Jack loosened his tie from his collar and said, "I'm sorry I interrupted your lunch. Do you mind if I grab a piece of pizza and eat with y'all?"

Uncle Dean said, "Not at all. Grab your pizza. We will wait for you."

Once Jack came back with his food and a soft drink, he reintroduced himself. He said, "I'm sorry about all that, but my publicity team has me traveling around our new Stopping Centers doing these local commercials."

While we were eating, Jack listened to me as I explained why we were in Houston. After Jack finished his pizza, he shared how he had built a truck stop franchise empire from nothing. He explained that he was born in Missouri and served in the US Army in the early 1950s. While he was stationed in El Paso at Fort Bliss, he met his bride. They pooled their money together and purchased a gas station there in El Paso. They did so well, Jack worked out a deal with Chevron to purchase a truck stop. In 1975 they opened the first self-service truck stop in the United States.

After taking a few sips of his drink, Jack continued explaining that his new station filled a void for truck drivers as they began to offer amenities for the truckers. Before Jack's station came along, truck drivers were not treated with much respect. Because Jack and his wife understood the truckers, they built their business on treating people with respect and dignity. They also let the truckers know that they appreciated their business. The franchise grew from their friendly reputation. Jack said, "We now have around forty Stopping Centers in several states."

I said, "That sounds like a pretty good business strategy."

Jack quickly replied, "If you want to be successful, Tim, this strategy applies to any business. It also applies to life. When you treat people with respect, you will be respected."

Uncle Dean could not resist when he asked, "So tell me, Jack, why did you pick me for your commercial?"

Jack laughed and said, "Well, I saw you when you pulled up. I knew you were the oldest person in the place because a flock of buzzards was circling overhead… I'm joking with you, Dean."

Uncle Dean replied, "Pretty smart. I take it that my 500 gallons of gasoline and free oil changes can only be redeemed at this particular Petro Stopping Center."

The wise business owner replied, "You are pretty clever yourself, Dean. When I do these giveaways, I always try to pick people with out of state tags on their vehicle." He then pulled out $300 in cash and slid it across the table. He said, "I know you will never be here again. Take this cash and use it on your trip to Florida. You gentlemen have been a delight. God bless you and safe travels."

***

Back on the interstate, I looked at Uncle Dean and said, "That Jack is somethin' else. It's easy to see why he is so successful. He has a great personality."

Uncle Dean pulled out the cash given to him by Jack and gave me $200. Although I initially objected, he said, "Take it. Use it to take your sweetheart out on a date." He momentarily paused and then said, "I guarantee you that Jack has worked his tail off. Nobody becomes successful like him without hard work."

After looking in the side mirror I said, "Speaking of hard work. I have been trying to find out what your big secret is."

Uncle Dean pulled out his pipe and continued to unravel a secret he had kept hidden for many years. He said, "Like I said before, it is complicated." He then inhaled a smoke from his pipe before he continued. "When your grandmother took your mother to Panama City Beach for a couple of days of vacation, my relationship with your grandmother went downhill in a hurry."

I asked, "What happened at Panama City Beach?"

Uncle Dean hesitated for a few seconds before he explained that on the first morning at the beach, my grandmother was walking near the water with my mother. While they were walking, my grandmother ran into a woman named Tessie Fisher. My grandmother recognized her from her days working in Birmingham. Tessie was not much older than my grandmother. When my grandmother was working as a waitress in Birmingham, Tessie was one of her regular customers. Tessie worked at a bank not far from the diner. She was one of the first professional women that my grandmother ever met. Every morning on her way to work, Tessie would visit the diner, order a cup of coffee, and talk to my grandmother. Although their conversations were mostly of a professional nature, they began to mutually admire one another. My grandmother wanted to become a professional woman like Tessie. Tessie wanted to find true love like my grandmother had found with my grandfather. Although they were not of the same social standing, my grandmother and Tessie had a mutual respect for each other.

This early morning coffee routine lasted for a few months until the Great Depression finally took its toll on the bank where Tessie worked. Unexpectedly, Tessie was forced to leave Birmingham when the bank closed its doors. She moved to Chattanooga through her political and social connections. Tessie's managerial skills allowed her to obtain a much sought-after position with the Tennessee Valley Authority."

I interrupted Uncle Dean and asked, "What in the world did this woman have to do with you and my grandmother?"

He shook his head with a shameful expression on his face. He said, "Several years later when I started workin' with the Tennessee Valley Authority, I met Tessie. She and I worked closely with each other as professionals. I'm ashamed to say but I sinned. She was married, and I was married. We fell in lust for each other; not in love with each other."

I almost pulled off the side of the road. For a moment I did not know what to say. Finally, I asked, "You had an affair?"

He looked me straight in my eyes, answering, "I did." He paused for a few seconds and continued explaining that nobody knew about the affair except my grandmother. She found out all about it while she and Tessie reunited on the beach of Panama City long after the affair had been over. Unbelievably, Tessie did not know that my grandmother was Uncle Dean's sister. While they were becoming reacquainted, Tessie decided to unload on my grandmother how she had an affair that caused her marriage to fail. As Tessie began to reveal to my grandmother how she confessed her sins to her husband, and how her husband could not forgive her sins, the story became more painful. My grandmother couldn't believe it when Tessie revealed the name of her former lover. After many more questions, they both were shocked once they figured it out.

I wanted to ask my great uncle a lot of questions, but instead I simply asked, "Did you ever tell your wife?"

He replied, "The last real conversation that Claire and I had with each other, she begged me to tell Emma Jean. I told Claire that it would devastate my wife. At first, she threatened to tell her. Once I convinced Claire that it would only cause heartbreak that could be avoided, she left it alone. As you may have guessed, this indiscretion has caused my relationship with your grandmother to be permanently strained."

I asked, "How long did the affair last, and how did it end?"

Uncle Dean paused before saying, "We saw each other for only a few months. That is when the Good Lord made me realize that what we were doing was wrong. I loved Emma Jean, and I loved my boys. Once the Tennessee Valley Authority projects were over, we parted ways; promising each other that we would never contact each other. I never saw Tessie again. I then promised God that I would change and become a better husband and father."

I asked, "Does my mother know about this affair?"

Uncle Dean replied, "Not to my knowledge."

All of a sudden, I began laughing uncontrollably. It was a nervous and unexpected laugh. I then looked at him and said, "Now I get it. You became religious after this happened. Once you found religion and became hooked up with the Church of Christ, you wanted your sister and the rest of your family to… Yes, I now understand. My grandmother was upset over your hypocrisy."

As we passed a huge cattle operation near Beaumont, Texas, he tried to change the subject when he said, "Look at all that money grazing in that field."

I was not about to let him off the hook. I replied, "My mother thinks you are a saint. I don't know if she would allow you to live with her if she knew…"

Uncle Dean interrupted me saying, "Tim, I am no saint. You don't know how much I hate that I messed up and fell to the sins of temptation and lust, but we all know, the only perfect person ever to live on this earth was Jesus."

I laughed even harder than before, shook my head, and said, "All these years, and you have kept this a big secret. Do you feel better now that you have talked about it?"

He slid up in his seat before replying, "It has been on my mind more than you can imagine. When Emma Jean was lingering during her final days, I came very close to telling her, but I didn't. I did not want her to leave this world with a broken heart. God knows that I pray every day that the Good Lord will not reveal all of this to her or my son up in Heaven. For the longest time, I felt like God took my first son away from me because of my sins. If that was my punishment for my sins, then the Good Lord applied the worst punishment a man could ever go through."

I said, "I don't feel sorry for you a bit. If there is any justice in Heaven, I have to believe your wife and son are watching you squirm right now."

With a somber face, he replied, "I guess it won't be much longer until I find out what they are doing up there in Heaven. My time on this earth won't be long."

I sensed that Uncle Dean was becoming a little emotional and decided to change the subject. Although I was shocked by what he had revealed to me, I tried to find some empathy for a man who was confessing his sins. Honestly, I could care less if the man slipped and sinned such a long time ago. I really did not know my Aunt Emma Jean and the only skin I had in the game pertained to his relationship with my grandmother. I laughed before asking him, "Speaking of Heaven… What do you think it will be like once we die?"

He replied, "I'm not really sure. I would like to think that it will be an incredible journey. I imagine it will be like flyin' on the most beautiful flight that anyone could ever dream about."

"No, that is not what I mean. What do you think it will be like once you arrive?"

He took off his glasses before replying, "Well, I'm pretty sure we are gonna have to answer for all of our shortcomings, and then we will live forever in eternity."

I asked, "What do you think we will be doing with all that time on our hands?"

Uncle Dean wiped his glasses and said, "That is a good question. I figure we will sing a lot, eat whatever we want, and visit with old friends."

I glanced over at him while saying, "You know that when I think of Heaven, I wonder how people who arrived before us feel about the life we have lived?"

He asked, "What do you mean?"

I replied, "I know it sounds crazy, but think about it. I sometimes wonder if there will be any resentment. I always imagine all those people who never experienced the wonder of television or using a telephone. I sometimes think about people who lived in a time when they were not able to experience the modern conveniences we have today. I know I would be mad if I never had the opportunity to experience air conditioning or an indoor toilet. I wonder if they will be resentful?"

He punched me on my shoulder while saying, "I don't know about any of that, but I have to admit that I always wanted to be able to play a few hands of poker with my grandfather; something that was never allowed in my house when I was a child."

I laughed at him before saying, "Maybe that is what Heaven is all about. If you live a good life, then for the rest of eternity you will travel to places you always wanted to see, be introduced to the famous people you wanted to meet, visit the relatives you never knew, and do all the activities that you wanted to do while you were alive."

He laughed at me and then said, "Doing what you just described would take up a lot of time."

"Yeah, once you were able to accomplish all those activities, you could always do it all over again. I know for a fact my Daddy would visit the Talladega Speedway every day if he could."

Uncle Dean shot back, "I bet my Emma Jean is shoppin' right now in some Paris looking boutique. She always wanted to do that."

I added, "I guarantee you that my mother would be eating lunch with Elvis Presley at least once a week and walking around on the beach with Tom Selleck every time there was an open spot on his social calendar."

Uncle Dean jumped on the Heaven bandwagon and said, "I would love to go deep sea fishin'. That is somethin' I have always wanted to do."

I kept it going by saying, "I would love to talk football with Vince Lombardi, the legendary football coach of the Green Bay Packers."

He asked, "I wonder how often we will get to visit with management?"

I asked, "Management?"

With a serious look on his face, he replied, "To me, management in Heaven would be the Good Lord and his disciples. I wonder if management in Heaven will ever have enough time to spend with the rest of us. I would have to believe that Jesus himself would have a pretty tight schedule. Think about all the people who would want to have a personal chat with Jesus much less having dinner or supper with him."

I couldn't help but laugh before saying, "I bet JC and his gang could put you on some really good fishing holes."

Uncle Dean responded, "Fishing with Jesus. I bet that has to be one of the most sought-after activities in Heaven."

I said, "I bet Jesus uses a modern bait caster rod and reel."

He replied, "I don't know, Tim. I would imagine that he would be more inclined to do a little fly fishing for trout in a cool mountain stream or stick to fishing on a small pond with a plain cane pole baited with crickets."

I couldn't help but laugh before saying, "You're crazy. JC would definitely be in Alaska, fighting a large salmon."

CHAPTER SIXTEEN

While we continued to talk about the what if's of eternal life, we drove through the city of Orange, Texas. Uncle Dean noticed a sign which read: Shangri La Botanical Gardens. He pointed to the sign and said, "Emma Jean loved those gardens. If you ever have some time on your hands, it is a sight to see."

I replied, "I don't think I will be coming back to Orange, Texas anytime soon."

On the outskirts of the city of Orange, Uncle Dean said, "If I remember correctly, once we pass these swamps we will be at the Sabine River. That, my friend, is the Louisiana state line."

A few minutes later we rode past a sign over a bridge that spanned the Sabine River. The sign simply read, "Louisiana State Line- Calcasieu Parish". While we were still on the bridge, a D&L Transport eighteen-wheeler passed us going at least eighty-five miles per hour. On the back doors of the trailer, the letters AU were painted in navy blue and outlined in orange. At the bottom of the doors, using the same color scheme, the phrase- WAR DAMN EAGLE was boldly displayed. I looked over at Uncle Dean and said, "Those Auburn people are everywhere."

He replied, "You know I don't know much about football, but whenever the University of Alabama plays, I pull for the Crimson Tide. I hate to admit it, but I really do like Auburn's head football coach. That Pat Dye seems like one of the good guys."

I turned down the thermostat in the U-Haul before saying, "I don't know much about Coach Dye, but I know his teams are always good. Some of the players at State told me that Coach Brown was pretty nervous about playing Auburn in the Sugar Bowl."

I took the opportunity to bring up the Sugar Bowl. I talked about the game and how much I wanted to be there. Uncle Dean patiently listened and then spoke up saying, "Tim, I would love for you to be at that game but waiting around in New Orleans until Monday is out of the question. Your grandmother is not doing well, and I really need to see her before it is too late. Parkinson's Disease is taking a toll on her body and her mind. I am praying that she will be able to speak to me once we see each other."

I decided not to argue because deep down I knew. I knew my grandmother was on the decline. I also knew I needed to take care of a few things before I had to go back to work at North Tallahassee High School.

A few minutes later, Uncle Dean insisted we take an exit into the oil town of Vinton, Louisiana and gas up at a Phillips 66 station and grocery store. He said, "It has been a long time since I ate in this place, but they have the tastiest boudin and crawfish you will find in Louisiana. These small establishments have some of the best food you will ever experience."

After we gassed up and parked the truck, we walked into a place that didn't look much different than when it opened in 1952. The place called Jimbo's was a cement block building with so much memorabilia on the walls that it appeared to be a museum. A short black man wearing thick glasses stood near the entrance and said, "Keep a movin' for da food- stay to your right and leave the aisles open. Better know what to order or get the hell on out da way."

While we were about to make our food order, a short scruffy looking man wearing an Auburn University hat stood off to the side of the counter waiting for his order. The man noticed my State windbreaker. He walked closer to me and pointed at my windbreaker before saying, "Y'all ain't bad, but y'all play in that sissy football conference. We play in the Southeastern Conference by God. We beat Bama this year, and now we gonna win the Shuga Bowl."

I was trying to order my food and did not know if the man was trying to be funny or if he was serious. I smiled at the man wearing the Auburn hat, but he did not respond. The man seemed a little agitated when he spoke louder by saying, "You do know that we are gonna kick your tails on Monday night. War Damn Eagle! How, you like that?"

I laughed momentarily before asking, "You keep saying we. How come you are not with the rest of the team practicing right now?"

The Auburn man cried out, "Look here, mister, we are all on the team at Auburn. Don't get scared when that Superdome be packed with nothin' but orange and blue this Monday."

Uncle Dean said, "Why don't you take your War Eagle rear end over there and eat your food?"

Before the Auburn fan could reply, another man walked over to us. I looked at Uncle Dean to make sure he was not pulling out Mr. .38 Special. The man politely said, "Ardale, leave these people alone. Go take ya food over yonder to our table and be nice." He then mumbled something Cajun so fast, we could not understand what he was saying. As Ardale began to walk away the man said, "Ca c'est bon. Ca c'est bon." (Meaning that it was really good.)

Ardale replied, "Ok, Bobby. I'll leave them old State people alone."

Once Ardale made it to his table, the man named Bobby whispered in a distinct, gravely Cajun accent, "Please forgive Ardale; he is as harmless as a toothless baby gator on Bourbon Street. He do love him some college football. The funny thing is that each week he pulls for a different team. A few weeks ago, he was wearin' an Ohio State sweatshirt. The week before that he was a South Carolina Gamecock. Through the years, different people in town have bought him different college football teams' clothing and hats. His wardrobe is amazing. Ardale may be the most popular man in town."

Uncle Dean asked, "Are you family?"

Bobby replied, "Not legally, but everyone in Vinton looks after him. He grew up pretty much an orphan. His mother did not know who was Ardale's father. She struggled with raising Ardale because he is autistic. Because his mother drank a lot, Ardale wandered around this town at a young age. When his mama passed away, he was a teenager. His life dramatically changed. The authorities said his mama ate some bad food. The official cause of death was some strange disease they called toxoplasmosis. Ever since she died, most everyone in this town considers Ardale like family. He lives in a small trailer on the back of the Renfrow property and works odd jobs."

I was stunned. I couldn't believe what I had heard about Ardale's mother dying of toxoplasmosis. I wanted to ask Bobby if the woman lived with cats, but I did not. I simply replied, "That is mighty nice of y'all to take care of him."

Bobby nodded with a smile and said, "I take it y'all are not from here."

I replied, "No, sir, we have been traveling from California. We are headed to New Orleans on our way to Florida."

Bobby smiled and then said, "When y'all pick up ya food, come over to our table and sit with me and Ardale. We would love the company."

Once Bobby walked away, Uncle Dean slightly punched me on my shoulder and then pointed to a huge poster on the wall behind us. I looked for a second and then said, "That is Bobby when he was younger. I knew he looked familiar."

Uncle Dean asked, "How do you know him? Is he some kind of football celebrity?"

I laughed and said, "That is Bobby Kimball. He was the lead singer for the band Toto."

Uncle Dean whispered, "Never heard of him or them. Are they a country band?"

I whispered back, "Get your food, old man. This is going to be special."

***

While we ate our Cajun food, we were thoroughly entertained by a world-renowned rock star, who was as down to earth as anyone you would want to meet. We were interrupted two times when several people walked up to our table to say hello to Bobby. While Bobby was talking to one of his friends, Uncle Dean and I could not help but notice how much tabasco sauce Ardale was putting on his po' boy shrimp sandwich.

Once Bobby was finally able to speak with us, he said, "I've been here a few days visitin' some of my kin. I live in Germany right now, but da road always seems to bring me back to Louisiana. This little Cajun town will always be special to me."

Bobby then explained how he moved to California early in his career with the blessing and support of his family and friends. He made it big after several rejections, some hard work, and a few lucky breaks. He told Uncle Dean, "California is beautiful, but after all my travels, there ain't no place like Cajun country. I love to perform, but I do not like the business part of da music industry."

I asked him, "I'm surprised that a big star like you would be eating here."

Bobby laughed before saying, "What you talkin' bout? These are my people. I love bein' round da people. Besides, they have the best jambalaya in da entire state of Louisiana. They also have a poster of me on da wall. The most important thing is that Ardale loves it here."

Bobby then began talking about once playing a style of music called Swamp Pop when he was young, and how he spent many of his nights in New Orleans playing and singing until the sun came up. He said, "Down here, we call that a Fais do-do or an all-night dance."

When Ardale found out that I had played college football, he wanted my autograph. Uncle Dean said, "Well, maybe we can do a trade for autographs." He looked at Ardale and said, "Tim will do it if Bobby does the same for Tim."

Bobby replied, "The only way I will do that is if Ardale can answer a trivia question about college football. He then paused before looking at me with a serious look on his face. He said, "Ask Ardale anything about football, and he will know da answer. This might be da most amazin' thing you will ever experience. Ask him a team's record, who da star player was, etc. It don't matter. Ardale knows da answer."

I thought for a moment and randomly asked, "Who was the head football coach at Army in 1928?"

Ardale smiled and replied, "That was too easy, Tim. Everyone knows that Biff Jones was the head football coach at Army in 1928."

I looked at Bobby and asked, "That is incredible. How did he know that?"''

Bobby laughed before saying, "Down here in da bayou, people around here sometimes call Ardale a 'Couyon'. In Cajun, it means he is a crazy person. Ardale ain't no 'Couyon'. He has a unique gift. Ask him another one. Ardale can't be stumped."

I asked Ardale, "Who won the Heisman trophy in 1959?"

Ardale looked at me like I was crazy before saying, "Everybody knows that was Billy Cannon from LSU. He played high school ball at Istrouma High in Baton Rouge."

Uncle Dean laughed and said, "Sign those autographs before he gets one wrong."

After we exchanged autographs, we shook hands and gave Ardale a hug before we walked out of Jimbo's. Bobby yelled at us across the parking lot saying, "Y'all have a safe trip. Once you make it to New Orleans, do what all of us Cajuns do. Laissez les bons temps rouler!! Let the good times roll."

***

Five minutes later, I was letting the good times roll, speeding down I-10 toward New Orleans. Through the bayous of Louisiana, we traveled in darkness. Uncle Dean was in rare form. He looked over at me and asked, "Do you know how to make Holy Water?"

"No, I do not."

Uncle Dean laughed at his own joke before saying, "You boil the hell out of it."

While I listened to Uncle Dean's corny jokes and his explanation about what exactly Cajuns were, I could barely hear a sports talk radio station out of New Orleans. Without being rude, I eased my hand on the knob of the U-Haul radio and slightly turned up the volume. When I heard, "Today, the team from State arrived in New Orleans." I quit listening to Uncle Dean. I focused my attention on the radio show. When I heard a clip of Coach Brown speaking about the upcoming game, I told Uncle Dean that I needed to find a phone and call my girlfriend, Maria. I could tell that Uncle Dean was not happy, but I went ahead and pulled off in Jennings, Louisiana. At the exit we noticed a large billboard that read, "Grand Opening Coming Soon: Chateau de Crocodile. Pet a live Crock- It will change your life".

I pulled over to a well-lit phone booth. I then called the Roosevelt Hotel in New Orleans and asked for room 319. Maria immediately picked up the phone. After telling her where I was located, I said, "Tell your family that I will miss being with them for the game."

Maria replied, "I understand. I will see you back in Tallahassee next week."

When I walked back to the U-Haul, I saw Uncle Dean standing next to the passenger side tire, smoking his pipe. I yelled at him, "Hop on in, and let's go."

He replied, "I hate you can't make it to that game, but I have a feeling one day you will make it to the Sugar Bowl."

***

We rolled into Baton Rouge a couple of hours later. Uncle Dean turned down the volume of the radio and said, "I need to let you know something before we make it to Florida."

"I can't wait to hear this." I replied.

"I want you to know that I am going to buy your parents' property."

I was stunned when I asked, "What did you say?"

He replied, "You heard me. I don't know how much your mother has told you, but their finances are in shambles. They are facin' foreclosure by the end of the month."

"What do you mean?"

He raised his voice and replied, "They are flat broke. Your mama is breaking her back tryin' to hold on, while your daddy guzzles beer all day and wonders why he can't find any new truckin' business."

I knew that finances were tight for my parents, but this revelation was something I did not expect. After hearing more details from him, I asked, "Are you sure you want to do this?"

"I can't think of a better way to spend my money. Your mother means the world to me."

It then occurred to me that my father might not be too happy with such an arrangement. I also worried that my cousins back in California would flip out when they learned that Uncle Dean was about to spend a considerable amount of his money for a seven-acre parcel of property in Shady Branch, Florida. I pondered about the details of such an arrangement. When I asked more about the particulars, Uncle Dean said, "I am going to buy the property from the bank. I'm pretty sure I will get a good deal since the property is already in foreclosure. Your parents will be able to stay on the property forever. It is the deal of a lifetime." He paused, looked at me and said, "Before I die, I will make sure that they will be legally protected."

I then realized why my mother had been so adamant about me bringing Uncle Dean to Shady Branch. She knew he would help her financially, and she had been making these arrangements in a roundabout way. It infuriated me that my mother had been so secretive about their financial dilemma. Then it occurred to me that my mother had done what she did best. She had closed another business deal with her ability to tell a good sob story and play on the heart strings of her uncle.

The sound of the radio and Uncle Dean urinating into a milk jug was all that was heard in the cab of the U-Haul until we came to a critical juncture of the interstate. I thought earlier that I might have a few minutes to visit with Maria and her family in New Orleans. I relinquished that idea. I decided to bypass the downtown area of the great city and kept driving toward the city of Slidell on I-12.

Uncle Dean said, "I didn't want to say anything, but I wasn't sure how you were gonna handle this U-Haul in downtown New Orleans. We can find a place to stay whenever you like. I am so thankful we are not going to have to cross over that bridge on Lake Pontchartrain."

A few minutes later, Uncle Dean later began saying, "Hotel, Motel, Holiday Inn."

His knowledge of those particular lyrics to a rap song surprised me as I could see a billboard in the distance, advertising a Holiday Inn near the city of Slidell. We unfortunately took a wrong turn off the exit near the Spanish Trail. We then realized the hotel was in the opposite direction. It was midnight when we were finally able to check in for the last overnight stay of our journey.

CHAPTER SEVENTEEN

Inside our motel room, I flopped down on my bed never considering changing my clothes. Uncle Dean, after changing into his worn-out pin striped pajamas, walked into the bathroom to find a cup to soak his dentures. I turned on the television and began watching a wrestling match between Hacksaw Jim Duggan and Andre the Giant. Uncle Dean walked out of the bathroom and said, "I love that Hacksaw. He is my kind of wrestler."

I asked, "You watch wrestling? I'm surprised. You do know it is all fake."

He replied, "There is nothin' fake about two men picking each other up and throwing each other around that ring. No, sir, I love Hacksaw. Look at him run circles around that Andre the Giant. Nothing fake about that."

All of a sudden, a blaring alarm went off outside of our room. We both thought that it was merely a system malfunction. We took our time to find out what was happening. As soon as I opened the door, chaos was taking place right outside of our room. Some people who were half dressed were running out into the parking lot. I could see the manager of the motel running past rooms, knocking on doors, and screaming, "Get out! There is a fiya! Get out right now!"

Like everyone else, Uncle Dean and I stood in the frigid parking lot as we watched the Slidell Louisiana Fire Department arrive along with several other emergency agencies. We couldn't see the fire from where we were standing; however, after noticing the thick black smoke coming from the other side of the building, we knew it was serious. When the emergency workers passed out blankets to everyone in the parking lot, travelers from out of town became acquainted while they watched the men of Ladder truck Number One fight a plume of smoke that climbed into a clear Louisiana night sky. While we sat on a curb, Uncle Dean looked at me and said, "I'd think we should go ahead and leave, but we need to get our suitcases, and I need my teeth."

I replied," Maybe they will let us back in since it looks like the fire was contained on the other side of the building."

A nice-looking middle-aged black lady standing next us began laughing and said, "Lord, I hope they let us back in. Like you, I need my stuff."

I asked, "Where are you from? You sure do look familiar."

She replied, "Jacksonville, Florida."

Uncle Dean asked, "What brings you to this part of the country?"

"My husband and I are headed to New Orleans to watch the Sugar Bowl."

Uncle Dean asked, "Which team are you pulling for?"

She replied, "State, of course. My daughter is a sophomore majoring in business there. She is also in the band. My name is Wanda Gibson."

Before Wanda could introduce us to her husband, Daniel, I recognized them both. I said, "Wait just a minute. I watch your commercials all the time in Tallahassee."

Daniel replied, "I hope you think the commercials are good. Our children think they are a little corny."

I shook Daniel's hand while saying, "Uncle Dean, these two are celebrities. Their commercials are so cool. I love it when you two pretend to fight about the style of upholstery for furniture in a house, or you argue about whether or not to buy a home with a swimming pool. Those commercials are classics. Who could ever forget that little jingle?... Don't make a mistake, Go with Gibson Real Estate."

The conversation kicked into high gear once they found out that I had played football at State. When I told them that I had a girlfriend, who was about to graduate from State, they seemed even more interested.

We soon learned that the husband-and-wife team owned one of the largest real estate agencies in the state of Florida. We listened with amazement as Wanda explained how they had built a successful business, all with the purchase of one rental property in Duval County years ago. One rental property turned into three. They hit it big when they began to secure beachfront property all down the Atlantic coast along with apartment complexes. It was a remarkable rags to riches story for a couple who were down on their luck.

Daniel explained that they had been in Slidell for a couple of days as they were closing a real estate deal for a well-known person from Slidell. Daniel went on to say, "Arthur Jones is the inventor of Nautilus weight equipment. He is from here. We met him years ago in Orlando. We now handle all of his real estate affairs."

A few minutes later, a fire brigade commander allowed all of us to retrieve our belongings but told us that we had to find other accommodations. After we wished the Gibsons a safe trip to New Orleans, we retrieved our belongings and Uncle Dean's false teeth. Not being able to find a place with a vacancy, we finally gave up and settled for something out of the ordinary.

We spent the rest of the night in the Slidell RV park. We were only able to catch a few hours of sleep before the sun woke me up. I had fallen asleep inside of Uncle Dean's Chrysler car. It dawned on me that this was not the best decision as I woke up shivering underneath a couple of Uncle Dean's old coats. I cranked up the car to generate some heat. When the car's radio came on, Uncle Dean woke up hearing the song, "Long Haired Country Boy" by the Charlie Daniels Band. He looked over at me and said, "I sure do wish I could grow a ponytail." He paused momentarily and then commented, "If I could, I would let my ponytail grow down to the crack of my ass." He then looked at his wristwatch and said, "Let's Slidell on out of here."

After we gassed up and looked at the Rand McNally Atlas, we sighed with relief. There was light at the end of the tunnel or rather light at the end of this journey. We drank our morning coffee and felt a jolt of energy. It was like our batteries had been recharged. We both realized that we were only about six hours away from Shady Branch, Florida. Although we both fought not having enough sleep, we were on the same page; we would sacrifice our own discomfort to make it to our final destination.

Further down the road, we stopped for a quick snack near Pascagoula, Mississippi. Uncle Dean started reminiscing, "When I was a teenager, I remembered a lady in church telling me that if you ever traveled through Mississippi, you needed to put your money in the bottom of your shoes in case you were ever robbed. To this day, when I think of Mississippi, I think about putting money in my shoes."

He then confided to me that he had actually spent a night in Pascagoula when a friend asked him to travel with him to purchase a truck. Uncle Dean smiled before saying, "I probably shouldn't tell you this, but that night was the first time I ever had a woman shoot me the squirrel."

I asked, "I have no idea what you are talking about. What in the world is shooting the squirrel?"

He replied, "You know. It is when a woman knowingly hikes up her skirt so you can see her underwear. We called that shooting the squirrel."

I asked, "What happened?"

He went on to say, "After she shot me the squirrel, she smiled and motioned with her index finger for me to come and sit next to her."

"Did you do it?"

He quickly responded, "Are you kidding me? Her husband was in the kitchen talkin' to my friend. That man was carrying a gun in his holster. I was scared to death."

I laughed at him while we walked back to the U-Haul. Before we jumped into the cab, I noticed an older man on a tall ladder taking down a Christmas decoration from the top of a light pole. I pointed toward the man while saying, "That reminds me of Shady Branch during Christmas. As a matter of fact, I'm pretty sure that decoration in the shape of a candy cane is the exact same type of decoration they use in downtown Shady Branch."

Uncle Dean said, "Speaking of Shady Branch, let's head that way."

A few miles down the road, he caught my attention when he said, "It seems like it was yesterday the last time I was here in Pascagoula. I had never been out of the state of Alabama in my life. I thought Mississippi was a foreign country before I took that trip. Time sure does go by fast."

I asked, "Speaking of time going by fast, how does it feel to be eighty-two years old?"

He replied, "You know, Tim, I wake up every day, and I can't believe I'm this old. There are days when I don't feel any different than when I was twenty-five. Then I look in the mirror and can't believe what I am lookin' at. I sometimes wonder who the hell is looking back at me. You will find out that the older you become, the longer your days seem but your years seem to go by faster than you can imagine. I can't explain it. The other odd thing that happens is that you will struggle with remembering what you did yesterday, yet there will be times when you can remember what you did twenty years ago."

I asked, "I hope you don't mind me asking this, but do you ever worry about when you… You know, when you are goin' to die?"

He gave me a strange look before saying, "Nobody wants to die. I'm no different than anybody else. All I can tell you is that I have traveled around the sun eighty-two times. I have made it through the Pandemic of 1918, the Great Depression, and a lifetime of regrets. I've watched people come and go. I have made friends and watched friendships disappear. I have watched many of my friends pass away long before their time.

There have been days when I have watched mothers cry over losing a child, and fathers shipped back home from overseas with a flag draped over their casket. But the beauty of this world is that I have been able to witness some of the most treasured things in life; like the miracle of birth, little children eating an ice cream cone in a park and taking trips halfway across this beautiful country.

I have met good people who became criminals, and criminals who became good people. I have encountered religious acting people who were the devil and devils who became sanctified. I have no idea what the Good Lord has in store for me as the clock is runnin' out, but I do know that when I wake up, I am thankful for another day.

You asked me if I was worried about when I was goin' to die. Dying does not bother me. What bothers me is my fear of becoming so helpless that someone has to feed me, bathe me, and wipe my rear end. I pray that when my time does come, I will not have to be taken care of like a little baby.

Years ago, when I asked my mother if she worried about dying, she told me that we don't need to worry about things we don't need to worry about. She explained that if all we did was to worry about dying we would miss out on livin'. I took that advice and have applied it to my life. I have tried to see each day as an opportunity to meet someone new and to learn something I didn't know before. I have tried not to worry about something that I don't need to worry about."

Right before we crossed the Alabama state line, the song "Sweet Home Alabama" by Lynyrd Skynyrd coincidentally began playing over the radio from a station in Grand Bay. I looked over at Uncle Dean, who was smiling like a little child going to the circus. Waiting for some profound words of wisdom about Uncle Dean's home state, I laughed when he remarked, "The roads here in Alabama tend to be a lot better than those in Mississippi."

***

We approached the George Wallace Tunnel in Mobile. He said, "I don't like long bridges, but for me, tunnels are the worst."

Once inside of the tunnel, I turned on the lights of the U-Haul, rolled down my window, and began barking like a dog. He thought I had lost my mind until I said, "You can hear the echo bouncing off these walls."

When we exited the tunnel, we took a long ride on the Jubilee Parkway Bridge which crossed Mobile Bay for seven miles. Halfway over the bridge, I began to laugh when I noticed Uncle Dean reaching for his milk jug.

We passed an Alabama State Trooper near the bottom of the bridge. I silently prayed that the patrolman hadn't witnessed Uncle Dean's indecent exposure. After he zipped up, Uncle Dean said,

"I don't know about you, but whenever you see a place to stop, I sure would like something to eat."

I replied, "Would that be dinner, lunch, or supper?"

He replied, "Right now I don't care what we call it. I'm hungry enough to eat roadkill on a saltine cracker."

A few miles later, we took an exit near Robertsdale, Alabama. We found a small meat and three place which also had gas pumps out front. It was an updated country store that served food. The Bama Biscuit House wasn't quite as large as a Cracker Barrel, but it was just as busy. After we filled up the U-Haul, we waited to be seated for a few minutes before the hostess told us to follow her to our table. She was a very pretty girl, who was wearing a Southern Miss t-shirt. Uncle Dean asked, "Do you go to Southern Miss?"

She answered, "No, sir. My brother goes there. I'm only in the tenth grade at my high school."

After we were seated, Uncle Dean whispered to me, "I could have sworn that little girl was about twenty-two or twenty-three years old. It amazes me how girls today look so much older than they did ten or twenty years ago."

While we waited to order our food, we heard a man sitting with some friends say, "That sign is not right. It should say Construction has ended."

While having a moment of Deja' vu, I took the lead by introducing myself and Uncle Dean. I said, "I apologize, but we couldn't help but overhear what you were saying about the road sign."

The man not much older looking than me, was wearing a Duke University sweatshirt. He asked, "What about the road sign?"

I replied, "You are not going to believe this, but we have been having conversations about that stupid road sign for several days. We have traveled all the way from California, and that sign has been a big topic of conversation during our trip."

The man laughed and then introduced himself. He said, "My name is Tim Cook. These are some of my old buddies from high school."

After the introductions were over, he said, "That sign has bothered me for years. It implies that we need to end construction; not that construction has ended. I know it sounds ridiculous, but there is a difference. My friends here always disagree with me, but I hope they change the wording of that sign one day. I guess you could say it is one of my pet peeves. I always see things differently than most."

Uncle Dean agreed with him and explained the story about his son pointing out the sign controversy to him years ago. He said, "Two Tims in the same place. What are the odds?"

Tim Cook replied, "The man who owns this place is also named Tim. Tim Payne cooks a mean pork chop. Take my word, you have to try his potato salad and pound cake. They are to die for."

Once we found out that Tim Cook had recently graduated from Duke University with his master's degree, we were impressed when he told us that he was working for IBM in management. He teased me when he found out that I had graduated from State. He said, "I completed my undergrad at Auburn a few years back. I wish I had time to go to the Sugar Bowl. It ought to be a good game." He then smiled and said, "War Damn Eagle."

The more Tim talked, the more we were impressed by his knowledge of an industry that he predicted was about to explode. He said, "I tell everybody I know they need to invest in computer companies. I predict that in the near future, not only will every business have a computer; almost every household will have one."

Uncle Dean laughed before saying, "I don't know about all that, but it sounds interesting."

I shook my head and said, "My girlfriend is a business major, and she says the same thing."

Tim interjected, "You better listen to her. From what I see and know, I hope you remember this conversation ten years from now. Invest now, and ten years later you will want to thank me."

Uncle Dean commented, "I can only hope that I can remember my name ten years from now."

A few minutes later, we finished eating and said our goodbyes at the Biscuit House. As we walked across the parking lot, we knew that we were on the very last leg of our journey together. As soon as we were in the U-Haul, I said, "I know that guy is smart, but I find it hard to believe that computers will be in every home."

Uncle Dean replied, "If you want to invest your money into something that will pay big dividends, invest it into a water farm."

"A water farm?"

Uncle Dean yelled out, "Yes, siree, bobcat tail. You could bottle water and sell it. Think about it. Bottling water has to be the biggest return on your investment you could ever find. Free water and a few bottles. What a great business."

I laughed at him and said, "You and I both know that nobody is ever going to buy bottled water. As far as that is concerned, I think that Tim Cook is dreaming some big dreams if he thinks every house will one day have a computer. I'm pretty sure that will never happen."

Uncle Dean laughed and then surprised me when he said, "Speaking of stock. I have a safety deposit box in Chattanooga, Tennessee where I have kept a good bit of stocks and bonds I purchased many years ago. My son knows all about it. If something happens to me, he will know where to find it."

I looked over at him and asked, "Let me guess. You bought stock in IBM."

He replied, "No, sir. It all came from the Bank of North Alabama. There is no telling how much it is worth today.

CHAPTER EIGHTEEN

During the last three hours of our drive to Shady Branch, we talked like we were trying to make up for lost time. We covered a wide range of topics not to exclude our best meal ever, the most fun we ever had as child, and how we remembered our first kiss.

By the time we had passed Pensacola, Florida, it seemed like we were best friends. The almost fifty-year difference in our ages did not diminish one word that was spoken. I thoroughly enjoyed conversing with one of the oldest people I had ever spent time with. Uncle Dean relished the fact that he had a younger relative who seemed to enjoy listening to his life experiences. We spoke about the past, and we verbally dreamed about the future. We laughed many times and cried together when Uncle Dean explained in detail about how his brother-in-law lost a leg in World War I in a place called the Argonne Forest.

As we continued to reminisce, I reminded him that the Berlin Wall had come down a month before. He told me he remembered when the Berlin Wall was built. He said he never dreamed he would be alive to watch it come down.

We thought back about the people we had encountered during our trip. We laughed at the fact that Uncle Dean promised he would practice shooting Mr. .38 Special before he unloaded it on another robber. I spoke about my relationship with my own father after he told me that he wished he could have spent more time with his father.

Uncle Dean talked about how much he hoped he would have some good quality time with his sister. He also talked in depth about how he regretted not having a good relationship with his younger son, Roy. He said, "When Roy was a little boy, I took him and Tom out to the barn to show them how to butcher a hog. I will never forget that look on Roy's face. He was horrified! After that day, he spent all of his time with Emma Jean. He never wanted to hunt or fish. He liked to read and help his mother in the kitchen. He and I were different, and I never allowed myself to appreciate his qualities. I know he loves me, but I also know he resents me to a degree. I certainly can't blame him."

Our conversation did not lack enthusiasm or emotion. It was heart-felt. Years later, I would wish that it had all been recorded so I could play it back to my other relatives. There was this one revelation, however, that was unexpected and shocking. I was so distracted by his words that I had to pull over at a highway rest area. I needed further explanations and details. I also wanted to be far from any distractions while I listened to what he had to say.

While we sat at a cement picnic table under an old oak tree smattered with Spanish moss, Uncle Dean poured out his tortured soul about something he had kept a secret for many years. He said, "As I was tellin' you in the truck, the other reason why I needed to leave California was because an investigator from the FBI has been callin' me askin' questions about something that happened so long ago, I had no idea that anybody even cared."

I was completely stunned when he revealed to me that he had once been involved in the illegal making and distribution of corn liquor moonshine when he was a sharecropper. He explained that times were tough during Prohibition, and that he and others in his community of Cool Shoals had worked together to produce a product that was in high demand and brought a lot more profit to them than the money they were making growing crops. He said, "That corn we put in a jar, gave me enough money to get married and buy my own farm."

He further explained that while he and a few others were making a good living, there were others that were threatened by this success and wanted it for their own needs and desires. He said, "There was guy named Veron Daniels who lived one county away."

As soon as Uncle Dean said the name Vernon Daniels, I remembered the conversation I had with Eston Harper on my flight to California. I yelled, "Are you talking about the man they found chained to a tractor?"

He replied, "That's him."

Uncle Dean then further explained in greater detail that Vernon Daniels had been threatening violence if Uncle Dean and his partners didn't stop selling moonshine. On a cold rainy night in 1927, Vernon drove his tractor eleven miles to a remote section of land near the Tennessee River. His intent was to destroy the still that was the backbone of Uncle Dean's moonshine operation.

Uncle Dean said, "He found out where we were making our moonshine and decided to steal our materials. When he arrived with a wagon on the back of his tractor, the only person there was your grandmother. He snuck up on her and caught her by surprise."

I interrupted him asking, "You mean to tell me that my grandmother was involved in the making of moonshine?"

He nodded yes while saying, "Vernon was a snake in the grass. He snuck up behind your grandmother before she could get to her gun. I was not there. I had been helping another friend butcher a hog a few miles away when Vernon caught your grandmother flat-footed. When I rode up to our makeshift shed on horseback later that evening, I had arrived way too late."

"What do you mean?"

"Vernon had already had his way with your grandmother. That sorry SOB beat the hell out of her and raped her in our shed.

When I entered the shed and saw him standin' over her, I knew what he had done. I ran toward him, but he turned quick, pulled out a revolver, and shot me on the side of my left leg. When I fell backwards up against a pile of corn husks, I could see him taking aim at my head. I closed my eyes and knew that this was my last day on earth. I heard the trigger engaged and a loud boom. However, I felt nothing. I opened my eyes, and unbelievably Vernon fell toward me deader than a door nail. Your grandmother had picked up her shotgun and unloaded it into the back of his head. She blew his brains out."

"My grandmother is the one who killed him?"

"Yes, but that's not the only part of the story that I need to get off my chest."

He explained to me that he and my grandmother spent the entire night moving a body, chaining it to a tractor, maneuvering that tractor into a ravine a few hundred yards away from their still, and covering it up with rock, clay, and small boulders, and brush. He then further shocked me by saying, "It wasn't long after that ordeal when we found out that your grandmother was pregnant. Unfortunately, it was the same time that she was being accused of having an affair with Little Cyrus. What I didn't tell you earlier was that a big part of her being sent away had to do with her being pregnant. In the backward minds of some of the people in our community, once the baby started showin' it would have appeared that Claire did have a fling with Little Cyrus."

"Are you trying to tell me that my mother is the baby produced from a rape by Vernon Daniels?"

"Nope. That baby born in 1928 was your uncle. The reason you haven't ever heard about him is because we put him up for adoption when he was born in Birmingham. It took me a lifetime to find this out, but he was adopted by a nice family in Pittsburgh, Pennsylvania. I discovered that his adopted name was Joseph Kelly. Joseph passed away before I could contact him. He died in a car accident in 1983. He graduated with honors from Notre Dame where he played football and baseball. He married a girl he met at Notre Dame, whose father owned one of the largest farm equipment dealerships in Indiana."

Uncle Dean paused and gathered his thoughts before continuing, "Joseph married her and became a successful salesman and vice-president of his father-in-law's dealership. He and his wife, who were good Catholics, had six children. The sad part of the story is that he had recently been named the new president of the company when he was killed. Ironically, he ran into a tractor on a rural road in Indiana on a cold rainy night."

I was stunned. Once again, I was learning about a part of my family that I never knew anything about. I then asked, "So what does the FBI have to do with this? Who contacted you?"

"Some guy named Drew Geddings."

It is a small world I thought. I then proceeded to tell Uncle Dean how I knew Drew Geddings. I found out that Uncle Dean's one phone conversation with Drew Geddings was enough to keep him from wanting to meet with a man who was digging to uncover facts about a murder that took place years ago.

Uncle Dean said, "I wasn't about to meet with him. He has been calling me for months, and I have avoided him like the plague."

Before we continued our journey home, we sat under that oak tree and talked about all that had been revealed. I wanted answers to several questions that were bothering me. I asked, "Did you send my grandmother to Birmingham to have a baby all by herself?"

He responded, "Not exactly. Once she was settled, I sent Emma Jean to live with her during the last few months of the pregnancy. She and two of her cousins were with your grandmother the night the baby was born. As you can imagine, your grandmother has suffered great emotional pain having to give up her son. Although that child was a product of a rape, your grandmother never forgave herself for agreeing to the adoption. Without your mother or other family members knowing, your grandmother has tried for years to find out about the child she gave away."

"You mean, who y'all gave away."

He snapped back, "That is correct. I was more guilty than any. I did not want her to keep that baby."

I then asked, "Does my mother know any of this?"

He leaned closer to me and replied, "I don't think so. As far as I know, I'm pretty sure your grandfather never knew. Your grandmother told me after your mother was born that revealing those family secrets would cause more pain than good. She begged me to never tell Sandy what I knew."

I was still stunned when Uncle Dean made me promise to never tell my mother about the brother she never knew. I made him promise that he would take care of my mother and father and make sure they had a place to stay after he passed away. We shook hands and headed for Shady Branch while I thought about the years of guilt that my grandmother suffered in silence all those years.

***

Before we knew it, we were passing the Apalachee County Welcomes You sign. We both noticed a large billboard advertisement a couple of miles away which read: Tuesday-January 24 is FRY DAY! Burn in Hell-Ted Bundy! At the bottom of the advertisement it read: Paid for by CFCP- Citizens for Capital Punishment. Uncle Dean said, "They are pretty serious down here about makin' sure that man is put to death."

I replied, "He may be the most hated man to ever set foot in the state of Florida." I then realized why Uncle Dean's opposition to the death penalty was so strong. He didn't reply, and I kept my mouth shut.

When we finally made it to the long dirt road which led to my childhood home in Shady Branch, Uncle Dean looked at me and said, "You did good, Timmy Boy. You don't know how long I have prayed that I would be able to make it. We made good time considerin'."

I thought that there would be a happy reunion or some type of celebration at my home. I quickly noticed that my mother's car was not parked in the yard. My father's pickup truck was also missing. I glanced over at the Styles by Sandy's Beauty Shop trailer. No cars were parked at the shop. I could sense that something was not quite right. Once I parked the U-Haul, we walked into the house. No one was at home. Unlike the special greeting I had received in California, Uncle Dean had nobody celebrating his arrival in Shady Branch.

I decided to take Uncle Dean to my room over the detached garage which was only a few yards away from our home. After helping him with his luggage, I showed him my old room which was filled with trophies, medals, and photographs which served as a reminder of my athletic accomplishments.

He said, "I promise I won't remove any of your stuff. I only need a bed to rest the weary bones."

While I helped him unpack, the telephone rang. I picked it up to hear my mother's best customer, Nancy Smith, on the other end of the line. She said, "Tim, this is Nancy. Your mother wanted me to call you. I hate to tell you this, but your grandmother has taken a terrible turn for the worse. We are all here at the nursing home. You need to get here as fast as you can."

I asked, "Is she still alive?"

Nancy paused before saying, "Tim, she's barely hanging on by a rat's whisker."

"Thank you, Mrs. Smith."

Not a word was said as I drove Uncle Dean in my Toyota pickup truck to the nursing home about twenty minutes away. Nancy and the minister from the Shady Branch Methodist Church were the first people to greet us when we arrived. Uncle Dean did not want to talk. He insisted that he be able to see his sister. An elderly-looking nurse with thick painted eyebrows and long gray hair took us back to my grandmother's room. My parents immediately hugged us when we came into the room. They were very emotional. My mother, with tears streaming down her face whispered, "They called us this afternoon. I can't understand it because she was fine and very alert yesterday. I don't know what happened."

Uncle Dean stood next to his sister as she laid motionless, gasping every few moments for her last breaths. He turned to me and whispered, "That is the death rattle. I have seen it many times. She won't be here much longer."

Five minutes later, the nursing staff, which had been instructed not to resuscitate, watched with the family as my grandmother gently passed from this world to the next. I couldn't help but watch Uncle Dean, who began to sob like a baby. I also fought back tears, knowing that my Great Uncle did not have the chance to ask his sister for forgiveness. Nobody in the room said a word. We stood around the body of a woman who had suffered with an illness that had wrecked her mind and body.

My mother was the first one to speak while she held my grandmother's hand. She said, "You rest now, sweet Mama. No more shaking, no more pain. God has you now."

This was my first experience with the death of a loved one. I stood still as I looked at my grandmother's face. To me she looked peaceful. I knew that she had suffered and was ready to go. Even knowing that, I silently grieved with a pain that I did not expect.

One by one we began to leave the room after individually saying goodbye. Uncle Dean asked us if he could be alone with his sister for a few minutes. I walked out with everyone else but stopped outside the door. I listened closely, trying desperately to hear Uncle Dean. The only thing I heard was, "You make sure to take care of Emma Jean, Tom, Mama and the rest of the gang up in Heaven. I will be with you all very soon."

***

By the time we made it back to the house, vehicles were parked all over the yard. Many of my mother's clients, close friends, and church ladies were inside arranging the food and drinks that had already arrived. My father, Hank, headed out to his shed to grab himself a couple of cold beers.

Uncle Dean whispered to me, "Back home we called these ladies the funeral buzzards. Every small town has them. God bless them, but they can be aggravating."

There was more fried chicken, pans of baked beans, and potato salad than an army could consume. Several ladies came up to me and said the same exact thing. "You know your grandmother is in a better place."

I thought back to my earlier conversation with Uncle Dean about death. I, too, did not want to hear their words of solace. I knew they meant well, but I didn't want to participate in their conversations. Instead of continuing to listen to people offer their condolences, I went outside to my old room over the garage and made a dreaded phone call to Maria. As soon as I told her the news about my grandmother, she told me that she would take the next flight back to Tallahassee. Although I wanted to be with her, I did not want to ruin her trip to New Orleans with her family. After finally convincing her that there was nothing she could do, we agreed that she should stay in New Orleans.

At first, my mother voiced her displeasure that Maria was not leaving New Orleans. Then after Uncle Dean agreed with me, she changed her tune and accepted the fact that her possible future daughter-in-law needed to stay with her family in New Orleans.

***

For the next two days, my mother frantically searched the house for any photos she could find of my grandmother.

Whenever she would find one, she would show it to Uncle Dean. He was grieving worse than anyone knew. However, like a good uncle, he sat next to his niece and listened as she reminisced about her mother. Occasionally, he would offer a positive story about his sister during their younger years, as this was easier to do than to reflect on their later relationship that was so strained.

Several times my father and I left everyone in the house to unload Uncle Dean's furniture from the U-Haul. Stacking it all in my father's trucking shed, we took our time not wanting to go back into the house. We never said a word to each other except to warn the other about watching their step or deciding which one of us would go down the U-Haul truck ramp backwards. Moving the furniture was a much-needed distraction.

While my father and I were unloading his furniture, Uncle Dean reluctantly called his son, Roy, telling him the dreadful news. Saddened but not surprised, Roy held back from telling his father, I told you so. As they were not able to attend the funeral, Roy told Uncle Dean that they would send a flower arrangement.

My father and I both were surprised about how many people kept bringing food. Whenever I was in the house, I watched closely as my mother would break down and cry for a few minutes and then suddenly stop when a new person would arrive; she would then break out in laughter as though nothing happened. I noticed my mother repeat these actions as if they were rehearsed. My father, on the other hand, kept a steady dose of beer flowing to the disgust of several church ladies and Uncle Dean. Whenever my father tried to console my mother, his words were inadequate or completely ignored. It appeared that my mother did not want to hear anything he had to say. While others talked to my mother, my father stayed glued to the television and continued to drink.

With decisions having to be made about the funeral arrangements, our family went to the Shady Branch Funeral Home to meet with the local funeral home director to work out the details. I wanted to slap the funeral home director, who kept telling my mother that she did not need to worry about the cost and the expenses. He kept saying, "We know y'all want the best for Mrs. Claire no matter the price. We have a no interest rate finance plan that will allow your Mama to enjoy her eternal rest."

Uncle Dean said nothing. However, I could tell as well that he was also perturbed by the high-pressure sales pitch. I also noticed that my mother was confused about what to do. I was shocked when my father stepped up and made the necessary arrangements without succumbing to the emotional distress. He told the funeral home director, "Let's put an end to the bullcrap and get this done. Mrs. Claire never drove a Cadillac, and she sure as hell ain't gonna be buried in one."

A day later, at 8:00 a.m., I stood with my family for almost two hours during the visitation at the funeral home. It was Sunday morning, so we had to work around local church services. I noticed that many of the people who came through the visitation line seemed to be hung over from their New Year's Eve celebrations the night before. A majority of the people I had seen at my home were the same people who walked through the visitation line. As I stood next to my grandmother's open casket, I would occasionally peek over at her. She was wearing glasses and a light green dress. I imagined that I caught a glimpse of her smiling. A reflection of light from her glasses and a quick shadow made it appear to me that she was winking whenever someone walked by her casket.

With people talking loudly and occasionally laughing with friends and family, it seemed disrespectful to me. I wanted more for my grandmother. I didn't know if I wanted people to cry or if I wanted a drawn-out service where everybody who knew her would stand up and testify about her kindness and how she loved to help others in the community. From the depths of my soul, I wanted to tell everyone about the trials my grandmother had been through during her life. I wanted to tell them about the man she killed in self-defense while saving her brother's life. I felt the urge to tell them about a child she never knew. It dawned on me; however, that my grandmother didn't want any fuss associated with her life nor her death.

She had kept her deep dark secrets from her family and friends for good reasons. Her wishes regarding her funeral had been simple. My grandmother had always been a humble person who did not like any attention on herself. I knew the service itself was only done for the sake of my mother. All my grandmother had requested was that one song be sung and a few scriptures read. Nothing more; nothing less.

After the very brief service concluded, I noticed my mother smiling while we rode in the Shady Branch Funeral Home limousine to Attapulgus, Georgia. My mother was pleased by the number of people who attended the visitation, considering it was New Year's Day. She kept naming names and asking if anyone had seen a few people she couldn't remember speaking to at the visitation. She commented on the flowers and the song, "How Great Thou Art", which was sung by a lady in the church who once accused my grandmother of having an affair with her husband.

My grandmother was buried next to my grandfather in a small cemetery that had long been forgotten. I became emotional when I noticed that there was absolutely no one at the graveside service except for my immediate family. The assistant pastor of the local Methodist church had to fill in for the full-time pastor who was out of town. Noticeably unprepared and somewhat nervous, the assistant pastor read a few scriptures before he quickly ended the graveside service which lasted a total of eight minutes. My father slipped him a twenty-dollar bill. The assistant pastor looked aggravated but quietly walked away when my father bucked up and gave him the evil eye. On a cold windy afternoon, in a small cemetery in Southwest Georgia, next to an old pecan tree, Claire

Lee Smoot was laid to rest right beside the only man she ever loved.

On our way home, my mother made the funeral limousine driver ride by my grandmother's old house in Shady Branch. The house which had long been sold to pay for my grandmother's nursing home care sat empty. My mother began to cry before she muttered, "Mama worked her tail off to keep that place. There was not a better lady on this earth. We will miss you, Mama."

CHAPTER NINETEEN

onday evening I sat on the couch with Uncle Dean and my father as we watched the Sugar Bowl together on my parents' RCA console color television. While we watched with great anticipation, my mother stayed on the phone in the kitchen most of the time talking to friends about my grandmother's funeral. I heard her say, "Thank goodness, Mama had that small life insurance policy. I don't know how we would have buried her. You know the price of funerals is outrageous."

Uncle Dean tried to talk to my father, but my father politely avoided any conversation. I didn't mind talking to Uncle Dean, but I was laser focused on the game. Even during the commercials, I anxiously waited for them to be over in hopes that the cameras would scan the crowd, and that against all odds, I would be able to catch a glimpse of Maria or her family. While we watched the game on television, we listened to it on the radio. My father and I loved to listen to the State sports radio play-by-play announcer.

When State scored on their opening possession, I, along with my parents jumped up and down together at the same time. We could all hear the announcer say, "Touchdown State!" in a golden voice which sounded like God was talking to us.

While we could hear the State band playing the fight song in the New Orleans Superdome over the radio transmission, my father and I joined in singing the fight song. We yelled out, "Go State!"

Uncle Dean looked at us like we were crazy.

At halftime, fourth-ranked State led Auburn 13-7 in a game filled with many mistakes. During the Sugar Bowl halftime show, Uncle Dean asked my mother to come into the living room. When she sat down beside him on the couch, he asked me to turn down the volume on the radio. He said, "I know this is not the best time to bring this up, but I wanted you all to know that I am going to the bank tomorrow to see about buying this place."

My father sat up in his Easy Chair recliner and asked, "Did Sandy tell me right? Are you going to let us live here rent free?"

Uncle Dean replied, "That is what I told her. You pay for the food and all of the utilities, and you can stay here with me."

My mother hugged Uncle Dean's neck before saying, "This will allow us to clean up our financial mess. We can't thank you enough. Lord knows, I feel like a big burden has been lifted off my shoulders."

Uncle Dean leaned up on the couch and replied, "You took good care of my sister. This is the least I can do for you."

The score of the game never changed as State intercepted a pass in the end zone on Auburn's last drive to secure the victory. I high-fived my father, hugged Uncle Dean, and kissed my mother when the game was over. For those few precious moments, I felt like my parents were the happiest I had seen them in quite some time. It appeared to me that Uncle Dean's arrival was a blessing for my parents.

***

Early the next morning, Uncle Dean asked me to take him to the Waffle House in Shady Branch. Uncle Dean had spied the only place that served breakfast in the town during the ride to my grandmother's funeral. He said, "When you go back to work tomorrow, I want to go out to breakfast so I won't disturb your parents so early in the morning. You know I love my eggs, grits, and bacon. I don't want your mother cooking for me."

While we sat at the bar of the Waffle House, Uncle Dean quickly struck up a conversation with a thirty-something brunette waitress, who had only been living in Shady Branch for a few months. The conversation with the waitress became more intense when she told us that she was from a small town in Alabama called Echo. Uncle Dean knew exactly where Echo, Alabama was located. Five cups of coffee later, Uncle Dean had found not only his new breakfast spot but a potential friend that he could talk to whenever he came to eat.

I was a little embarrassed as his conversation with the waitress became quite lengthy. When I finally convinced him to pay the bill, I noticed that he left the waitress a tip much greater than the cost of the breakfast.

I asked, "Why did you leave her twenty dollars? I have been with you all week, and I have never seen you tip like that."

He replied, "If this is going to be my regular breakfast place, I want the best service possible. My advice to you is that a good tip eventually pays for itself."

One block away from the Waffle House, Uncle Dean and I went to the Bank of North Florida. Thirty minutes later, he had secured the paperwork associated with purchasing my parents' property from the bank. The only loan officer in the bank said, "We look forward to doing business with you. Now, you go and see Walter Barrineau. He is the only lawyer in town who handles real estate closings. Once you work out all the details with him, we will put all of the wheels in motion."

Uncle Dean replied, "I sure do want to make this happen quickly. All I have to do is write a check. You don't need to worry about any financing."

The loan officer stood up from behind his desk and asked, "Did you say you will be paying the full amount with a check?"

"Yes, siree, bobcat tail. Tell me the price, and I will write you a check right now."

The loan officer's demeanor quickly changed. With a big smile on his face, he said, "Seventy-two thousand dollars is the asking price."

Uncle Dean pulled out his checkbook. Before he began writing, he said, "Seventy thousand and you have a deal."

The loan officer cried out, "Sold."

Uncle Dean wrote the check. With great enthusiasm, the loan officer said, "Technically, we have to go through the foreclosure process. By the time your check clears the bank out in California, all of your paperwork should be in order. You will need to be at the steps of the Apalachee Courthouse two weeks from now on Monday morning, January 15, so you can bid on the property. You don't need to worry because I know for a fact that nobody in all of North Florida would ever purchase that property for that amount. You have my word, in two weeks you will be the owner of the Jackson place.

***

The next day, while Uncle Dean paid a visit to Shady Branch's only real estate attorney, I went back to work at North Tallahassee High School. During a break at the school, I pulled out my wallet to see if I had enough money for a soft drink. When I pulled out my wallet, I saw the business card of Don Frost from the Carnation Division of the Nestle Corporation. At first ignoring the card, I began to think more about a possible career change during the rest of the school day.

While my physical education students played multiple games of badminton in the gym, I pondered over the possibilities. At the end of the school day, I decided to make that call. Three calls later, Don Frost was finally available to speak to me.

Don said, "Let me check our schedule, but I am positive we can meet with you in Tallahassee next week. I will have my secretary call you back tomorrow with all the details. Whatever you do, make sure you dress snazzy."

I asked, "Tie or no tie?"

Don snickered over the phone before replying, "You better wear a tie, Big Boy."

***

The next Saturday morning, my mother called me at my apartment in Tallahassee. I could tell that she was calling from the beauty shop because I could hear an Elvis song playing in the background. I could also tell she needed to unload on me because whenever she began a conversation by saying, "I don't know why I can't lose weight", I always knew something was up. After explaining to me that she had finished with her only customer of the day, she began by saying, "I don't know what to do."

I asked, "Do about what?"

My mother muttered in almost a whisper, "Uncle Dean." She paused momentarily before saying, "He went on a date last night. Can you believe that?"

I began laughing before replying, "I didn't think there was anyone left in Shady Branch that was old enough to go out with him. Was it Mrs. Ollis, the widow who lives on Creek Road?"

My mother yelled, "You're not even close. It was that new waitress at the Waffle House. Her name is Tracy Lynn Sherer. That wild child from the 1960s has put a spell on my uncle."

I interrupted my mother, "Hold on, Mom. I'm sure it's all innocent. Uncle Dean probably wants to help her out. She is new to town, and I think he enjoys talking to her."

My mother continued screaming on the phone, "That little whore is after his money."

I yelled back, "Whoa, Mom. You need to calm down. You don't know a thing about that woman."

My mother lowered her voice saying, "I know all about her."

"How do you know about her?"

My mother replied, "Nancy Smith knows Tracy Lynn's cousin Amy Sparks. Amy told Nancy that this waitress has bounced around Alabama and Florida like a common street whore. For God's sake, the woman has three children by three different men. On top of all that, the woman has a tattoo of a snake on her shoulder along with more piercings than the law allows."

I said, "I wouldn't be too worried."

My mother screamed again, "He brought the little whore to our house so we could meet her before he took her to the movies."

"So what if he took her to the movies. I promise it is no big deal. He loves talking to people."

My mother screamed, "That's not all he likes to do. They walked off our front porch holding hands. Can you believe that? For God's sake, it looked like a little girl holding on to her grandfather. I wanted to puke. I don't know what to do about him."

I kept trying to calm my mother down. I couldn't remember the last time she seemed so bent out of shape. The more she talked, the more upset she became. The conversation blew up when my mother said, "He threw me for a loop this morning. Uncle Dean told me that he was going to invite that woman to go with him to the Church of Christ on Hickory Street. You know, it's that little church which hardly ever has any people attend. I told him I thought he was moving way too fast. I also told him he needed to slow things down with this woman. He told me to mind my own business."

After hearing that, I became a little worried. I asked, "How is Daddy taking all of this?"

My mother snapped back at me, "Your Daddy doesn't care what Uncle Dean does as long as we don't have to pay any rent. He told me to leave Uncle Dean alone. He told me that if Uncle

Dean wanted to have a good time then he didn't see anything wrong with it. A few hours later, your Daddy came over to the shop and told me that he didn't know if this arrangement was going to work out. He said that Uncle Dean was driving him crazy. When your Daddy walked into his shed and found the place cleaner than a whistle he couldn't believe it. Uncle Dean had put away all of your Daddy's tools and spare truck parts. He even organized your Daddy's work bench. The man welded together your Daddy's old delipidated tire rack and is using it to store all of his small furniture and knick-knacks. He then gave your Daddy a sermon about the evils of drinking. To top it all off, he told your Daddy he needed to join the Church of Christ. You can imagine how that went over. I swear, I don't know what to do."

After I was finally able to calm down my mother and end our conversation, I drove to Lake Ella to meet Maria for a mid-morning jog. Because it was cooler than normal, we cut our jog short and only ran for about a mile. While we sat on a park bench next to the lake, Maria gently squeezed my hand before saying, "It sounds like your great uncle is getting on your parents' nerves."

Still trying to catch my breath, I replied, "Uncle Dean can be a strange bird, but I know that this financial arrangement is a blessing that my parents can't ignore. There is no way that the woman from the Waffle House is serious about him. Their age difference is shocking. But then again, who knows these days?" I paused for a moment, and caught my breath before saying, "She probably needs his help. I don't see any reason for them to quit seeing each other."

Before Maria and I left Lake Ella to go clean up and shower, Maria informed me that she made plans to take me to the notable Silver Slipper Restaurant in Tallahassee later that evening. Although it was one of Tallahassee's most upscale dining venues, Maria decided she needed to treat me to a nice meal at a place that had an outstanding atmosphere. She had also made plans for us to attend a concert after dinner at one of Tallahassee's best night spots.

When we kissed each other goodbye, I thanked her for arranging our evening activities and footing the bill. Maria then drove back to her apartment because she had a hair appointment later. I drove back to my apartment near Monroe Street.

As soon as I entered the parking lot of my apartment building, I almost wrecked when I saw Uncle Dean standing next to his Chrysler. I quickly parked my Toyota truck and began walking over to Uncle Dean. I yelled across the parking lot, "Man, you sure are full of surprises. What brings you to Tallahassee?"

He said something, but I could not hear him. Once I was close to him, he said loudly, "We need to talk."

Inside my apartment, he informed me that he was making plans for his new girlfriend, Tracy Lynn, to move in with him. Needless to say, my head began throbbing. I suddenly felt sick to my stomach. I looked at him and yelled, "Have you lost your mind? Where will my parents live?"

He replied, "I'm not going to disturb your parents. Tracy Lynn will move into my room above the garage."

I was beyond perplexed when I asked, "Why are you doing this so fast?"

He replied, "You don't understand. That little lady turns me on like I have never been turned on before."

Like my mother, I wanted to puke. Listening to him was painful. Reasoning with him seemed impossible. After listening for a few more minutes, I interrupted him and said, "Please don't tell me that you have slept with her."

He smiled big before answering, "That is why I want her to move in with me. That wildcat of a woman has taught me things I never knew were physically possible."

After almost vomiting, I asked, "Have you told my Mom?"

He paced around my apartment living room for a few seconds before asking, "Do you think I should tell her that we have slept together?"

I yelled, "Heck, no. I was talking about her moving in with you." I then paused and gathered my thoughts for a moment before asking, "When do you plan to move her into the garage, and what about her children?"

He replied, "I want to move her and the children in with me as soon as possible."

I did not know what to say. I walked into the kitchen and poured myself a drink of water. I then asked, "Why are you here?"

He sat down on a barstool next to the bar that separated the kitchen from the living room before replying, "Because I wanted you to be the first one to know. I didn't want you to hear this from your mother."

He then explained that Tracy Lynn was behind on her rent and needed some financial help. I painfully listened as he further explained that he intended to help her look after the children when she was away at work. When he asked me if he thought my father would mind helping out a few days babysitting the children, I screamed, "Daddy will shoot you! He hates little kids."

I finally convinced him that he needed to wait a while before allowing Tracy Lynn to move in with him. I told him that it was not good timing. I explained to him that my mother was still grieving over losing her mother. He shook his head and agreed with me. I then told him that he could pay for Tracy Lynn's rent for a few months and visit her instead of having her move in with him.

Before he left that afternoon, he looked at me and said, "I sure do trust you. I'm glad I came here to talk. You make perfectly good sense. Thank you, Timmy Boy."

CHAPTER TWENTY

I was still visibly aggravated by Uncle Dean's surprise visit when Maria and I were being seated in the Silver Slipper Restaurant later that evening. As I stepped up into one of the private curtained alcoves, I did not even notice the hostess because of my preoccupation with prior events of the day. As the hostess was leaving and pulling our booth's curtain shut, Maria took hold of my hand and said, "You seem like you are a million miles away from here. You do realize that this is one of the nicest restaurants in the state of Florida?"

Before I could respond, the curtain abruptly opened. A tall, skinny, waiter sporting a tight-fitting tuxedo greeted us. Speaking with a deep voice he said, "Welcome to the Silver Slipper. My name is Romano. I will be at your service tonight. Before we begin, please note that this establishment has been in operation since 1938. Our unique private booths have served some of the most prominent people of this state for fifty years. Senators, governors, a vast array of politicians, and celebrities have dined with us in a most intimate atmosphere. If you are ready, let's start with your drink order."

Maria smiled at the waiter before saying, "He will have a Bacardi Rum and Coke with a lime wedge. I think I would like a martini shaken, not stirred."

After ordering our drinks, I explained to Maria why Uncle Dean had decided to make a surprise visit to Tallahassee. By the time our waiter came back for our appetizer order, I had not even glanced at the menu. Maria took it upon herself to make the decision for the two of us. She said, "For appetizers, he will have the Fresh Shrimp Cocktail, and I will have the Pickled Bismarck Herring. For our main course, I will have the Baby Lamb Chops, and he will have a medium-rare Porterhouse steak.

I whispered to Maria asking, "What is a Porterhouse steak?"

She laughed at me before saying, "Trust me on this one, Coach. You will love it."

As we dined at our table beneath the low lighting, I told Maria about my upcoming interview with the Carnation Milk Division of the Nestle Corporation. Earlier, I had told her the story about how the interview came about. I was excited to share with her that I would be meeting with Don Frost and another man after school on Monday.

Maria, who wanted to be supportive of the possibility of me changing careers asked, "Do you know where you would have to work if you were hired?"

I kept cutting my steak while answering, "I have no idea."

The conversation then quickly changed when Maria began to inform me of her unexpected career news. She said, "I don't know if you remember, but last month I was chosen to interview with several of the top business accounting firms here in a job fair hosted by the College of Business. One of the largest firms, Price-Waterhouse, has offered me a position in their San Francisco office when I graduate this spring. I will be flying out there in a few weeks to decide if I want to take the position."

I was stunned. I didn't know what to say. I pretended to be excited for her, but deep down I never thought Maria would consider moving that far from her parents. I had imagined that one day we would be married. My dream job was a coaching job in Pensacola, and then we would live somewhere near her parents. With one bite of a Porterhouse steak that dream seemed to fizzle.

Maria continued to explain how lucky she felt to have such a wonderful opportunity. I began eating my dessert to divert my attention away from the conversation. Our waiter Romano had inadvertently left the curtains pulled apart after dropping off our slices of cheesecake. Across the room, I immediately noticed Coach Brown coming out of another curtained alcove with two of his coaches from State. At the same time, Coach Brown caught a glimpse of me. He stopped and turned toward his coaches. He then punched one of them on the shoulder and pointed at me. All three of the coaches made their way over to our table. Coach Brown said, "Dadgum, Jackson, they must be paying you a fortune over there at North Tallahassee High." Before I could respond, Coach Brown introduced himself, Coach Mike Morris, and Coach Dave Stevens to Maria.

Coach Stevens, who had been my position coach at State, gently slapped me on my back and said, "I see that you have definitely out-punted your coverage with this young lady."

I replied, "Thanks, Coach. Congratulations on the Sugar Bowl. What a game!"

Coach Brown interrupted, "Those Auburn rascals just about pulled it off. We were a lucky bunch in New Orleans."

I asked Coach Brown, "Do you come here often?"

He replied, "Heck no! Only on special occasions."

I asked, "I guess you are celebrating the big Sugar Bowl win?"

Coach Brown laughed and said, "No, we are not, Tim. We almost got our tails whipped. Actually, we are celebrating Coach Steven's promotion as the Offensive Coordinator for next season. Don't say anything. It won't be announced until Monday."

I immediately stood up and gave Coach Stevens a handshake and a hug. I said, "Congratulations, Coach. You deserve this. You know that I have always been a big fan of yours."

***

As we drove down Monroe Street heading for the Musical Moon, I was now in no mood to go to a concert or a club. I wanted to talk. Maria, however, wanted to celebrate along with others in her class, who were looking forward to hearing the Red Hot Chili Peppers band at Tallahassee's most popular night spot. It would be only the second time the nationally known band had played since the death of their lead singer six months prior. When the funk rock band played their hit song, "Fight Like a Brave", the mostly State student crowd went absolutely wild.

It was almost midnight when the band quit performing, and Maria asked me what was wrong. I did not reply. She then said, "You haven't hardly said a word. I know you. What is the problem?"

I held tightly to her hand and replied, "I am so happy for you, and I know we have something special. I hate to think what might happen when you move away to San Francisco."

Our talk became serious as we ended up at Maria's apartment. Through tears and occasional laughter, we made a pledge to one another that neither one of us thought we could keep. The reality of a long-distance relationship, all the way across the country, weighed heavy on both of us. As I began to fall asleep around four in the morning, I held Maria tight on her apartment couch. I sensed the beginning of the end. The indefinite ending of our relationship was all I could think about. I felt that I was about to lose the most incredible woman I had ever met.

***

Monday after school, I met Don Frost and Bill Kelso of the Nestle Corporation at the Governors' Inn located two blocks away from the Florida State Capitol building. I was not comfortable wearing a necktie. I felt somewhat awkward speaking to two sophisticated business executives. Before a word was ever spoken, I was intimidated by their expensive suits, polished shoes, and wristwatches that I estimated all cost more than my truck. As we sat in the dining area of the elegant hotel, Don Frost began a five-minute sales pitch about the great company he worked for in California.

Bill Kelso, a short red-headed man in his forties, sat at the table ready to take notes. Without speaking a word or offering any facial expressions, he appeared to be all business, lacking personality or a sense of humor. When I was asked by Don Frost to tell Bill about myself, I was noticeably nervous. I slightly pulled on my necktie before I began. A little more than halfway through my personal story, Bill Kelso from Virginia rudely interrupted me and asked, "Bottom line, Tim. Why should we hire you at our company?"

I thought he was rude, and I was startled. At that point, something boiled inside of me. In a knee jerk reaction, I pounded my fist on the table so hard it rattled the silverware. I then raised my voice and said, "Why should you hire me? I will tell you why. Because I would be the hardest working person your company ever hired. If you want a 'yes man' that will lick your tail, don't hire me. If you want a person who will try to sweet talk his way up the corporate ladder, I'm not your man. But if you want someone who will be loyal, trustworthy, honest, and the hardest worker you have ever met, you have found your man."

Kelso looked at Frost and said, "You were right. This young man is a diamond in the rough. Now let's find out how we can hire Tim Jackson."

I sat upright in my chair as I listened to a compensation offer that made my head spin. I couldn't believe the offer because it was more than double what I was making at North Tallahassee High School. They threw in a company car and an annuity program that sounded too good to be true. When they told me that I would be based out of Los Angeles, I began to smile. I immediately asked, "How far is that from San Francisco?"

Don Frost informed me that it was about a six-hour drive. I wasn't overly excited, but I felt a glimmer of hope regarding my relationship with Maria. Bill Kelso then upped the ante when he said, "After you complete your training in a year, you will be making a base salary of eighty-five thousand dollars. With bonuses, you could make up to 200k per year."

When they said they would fly me to Los Angles in a few weeks to tour the corporate office, I felt like I had hit the jackpot. After we ended our meeting, I could not wait to talk to Maria and my mother.

CHAPTER TWENTY-ONE

As I ran up the steps to my apartment, I dropped my keys twice before I was able to unlock my door. I dove on my bed and quickly dialed Maria's number. After calling her three times without an answer, I called my mother. She answered the phone saying, "Hello, Styles by Sandy. How can I help you?"

"Hey, Mom, it's Tim."

My mother, sensing excitement in my voice, replied, "I guess you have heard the news."

Confused, I asked, "What news?"

My mother yelled, "Uncle Dean has definitely lost his mind."

"What now?"

My mother, almost yelling, replied, "He went and bought that little whore a red convertible Corvette today."

"How do you know that?" I asked.

My mother lowered her voice when she replied, "To begin with, Nancy Smith saw Tracy Lynn driving Uncle Dean in the new car on her way to the grocery store. Right after Nancy called me and told me what she had seen, I happened to look out the shop window and there they were, parking that new car next to the shop. That little whore and Uncle Dean pranced right into this shop, full of customers, and declared to us that he had surprised his 'honey' with a new car. You can imagine how horrified my customers were as they sat there hiding their true feelings behind their polite smiles and snickers. Lord knows, I didn't know what to say! Uncle Dean was smiling and carrying on like a little boy who had just found the golden egg at an Easter egg hunt! He then made all of us walk out to take a look. I haven't been that mad since your Daddy was locked up at the race in Talladega. That's when he and crazy Buddy Turner became so drunk they tried to jump into Richard Petty's race car to take it for a spin."

I interrupted my mother and said, "Mom, I hate it for y'all, but Uncle Dean can spend his money on whatever he likes. Don't forget he is helping y'all out in a big way."

My mother paused for a moment, taking in a deep breath. After calming down, she said, "You're right, son, but it pains me to watch my uncle being taken advantage of by a woman who only wants him for his money."

Not knowing what to say, I agreed with my mother and listened as she continued to rant about her uncle's money. Before we ended our call, my mother said, "I wonder how much money he actually has. Did he hint at any of that when you two were traveling across the country?"

I replied, "It never came up."

***

The next morning Tallahassee was buzzing as the execution of Ted Bundy occurred while I was on my way to work. I had forgotten all about it until I walked into the gym at North Tallahassee High School and saw some of the students wearing T-shirts that read: Tuesday is FRY DAY. Most everyone in Tallahassee knew about Ted Bundy.

His real name was Theodore Robert Bundy. He was one of the most notorious criminals of the late 20th century. He confessed to twenty-eight murders in the states of Washington, Oregon, Colorado, Utah, and Florida between 1974-1978. He sexually assaulted girls and women and decapitated several of his victims. On January 15, 1978, Bundy broke into the Chi Omega sorority house in Tallahassee, raped, strangled, and bludgeoned two students to death. Two other students were also attacked but survived. The same night, he attacked another woman several blocks away who also survived. His last victim was a twelve-year-old girl in Lake City, Florida. Bundy picked her up near her school before he raped and killed her on February 9, 1978. The trial of Ted Bundy for the Florida murders was the first nationally televised trial in the United States.

Inside the coaches' office, all of the coaches were standing around a television watching the live reports coming from the Florida State Prison in Raiford, Florida. As a local news channel film crew broadcasted the scene outside of the prison, I noticed a large crowd assembled when a prison official made the announcement of Bundy's death at 7:25 a.m., January 24, 1989. At this precise moment the entire crowd erupted into a celebratory yell.

Back in Tallahassee, on the State House steps, the local news crew filmed two opposing groups cheering and chanting as the announcement was made. When the camera spanned across the street into a small crowd of anti-capital punishment protesters, I almost dropped my cup of morning coffee when I saw Uncle Dean singing while holding a lit candle. As the other coaches in the office cheered Bundy's death, I was too embarrassed to tell them my great uncle was protesting the execution. I wanted to call my mother, but without any privacy I decided against it.

That afternoon, while many of the bars in Tallahassee threw huge parties celebrating Bundy's execution, all hell broke loose at my parent's home in Shady Branch, Florida. By the time my mother was able to reach me, she was close to having a mental breakdown. At first, I couldn't understand her as she yelled loudly over the phone. I then heard her plainly say, "He has moved that little whore and her children into your old room."

After I was unable to calm my mother, I asked her to put my father on the phone. My father said, "I had to call Nancy Smith over here to calm your mom down. Your mom is about to lose her mind over this. You might need to take a day off and come home tomorrow. It's been a long time since I've seen your mother this upset."

***

I took a sick day and began driving to Shady Branch early the next morning. While I drove down a curvy back road lined with oak and pine trees, I tried to think about what I was going to say to Uncle Dean when I confronted him about a move we both had agreed was not a good idea. I also did not know what I would say to my mother, who appeared to be losing her patience with the man she idolized as a child.

Before I made the dreaded turn down the dirt road which led to my childhood home, I noticed several cars turning before me. By the time I approached the house, cars and emergency vehicles were parked with their lights flashing. A small crowd of people had assembled in the yard. When I opened my truck door, my father approached me. He said, "I hate to tell you this, but Uncle Dean died this morning. He is in your old room."

In total disbelief I began slowly walking toward my old room while I ignored my mother and Tracy Lynn yelling and screaming at each other on the other side of the property. At the bottom of the steps of the detached garage, Jared Bowman, the Apalachee

County Coroner said, "Tim, you may not want to go up there right now. Your grandfather is in no condition to be seen."

I shot back at the old family friend, "He's not my grandfather, Mr. Bowman."

He apologized saying, "That's right. He's your mother's uncle. I'm so sorry."

I simply replied, "I want to see him right now."

He held up his hand and replied in a soft voice, "That is up to you, but I must warn you. It is not a pretty sight."

I asked, "Did he shoot himself?"

Jared fought hard not to laugh. He said, "Not exactly, but from all appearances, he left this world with a big bang."

Confused, emotional, and mentally strained, I dispensed with the small talk and quickly walked up the stairs. When I entered the room the sight I saw was one I would never forget. Uncle Dean was lying on my State bean bag, with his eyes and mouth wide open; he was only wearing a white pair of socks. That sight of him being naked was bad enough, but what I and everyone else who had entered the room noticed was that Uncle Dean, although deader than a doornail, was still aroused in an upright position. It was jaw dropping; it was revolting; it was in my mind; Obscene.

As I stood next to Uncle Dean, I had no words. The first thing that came to my mind was that Tracy Lynn had unintentionally killed her sugar daddy. I became embarrassed when I heard one of the EMS workers downstairs say, "Now that's the way I want to go out when it's my time."

I knew without a doubt that everyone in Shady Branch would be talking about this for many years to come. I wanted to say something of spiritual importance. I suddenly began to think about the legal implications. I realized that if Uncle Dean had altered his will to include his new girlfriend, my parents may be on the street. I immediately scanned the room for Uncle Dean's brown folder case. I then saw Uncle Dean's car keys lying on top of the dresser next to the bed. As I walked out of the detached garage, I noticed what should have been a sad and solemn occasion was already becoming nothing more than a spectacle for laughter and small-town gossip. Uncle Dean was dead, but all anyone could talk about was that he was leaving this world with a big smile on his face.

Before I could walk to Uncle Dean's Chrysler, Tracy Lynn came running up to me. Without any hesitation, the lady, with a snake tattoo on her neck, grabbed me and began hugging me with a tight grip around my back. She said, "He loved you more than anything. I am so sorry."

I gently pushed her away as several of the people in the yard, including my mother, watched our interaction with great interest. I then asked without thinking, "What happened…I mean when did this happen?"

Too much information was given when Tracy Lynn answered me. With a good dose of crusty mascara flowing down her cheeks, she replied through her tears, "We were making love like we do every morning. It was dark, and I couldn't see his face. After a few minutes he didn't say a thing which I knew was unusual. I asked him if something was wrong. When he did not reply, I turned on the lamp next to the bed." Sniffling and then blowing her nose, Tracy Lynn then continued by saying, "Tim, I knew he was gone. That is when I called 911." She then began hugging me again. Before she let go of me she whispered, "Your Uncle Dean promised me that I could live here forever. He told me that he had taken care of everything with his attorney."

I gently pushed her away and asked, "Which attorney?"

Tracy Lynn replied, "I don't know his name. It is the same one he used to purchase this property."

Once I finished talking with Tracy Lynn, I walked over to my mother and father who were sitting on the front steps smoking cigarettes. My mother asked, "What did the little whore have to say?"

I did not want to tell her. I simply said, "She's just upset."

My father, who never said much, spoke up and said, "I bet she is. She's done rode her gravy train off the tracks."

My mother took another drag off her cigarette and said, "I don't think I can call Roy and Linda in California. You know this is going to be a big mess."

I reluctantly volunteered to make the phone call to my cousins in California. After going inside the house to make the call, I remembered the time zone difference and opted not to wake them so early. I then avoided everyone who had begun to gather inside the house. I walked outside to Uncle Dean's Chrysler. I found the brown folder case in the same spot I had last seen it. I took the case into my parents' bedroom to search for Uncle Dean's Last Will and Testament.

After quickly thumbing through all of the files, I couldn't help but notice the file which read: Florida Payments. I dug into it with intrepid anticipation and pulled out a small notebook which began to reveal a secret Uncle Dean had kept for years. Uncle Dean had recorded several years of payments to a woman named Patricia, who was living in Live Oak, Florida. At first, I thought that Uncle Dean had another woman on the side. However, when I found copies of canceled checks, I realized Patricia was not a secret lover; she was his daughter.

I suddenly remembered the name Tessie Fisher from Uncle Dean's admission about his one-time marital affair. I was stunned when one of the older checks was written to Tessie Fisher. At the bottom of the check it read: For Patricia Fisher on my baby's 16th Birthday. As I dug further, I found two letters written to Uncle Dean by Tessie. One of the letters revealed that although Patricia appreciated all the money he was sending her, Uncle Dean's daughter really did not want to have a relationship with her biological father. I dropped the letter like a hot potato. The necessity of finding Uncle Dean's Last Will and Testament became even more crucial. A hundred thoughts crossed my mind as I frantically dug through those records. When I opened the file which read, Insurance, I became excited when I saw at least a dozen life insurance policies. When I looked closer, I realized that every one of the policies had been cashed out. I then opened Uncle Dean's checkbook. I was surprised to find that he only had a little more than five thousand dollars in his account.

After searching through all of the financial records, it became clear to me that Uncle Dean had spent most of his money. The man my mother once described as a financial genius had been sending large sums of money to a daughter that nobody in the family even knew existed. After buying a seven-acre parcel of property in Shady Branch his account had dwindled. Uncle Dean also spent a great deal of his money on a woman in Shady Branch which helped him die with a smile on his face.

Before giving up on my quest to find the most important document, I decided to inform my father about what I had found. I then asked my father to help me with the search. My father immediately realized the importance of the task at hand and went into action searching for the Last Will and Testament as if his life depended on it. When my mother came into the bedroom and saw us going through Uncle Dean's financial records, I had to stop and explain it all to her. For the next thirty minutes, we all frantically searched for any evidence of Uncle Dean's Last Will and Testament. After finally giving up, my father looked at me and said, "We need to pay a visit to that real estate attorney before this thing gets out of hand."

***

My father and I waited for more than thirty minutes for Attorney Walter Barrineau in a small waiting area that was filled with ducks and deer heads mounted on the walls. The receptionist, named Pinky Little, put out a cigarette in an ashtray on her desk before saying, "The boss man says he can see you now."

Walter, who grew up with my father, told us in a very country sounding voice to have a seat. The only real estate attorney in Shady Branch sounded more like he was from Tennessee than Florida. Once we were seated, Walter said, "I just heard the dang bad news about Sandy's uncle. I'm awfully sorry. Goodness sakes alive, y'all have been through the ringer these past few months."

My father thanked him before saying, "Walter, I think you know why we are here. We need to take a look at Dean Lee's will."

Walter picked up a tooth pick off the top of his desk and began picking his teeth before saying, "Now, Hank, I would love to do that for you, but Mr. Lee gave specific instructions that nobody, and I mean nobody, is to view his Last Will and Testament and codicil until all parties that are involved meet here at my office all together."

My father asked, "What did you say about a codicil?"

Walter replied, "Shoot, Hank. I'm sorry. A codicil is simply an amendment to the original will. I can tell you that he did amend his original will in this office."

As I watched my father's reaction, I could tell he was unusually nervous as he kept rubbing his forehead. After rubbing his head several more times, my father said, "Walter, you and I go way back. To be honest, all I need to know is whether Sandy's uncle left us the property or not. Surely as an old friend you can at least tell me yes or no."

Walter smiled and said in a slow drawn-out tone, "Man, I wish I could tell you everything I know, but there is more to this story than I wish to be involved with. Let's just say there are other people involved in this legal mess that you may or may not be aware of. I have been instructed to contact all parties involved and have them meet here at a designated date and time. By law, I must do everything in my power to grant my client's wishes."

My father asked, "Are you talking about his daughter in Live Oak?"

Walter replied just as slowly as he had done before by saying, "I'm not at liberty to say. All I can tell y'all is that several people will be asked to join me for the reading of the will. Of course, whatever is revealed will not be able to be acted on until the Probate Court finalizes everything." He then paused before saying, "Once the funeral is over, and I have had time to contact everyone, I will let you know when we will meet."

Later that afternoon, when I was finally able to reach my cousin Roy to give him the sad news, Roy seemed very matter of fact in his reaction to his father's death. When Roy asked me to tell him all of the details regarding Uncle Dean's demise, I did not know what to say. I kept flashing back to what I had witnessed earlier that morning. I finally told Roy, "He died peacefully in his sleep."

A few minutes later, Roy began to ask me about Uncle Dean's finances. I told him that my knowledge of such matters was limited; however, I did reveal to Roy that Uncle Dean had bought my parent's home. Roy's demeanor quickly changed. He seemed agitated. He wanted to know what legal arrangements his father had taken. He also wanted to know about his father's insurance policies. Roy said, "I know Daddy had several policies he kept with him. He always told me there was plenty of money to bury him."

When I did not immediately answer him, Roy inquired, "I sense there is something you are not telling me. What is going on?"

I did not want to shock Roy, but I eventually had to tell him what I had discovered. I said, "Uncle Dean told me that he had purchased a lot of stocks and bonds. He said you would know how to access them in Tennessee."

Roy shot back, "I have no idea what you are talking about."

I simply said, "All I know is that he told me that he purchased a lot of stock and bonds from the Bank of North Alabama and that you would know where to find the records in some safety deposit box."

Roy thanked me after I explained all the details about his father's exploits since he arrived in Florida. I could tell Roy was emotionally crushed after learning about Tracy Lynn. Roy then ended the conversation by saying, "Once I contact our funeral home, we will have his body flown here to California so he can be buried next to Mama."

I immediately thought back to a conversation I had with my California cousins who had told me that their GP would end up in the place he was trying so hard to escape.

CHAPTER TWENTY-TWO

ater in my life, I would refer to the couple of weeks after Uncle Dean's death in 1989 as the beginning of the Shady Branch Civil War. Tracy Lynn started the war when she insisted that she be the one to plan arrangements for some type of funeral service before Uncle Dean's body was shipped to California. After my mother heard what Tracy Lynn was planning, she marched into the Shady Branch Waffle House and attacked the woman she called the "little whore". My mother was arrested and charged with assault and battery. She spent fifteen minutes at the Shady Branch Detention Center before her friend, Nancy Smith, bailed her out. Nancy knew the Chief of Police intimately when she was in high school. This helped expedite the process.

After being allowed to leave the Waffle House sporting a black eye, a few cuts, and scrapes, Tracy Lynn walked across the street to the Shady Branch Hardware Store. She purchased a few items and went back to the detached garage. She immediately began making signs which advertised a garage sale to sell Uncle Dean's furniture.

When my father later saw one of the homemade signs posted next to the Styles by Sandy's sign at the end of our dirt road, he quickly informed my mother there was a problem. My mother took matters into her own hands. She tried to break down the door to my old room over the detached garage. She threatened to skin Tracy Lynn alive. A few minutes later, two deputies from the Apalachee County Sheriff's Department arrived to sort out one hell of a shouting match.

Even though things at home were still in an uproar, I had to make it back to work. No sooner than I had returned to Tallahassee, my father called me to come back home to help calm down my mother. My mother, who barely avoided being arrested twice in one day, was beside herself. Despite all of their efforts he and other friends could not calm her down. When I made my way back home after a forty-minute drive, I found my mother so emotionally distraught, I thought she needed hospitalization. Finally speaking to her about the situation, Nancy Smith, my father, and I agreed that it was in her best interest that she should remain at home.

After I made sure my mother was sleeping comfortably, I walked over to the detached garage to speak to Tracy Lynn. When I went inside, I was shocked by the way she looked. Tracy Lynn was not recognizable. She looked like she had been attacked by a wild cat. She quickly told me that she intended to sell everything Uncle Dean owned including his Chrysler. When I told her that she could face possible jail time if she proceeded, she immediately became hostile and asked me to leave. While her children cried, Tracy Lynn ended her conversation with me when she said, "You may be right, Tim. I guess we will have to wait and see what the courts decide about all of this. But you need to know that your Uncle Dean made a promise to me, and I intend to collect on that promise."

***

Before lunch the next day, I drove my mother and my father to the Shady Branch Funeral home to say one last private goodbye to Uncle Dean. Upon our arrival, we avoided another embarrassing scene when I noticed Tracy Lynn exiting the funeral home while we were about to park the car. I drove past the funeral home entrance. My mother screamed at me that I had missed the turn. I played it off by telling her I wanted to stop and purchase a soft drink before visiting Uncle Dean. When I parked at a convenience store across the street, my father winked at me acknowledging that I had avoided another possible altercation.

Uncle Dean's body was scheduled to be flown back to Los Angeles in a cargo jet from Tallahassee late that afternoon. He was dressed up in his only church suit along with a pair of P.F. Flyer tennis shoes. My mother was very pleased with his appearance.

She said, "The funeral people did a good job on him. He looks marvelous."

My father whispered to me, "He looks dead."

As we all stood next to Uncle Dean's open casket, none of us said a word. We all had mixed internal thoughts and emotions for this man whom we all revered and for this man whom we had experienced watching his fall from grace.

I closed my eyes and prayed briefly and silently for a man who had unexpectedly become a friend. Then I opened my eyes and laughed to myself after thinking about the incredible trip the two of us had made across the country. I thought about all of the stops and the different people we encountered on our journey. I then thought about the conversations we had with one another. To me, those conversations were priceless. I realized that Uncle Dean had lived a pretty amazing life. An accomplished self-taught attorney and welder, the man with an eighth-grade education had started plowing with a mule when he was fourteen-years-old. He helped build the Wheeler Dam and was a leader in the early days of the Tennessee Valley Authority. He was a man who legally fought for the poor people of his community, while paying and sending his two sons to the University of Alabama. He was a man who grew vegetables for some of Hollywood's celebrities. He was never afraid to talk to someone he did not know or take a motorcycle ride with a stranger; Dean Lee lived a rich and fulfilling life.

I reached into my pants pocket. I slowly pulled out a Polaroid picture that was taken of Uncle Dean sitting on that motorcycle while we traveled through Texas. I gently placed it on top of Uncle Dean's chest. Again, I closed my eyes and thanked God that I was able to learn more about my grandmother's only brother and our entire family. I opened my eyes, smiled, and thought about my Grandmother, Emma Jean, Tom, and the gang in Heaven greeting Uncle Dean. I knew in my heart that there would be a special fishing trip planned for Uncle Dean and Jesus.

Everyone stayed silent for a few more minutes. My mother finally spoke up and said, "If you are the man I think you are, I pray right now that you worked it out so we could stay in our home."

My father surprised us both when he ended our visit at the funeral home by saying, "Rest easy, Bama Boy. Rest easy. Have the most wonderful flight to Heaven you could ever imagine. I know you will be flying in first class!"

***

Later that afternoon after I drove back to Tallahassee, I took Maria to the Whataburger fast food restaurant for a bite to eat. While we dined outside on a wooden picnic table, Maria listened to me tell her all about my family's affairs. She then looked at me and said, "Waiting to find out what is going to happen has to be awful for your parents. There is no telling what arrangements your Uncle Dean made in his final days."

I took a sip of my diet drink before saying, "Yeah, it is a total mess. I have a bad feeling about all of this."

We talked a few more minutes about my family situation. Maria then abruptly changed the subject when she said, "I've been doing a lot thinking and praying about our situation."

The more she talked, the more I felt that our relationship was unraveling. Maria talked about long distance relationships while I countered by promising to drive six hours from Los Angeles to San Francisco. My words were all in vain when she said, "If it is meant to be, it will work out. In the meantime, we need to end our relationship for the time being."

I asked, "Are you breaking up with me?"

Maria smiled before saying, "It's not a breakup! It is only a time out."

Stunned, I replied loudly, "It doesn't matter what you call it. You are breaking up with me."

Maria took hold of my hand and said, "Tim Jackson, you know I love you more than anything, but right now we need to find out where we both are headed. You may end up staying right here in Tallahassee. Two or three years from now, I may end up in New York or Miami. I think we both know that you and I were not meant to be followers. If you followed me to San Francisco, you would end up hating me. If I did the same and followed you to Los Angeles or stayed here with you in Tallahassee, I know I would always regret not taking a chance."

After dropping Maria off at her place, I drove to my apartment. When I closed the door of my apartment, I suddenly heard a knock on my door. I opened it. An older man with gray hair wearing a white shirt and a blue tie asked, "Are you Tim Jackson?"

"Yes, sir. How can I help you?"

"My name is Drew Geddings. I'm an agent with the FBI. If you don't mind, I would like to ask you a few questions."

For the few minutes, I allowed Drew Geddings to sit in my apartment while he explained why he was in Tallahassee. He said, "I have been working on an unsolved murder case for many years. My very last hope of solving this murder all rested with speaking to your great uncle Dean Lee. I had tracked him down and arranged to meet with him to discuss the case the morning he passed away. After speaking to your father on the phone, he suggested that I talk to you since you and your great uncle spent a few days together on your trip from California."

I was really in no mood to talk, but I felt sorry for a man who had devoted his life to finding out the truth about a murder that had been committed over fifty years ago. Before I answered any questions, I told Mr. Geddings that I knew of him from a mutual friend in Los Angles. He smiled and seemed relaxed when he said, "Well, how about that! It is a small world. Eston Harper has been helping me with this case for years. I guess Eston is right. It looks like I will never solve this thing."

I answered a few simple questions before saying, "I know the truth, Mr. Geddings, but whatever I tell you, is off the record. I want you to know what happened so many years ago, but I do not want my relatives' names used in any official documentation or news release. What I will share with you is for you and Eston Harper's information ONLY - not be discussed with anyone else."

An hour later, Drew Geddings walked out of my apartment a changed man. His quest to resolve an unsolved murder was finally over. He thanked me and wished me luck.

After he left, I began looking at all of the photographs, notes, letters, and any memorabilia that represented my relationship with Maria. I was emotionally crushed. A sadness I had never experienced overcame me like a ton of bricks falling on my chest. Losing two close relatives had been a shock to my system. Losing the love of my life was painfully indescribable.

***

Two days later, as I moped around my students and staff members at North Tallahassee High School, my boss asked me to join him in his office. Head Coach Riley Upshaw, the first black Athletic Director and Head Football Coach at North Tallahassee High, was a local legend. The former All-American at Florida A&M University asked, "Are you happy working here?"

I immediately replied, "Yes, sir." I then asked my boss, "Is there something wrong?"

Coach Upshaw leaned back in his large office chair and said, "You tell me? I just received a phone call from the Superintendent of Schools in Alapaha Station, Georgia. She informed me that they were going to ask you to interview for their head coaching position at Alapaha Station High School. She wanted me to know out of courtesy. I don't mind telling you that I was shocked. In all of my years, I have never had anyone call and officially tell me that they were going to interview one of my coaches. The other thing that shocked me was that I have never had a coach on my staff that didn't tell me first that he was applying for another position."

I leaned forward in my chair across the desk from a man I held in high esteem and replied, "Coach Upshaw, I have no idea what you are talking about. I don't even know where Alapaha Station, Georgia is located. I promise, I have not applied for another coaching job."

Coach Upshaw, not convinced, replied, "Well, let's get to the bottom of this right now."

After Coach Upshaw was able to reach the Superintendent of Alapaha Station Schools on the phone, he asked Mrs. Dona Felder, when exactly did she receive the application for employment from Coach Tim Jackson. He listened to her explanation of why they were contacting one of his coaches. Coach Upshaw finally responded to her by saying, "Yes, ma'am, you couldn't hire a better young man."

After hanging up the phone, Coach Upshaw looked at me and said, "I owe you a big apology. It seems that you have a friend from that town who told the Superintendent that you would be the best candidate to fill their vacancy. All she kept saying was that if Eston Harper recommended you, then that was good enough for her. It looks like you have some decisions to make."

I agreed and thanked the man who had taken a chance on me less than a year before. I explained to Coach Upshaw how I knew Eston Harper. I also revealed the details of my recent job offer with the Nestle Corporation. Coach Upshaw, with a look of amazement on his face, laughed before saying, "Now that is one incredible story. You evidently made a very good impression on that Harper man. It's hard to believe that one plane ride to LA has blessed you with opportunities you never knew existed. Don't get me wrong. I think you are a very good young coach, but I can assure you that Alapaha Station High School will never come close to offering you the kind of money that they are willing to pay you in Los Angeles."

I replied, "Yes, sir. I'm not sure what I'm going to do."

Coach Upshaw stated, "I don't know what to tell you. It sounds like you have some big decisions to make." He then paused and said, "The real question for you is now pretty clear. Does money buy true happiness or does true happiness come from doing something you really love? I'm afraid this is a question that goes all the way back to the beginning of time."

CHAPTER TWENTY-THREE

The next day, my life became even more complicated when three different phone calls forced me to make plans to use most of my paid leave that I had accrued from the Tallahassee School District. An early morning phone call from Don Frost ended when I found out that I was scheduled to visit the Los Angeles office of Carnation Milk the next Monday.

During my lunch break, Alapaha Station School Superintendent Dona Felder called and invited me to interview for the football head coaching position at Alapaha Station High School the next Wednesday. Ten minutes later, the receptionist for the law office of Walter Barrineau in Shady Branch called me and said, "This is Pinky Little down at the Barrineau Law Firm. The boss wanted me to call you and let you know that you, your mother, and your father need to be here at the office next Friday afternoon at 5 p.m. You should have received a letter stating what I just told you. He also told me to make sure that you understand it is imperative that you attend this meeting."

***

The next Sunday morning, I found myself back at the Tallahassee Airport preparing to check in my Samsonite suitcase for another flight to Los Angeles. This time, after checking in my suitcase, I waited next to the boarding gate with my father, who had driven me to the airport. Unshaven, and wearing a black and white Independent Truckers Association hat, my father sat down next to me and said, "I want you to know how much I appreciate everything you have done to help me with your Mom these past few weeks."

I leaned back in my terminal gate seat before replying, "Daddy, you need to think about what you and Mom are going to do if Judgment Day doesn't turn out the way we want this Friday."

My father replied, "I know you are right, but your Mom won't talk to me about it. It is hard to start all over again at our ages."

I couldn't look at my father when I replied, "I know it is."

Ten minutes later, a male Delta Airlines attendant picked up a microphone and said, "Delta Airlines Flight 351 to Los Angeles will now start boarding at Gate Number Two. Please make sure your carry-on luggage will be able to fit in our overhead compartments before boarding. If you are not sure, please check in your carry-on."

After telling my father goodbye, I showed the attendant my ticket. The attendant said, "Welcome to Delta Airlines. Thank you for flying with us."

I replied, "Thank you, sir."

The attendant laughed before replying, "Sir? Do I look like a sir?" He then winked at me with a big smile on his face before saying, "Honey child, aren't you a cutie pie?"

Nobody sat next to me on this flight. I had plenty of room to stretch out my legs as I sat next to an exit aisle. I tried to nap several times, but my thoughts concerning my future would not allow me to doze off. Unlike my last flight to Los Angeles, this one seemed long and very boring. When a lady sitting behind me began throwing up in a Delta Airlines vomit bag halfway through the flight, I couldn't wait for the flight to be over.

Once the flight finally landed at LAX, I quickly headed toward the large terminal. As I walked past the male flight attendant, I said, "Thank you, sir."

The attendant replied with a smile, "Welcome to LA, the city where dreams come true."

***

After retrieving my Samsonite suitcase at the luggage terminal, I found my way over to the Hertz Rent a Car booth. I had already made plans with Cousin Roy to spend the night with him and Linda in Bell Canyon. Although Don Frost offered to pick me up from the airport, I decided that I wanted to drive around Los Angeles on my own before spending the evening with my cousins.

As it was still Sunday morning due to the time zone changes, I used Uncle Dean's Rand McNally Atlas to navigate through LA in my rental car. Not having the opportunity to see the Pacific Ocean on my last visit, I left LAX and headed to Marina Del Rey only a few minutes away. As I drove around the massive marina, I concluded that I had never seen so many boats parked in one spot. After riding around viewing the various luxury sea vessels docked near some of the most expensive condos in LA, I drove to the famous Santa Monica Pier.

I parked my rental car and walked down to the historic site which had been in operation since 1909. I watched a group of children eating ice cream cones while they waited in line to ride the Carousel in the amusement park portion of the pier.

I found a set of wooden steps which led to a small area of the beach. I walked down to the Pacific Ocean and reached down and touched the water. I stood unimpressed as I compared this view of the ocean to my childhood beach adventures at Panama City Beach, Florida. I then realized it was February. Although it was February, people were sunbathing. This would not have been the case at Panama City Beach. I glanced over at two girls in string bikinis and thought to myself, "Dang. Is this really February? It is supposed to be too cold to be at the beach."

I walked back up to the pier. I stopped when I noticed steam rising next to a middle-aged man selling food from a portable hot dog stand with wheels. I ordered two dogs all the way. The man, who had a thick Slavic accent, said, "Zat will be chetyre dollars." Before I could ask him to repeat what he said, the hotdog vendor held up four fingers. He then pointed to the cooler of drinks on the side of his cart.

I said, "I'll have Diet Coke."

The hotdog vendor shook his head and said, "Zat will kill you." He then pulled out a clear glass bottle of water which had a label that read: California Gold. He pointed at the bottle and said, "Zis give you life."

I laughed before asking, "How much does the life water cost?" The hotdog vendor held up five fingers without saying a word. I said, "I'll take the Diet Coke." I could not help but laugh and thought back about Uncle Dean trying to persuade me to invest in a water farm.

As I was finishing my hot dogs on the Santa Monica Pier, I decided that I would take my own tour of UCLA. I had always wanted to visit the campus. I knew that it was not far away in Westwood.

Upon entering the beautiful campus, I noticed many flags and banners with the UCLA colors of light baby blue and gold. When I drove past UCLA's signature building, Royce Hall, I jokingly wondered if the name on the building had anything to do with my cousin Roy. After passing the Main Quad, I rode by a statue of UCLA's mascot, the Bruin Bear. A short distance away, I ended up parking next to Pauley's Pavilion.

Once I parked, I walked next to the iconic basketball arena. Outside of the building I stopped to read a plaque about the revered basketball coach, John Wooden. He won ten NCAA National Basketball Championships. Although the doors of the building were locked, I could see the NCAA National Championship trophies on display through the modern glassed arena. As I pressed my hands and face up against the glass exterior of the building, I was startled when a door not far from me opened. I immediately recognized the retired coach, John Wooden. Coach Wooden yelled at me, "Don't put your fingerprints all over the glass." The famed Wizard of Westwood then motioned for me with his arm as he held the door open. He said, "Well, come in if you want to see the place."

I was speechless. I did not know what to say or how to react to one of the most recognized figures in the world of basketball.

With great excitement, I entered the grand lobby. Coach Wooden turned toward me and smiled before saying, "I assume you are not from around here, wearing that tacky looking State hat."

I took off my hat and asked, "You are...?"

He interrupted me and said, "That's right, I'm Coach Wooden."

Several minutes later, I found myself being given a tour of Pauley Pavilion by the very man who had made the place famous. As we walked, Coach Wooden explained that since his retirement from coaching, UCLA had allowed him to stay on in a limited administrative role. He told me, "I'm glad they still allow me to come by here every now and then."

He then explained that his limited administrative role had more to do with him visiting with alumni who had deep pockets. The more Coach Wooden talked, the more I thought I was listening to the voice of God.

Coach Wooden asked me about my visit to Los Angeles. When I explained all of the particulars, Coach Wooden said, "My parents wanted me to be anything other than becoming a teacher and a coach. I coached at the high school level for years. During those early years, I had many different opportunities to do other things. I chose coaching because I loved it. Whatever you decide, you remember that you are lucky if you have the opportunity to do something you really love."

We ended up back at Coach Wooden's small office near the lobby. I said, "Thank you, Coach. I can't believe that you would take the time to show a stranger around this beautiful facility. Nobody back in Shady Branch, Florida will ever believe that I had the opportunity to meet you."

Coach Wooden laughed before saying, "I'm not God, Tim, but God does allow us to cross paths with individuals in the most peculiar of circumstances; like when someone has their face pressed up against a clean window." He then laughed before continuing, "I've been out of coaching so long; I'm sure that nobody in Florida remembers me."

I immediately replied, "Are you kidding me? In our coaches' office we have a poster of your Pyramid for Success. I also remember watching the 1970 National Championship game on television. The whole state of Florida watched on that Saturday afternoon when you beat Jacksonville University and their superstar Artis Gilmore."

Coach Wooden smiled before saying, "If I were a betting man, I would guess you were pulling for Jacksonville."

I replied, "I was a little too young to remember much of it except that my father, and everybody else in the state of Florida were pulling for Jacksonville that afternoon."

Coach Wooden then reached down behind his desk and pulled out a clean sheet of stationery from a bottom drawer. The stationery had a UCLA Bruin logo at the top along with the words- *from the Office of John Wooden* printed on it. He then picked up a pen and wrote: *Thank you, Tim. Best wishes for a Successful Career. God Bless, Coach John Wooden.* He handed it to me and said, "Hopefully this will help you when you tell your friends you met me at the greatest campus on earth, UCLA."

***

After having met one of the most famous coaches in America, I didn't care what else I saw as I pulled away from the UCLA campus. As I drove by the Los Angeles County Museum of Art, the building and its sign caught my attention. At the next intersection I decided to turn around and make my first visit to a real museum of art. My only other visit to a museum was at Mr. Ralph Compton's Museum of Natural History located near Shady Branch. Mr. Ralph's "museum" was actually a taxidermist shop which had a few live snakes, turtles, and baby alligators housed in several large aquariums behind his shop.

Although completely out of my element, I found myself amazed by the beauty and complexity of the art I viewed. Inside the Robert O. Anderson Building, I viewed modern paintings that were very thought-provoking. In the newly opened Pavilion for Japanese Art, I became enamored by a series of sketches and paintings depicting various interpretations of the Japanese landscape and ancient fishing villages. As I walked through the new exhibits of sculpture in the B. Gerald Sculpture Gardens, I was fascinated with different life-sized sculptures surrounded by a series of well-manicured gardens.

While I was standing next to a small stream, I suddenly felt a tap on my shoulder. Before I could fully turn around, a gorgeous blonde woman about my same age asked, "Excuse me, can you tell me anything about those ferns on the other side of the stream?"

Somewhat startled, I replied, "I'm sorry, I don't work here."

The woman laughed and said, "I know. I didn't mean to scare you, but I've been watching you for the last ten minutes."

"Oh, you have?" I replied.

She nodded in affirmation while replying, "My name is Sharon; Sharon Fedorov."

For the next hour, Sharon and I sat on a wooden bench in the middle of the sculpture gardens, becoming acquainted with each other. We then decided to walk across the street to a TCBY yogurt shop. The more we talked, the more I became interested in what she had to say. She informed me that she grew up in Schenectady, New York. She had graduated with a degree in finance from the University of Georgia. Sharon now lived in a small apartment in Beverly Hills. When the former cheerleader for the University of Georgia told me that she was working at Carnation Milk in Los Angeles, I almost spit out my mouthful of chocolate yogurt. When I told her that I had a scheduled tour of the facility the next day, for the possibility of taking a job offer, she reached across the table and punched me in my chest. She cried out, "Get out of here. No way."

Later, in our conversation, Sharon explained to me how she had been recruited to work for Carnation while she was finishing her degree in Athens, Georgia. Her story sounded familiar to another girl I knew in Tallahassee.

I learned that Sharon's father was a Vice-President for General Electric. After she revealed that her mother was a former dancer with the Rockettes in New York City, I was even more interested. I listened to her tell the story about how her immigrant grandfather from Russia came to the United States through Ellis Island at the turn of the century, and I was moved. As soon as I revealed that I was a high school football coach, who had played college football, I could tell Sharon was interested in me.

Less than thirty minutes later, I agreed to follow Sharon in my rental car to her apartment. Once we arrived at her apartment in Beverly Hills, I called my cousin Roy and informed him that I would not be able to spend the night. I lied when I claimed that my future boss insisted that I go to dinner with several others of the Carnation Milk sales team. I told Roy it would be too late for me to drive all the way to Bell Canyon. After calling my mother in Shady Branch, to let her know I had made it to California, I listened to Sharon tell me more about herself.

Sharon explained in great detail how expensive it was to live in Beverly Hills. After she told me what her parking garage fees were, I knew I was out of her league. Those parking fees were higher than the rent for my apartment back in Tallahassee.

Later that evening, Sharon ordered Thai food from a local joint that she thought was the best. I had never eaten Thai food and was excited about it. However, I had other things on my mind that had nothing to do with eating Thai. When the food arrived,

Sharon insisted that we eat on the floor of her apartment's tiny living area. She showed me how to properly use chopsticks. I was totally mesmerized by this blonde-haired stranger that I was unexpectedly blessed to have met. As I was staring at her with amazement, I noticed a speck of food on the corner of her face. I gently took my napkin and wiped it away. I did not care that she knocked over a glass of wine when we quit eating and spontaneously began kissing. We were listening to the MTV channel on her television, when I unexpectedly began laughing. The music video of the song "Wild, Wild, West" was playing. She squeezed my hand and asked, "What is so funny?"

I laughed out loud and told her, "It's that song. You wouldn't believe the significance of that particular song and the big part it has played in my journey to Los Angeles over the past few weeks."

We stopped making out and talked late into the night. I shared with Sharon my earlier adventure to Los Angeles and my cross-country road trip. I explained to her what seemed like my life story and then she shared hers as well. I learned that she had recently broken up with a semi-professional surfer and model from San Diego. For some reason I felt the need to share with her the ending of my relationship with Maria. Much deeper into the conversation, a girl named Maria had temporarily vanished from my mind.

I finally fell asleep. Later, I was awakened by the smell of breakfast. Sharon was cooking scrambled eggs and bacon. I yelled across the room, "What are you doing?"

She bounced over to the couch and handed me a plate before saying, "You will never forget the first time you had breakfast in bed or should I say on a couch in Beverly Hills."

I smiled but never replied. I quickly ate my breakfast before both of us began getting ready to face our day at Carnation Milk. While I shaved, I could see Sharon's reflection in a small mirror hanging above the sink. As I watched her iron a blouse on the side of her bed, I was convinced that she was special. I was not sure about our future, but I was sure I wanted her to be in mine. I jumped into the shower and began singing. I didn't know she was listening until she yelled from the bedroom, "Your Southern accent kills me even when you are singing."

At 7:30 a.m., I followed Sharon to the Carnation Milk office near the Los Angeles International Airport. I had to drive by two construction zones in Beverly Hills. I began laughing each time I saw an End Construction road sign. Subconsciously, I could hear Uncle Dean laughing along with me.

We parked next to each other on the fifth level of the Carnation Milk parking garage; Sharon was still applying her makeup while she glanced in her rear-view mirror. I walked over to her car. She quickly grabbed her car keys and opened her door before saying, "I am going to let you go ahead and take the elevator by yourself. Don's office is on the third floor. Whatever you do, do not mention my name. These people are funny about the whole company fraternization thing. Go take this job, Tim Jackson, and we will deal with our 'relationship' when the time comes. Good luck. Call me when you make it back to Florida."

CHAPTER TWENTY-FOUR

When I stepped off the elevator, I was impressed with the Sales Division Floor of Carnation. Before I could say anything to the receptionist, she stood from behind her modern looking glass desk and said, "You must be Mr. Jackson. Follow me. Mr. Frost is expecting you."

As I entered the office of one of Carnation's most powerful executives, I couldn't help but notice all of the various sports and Hollywood memorabilia. Autographed baseballs, footballs, and basketballs sat on expensive looking glass shelves. One wall of the office was filled with autographed photos of celebrities. When I noticed a basketball signed by Coach John Wooden, I laughed to myself, noting that Don's office was much larger than Coach Wooden's.

Don motioned for me to take a seat while he continued to sit behind his desk talking to someone on the phone. He told the person on the other end of the call, "They can kiss my ass if they think they can find a better deal than what we are offering." He then smiled at me before he abruptly hung up the phone. He stood up, extended his hand toward me while saying, "Welcome to Carnation. I hope you are ready to do some walking."

For the next two hours, Don introduced me to every manager in every department of the massive operation. In between introductions, he tried to explain the specifics concerning each department. By the time we had walked our way to the other end of the warehousing department, I had already seen enough. As we strolled through Finance, we walked right by Sharon, who was busy trying to feed a pile of green and white computer paper into a large printer. Don nudged me on my shoulder and winked at me as if to say that Sharon was a looker. Sharon never looked up or noticed us as we made our way through her department.

We later made our way back to Don's office. It became clear to me that Don was preoccupied with other matters when he took a phone call which eventually turned into three more. During the third call, Don held his hand over the mouthpiece of the telephone receiver and said, "Why don't you walk around the building for a few minutes, and then we will go to lunch."

As I walked into the reception area, I asked the receptionist if I could use a private phone and borrow the Los Angeles phone book. The receptionist showed me into a break room down the hall, pointed at the telephone book on a table and left me alone. I immediately began searching for the phone number to the LA

County Coroner's Office. Luckily, I was able to quickly reach Eston Harper.

After a fair amount of small talk, Eston said, "Don told me you were scheduled to meet with him today. I thought you may have had second thoughts."

I replied, "That is one reason why I am calling you. I am confused as to why you contacted your friend about me coaching high school football in Georgia. You really don't know anything about my coaching ability."

Eston replied, "I know that my old high school needs new blood as far as coaching goes. For the past fifteen years all of their coaches have been old-timers. After meeting you, I felt that this might be a great opportunity for a young coach to bring a spark back to a place that once prided itself with good football teams."

I asked, "Knowing that your friend at Carnation had already offered me a job, why did you feel the need to throw my name into the mix at Alapaha Station High?"

Eston paused before saying, "Because something tells me that you were born to coach. Coaching is something God calls you to do. It's not much different than being a pastor. I know this - Not everyone can preach, and not everyone can coach. Anyone can sell milk."

I didn't know how to reply. I simply said, "I see." I then gathered my thoughts and asked, "Did your friend Drew

Geddings call you and give you the good news about solving his case?"

"He sure did. It is definitely a crazy world we live in. Who would have ever thought that your family members would be involved. Don't worry; this will always be our little secret."

After thanking him and talking a few more minutes, Eston ended our conversation by saying, "I recommended you for the coaching job because I know that you will do everything in your power to help my alma mater have a successful football program. I stand by my recommendation and don't have one regret in doing so."

As soon as I hung up the phone, the receptionist walked into the break room and said, "Mr. Frost is ready for you, now."

***

While I ate lunch with Don in the Carnation cafeteria, I had a hard time concentrating as I noticed Sharon eating with a group of women a few tables away. In mid-sentence, Don changed the subject when he noticed me looking over at the table of women. Don said, "We do have some good-looking ladies in this facility. But let me warn you, we at Carnation have a strong belief that workplace relationships are a big no-no." He then asked me, "So what do you think about our California piece of heaven?"

I replied, "It seems too good to be true."

Don leaned back in his chair and said, "I knew you would love it. We would like to have you working here by the first of June.

This will give you enough time to make the move, find a good place to live, and get settled before you start. It also gives us plenty of time to assemble the rest of our trainee team. You do realize that you will be one of seven young trainees we have selected from all over the country?"

I nodded and did not reply.

Don told me that he wanted me to go ahead and sign a contract. I did not know how to respond. After a long pause, I finally said, "If you don't mind, I would like to take the contract back with me and do some real soul searching before I make a commitment."

Don raised his eyebrows before asking, "Are you having second thoughts?"

"No, sir. But hopefully you can understand that this is a big commitment. Moving all the way to Los Angeles is a big decision. Surely you understand."

I could tell that Don was not happy, but he said, "I certainly understand. It is a big commitment. Take a few days and call me no later than next Monday. You do understand that we are anxious to hire the most qualified people to fill these positions." Don then stood up and continued saying, "If you would like to spend another day or two here to learn more about our operation, I can have your flight plans rearranged, and I will pay for you to stay in a nice hotel here in Los Angeles."

Our conversation ended when I convinced him that I had seen enough, and that I needed to make my way back to Tallahassee. I desperately wanted to say something to Sharon before I left. I briefly entertained the idea of calling from a payphone at the airport, but I had second thoughts as I did not want to make her uncomfortable by calling her at work.

***

That afternoon as I sat on a flight, cramped next to two elderly women, who didn't speak a word of English. I had plenty of time to process decisions that had to be made about my future. More confused than ever, I looked out of the window, glanced down at the Los Angeles skyline, and prayed for some type of providential guidance.

Six hours later when I landed in Tallahassee, I still had no idea where my career and life were headed. As I walked toward the luggage area of the Tallahassee airport, I noticed a familiar looking man sitting at a table in the airport's lounge area. The man was dressed in a suit and smoking a pipe, while thumbing through a stack of papers. I turned around and took a second look. I then knew I was looking at Coach Howard Snellenberger, the National Championship football coach for the University of Miami, who was now the head coach at the University of Louisville. I decided to take a chance and walked over to the coach who was known for being the best dressed coach in college football.

I then spoke to him saying, "Coach Snellenberger, I hate to disturb you, but I am Tim Jackson. I am a high school football coach here in Tallahassee. I just wanted to tell you how much I have admired your coaching."

I did not want to act like a stupid fan and did not want to sound like an idiot. I became excited when Coach Snellenberger replied, "Thank you. Why don't you sit down and talk to me for a while? My plane back to Louisville has been delayed."

After a few minutes of conversation, I could not help but think that if Coach John Wooden sounded like God, Coach Snellenberger looked like God. With his grandfatherly flowing white hair, and his sophisticated looking smoking pipe, Coach Snellenberger soon turned out to be one of the most pleasant people I had ever met. The championship coach, who had become famous at the University of Miami for only recruiting what he called the 'State of Miami', explained that he had been in Florida for a week trying to find new talent for his rising program at the University of Louisville.

He said, "It was always a challenge trying to out recruit the other Florida schools while I was at Miami. It's almost impossible now to snatch away any of the best players from this area since I am at Louisville."

This down-to-earth coach not only shared with me more information than I expected, but he also listened to me while I explained the dilemma about my career. After I talked about my upcoming coaching interview, Coach Snellenberger said, "One thing I have learned through the years is that when you are being interviewed, do not try to be someone else. Always be yourself, and you will never have any regrets."

Coach Snellenberger looked at his wristwatch and said, "I hate to end this conversation, but my flight is about to depart."

I then thanked him for taking the time to speak to me. The wise coach then wished me the best of luck.

Before he began walking away, Coach Snellenberger said, "I'll leave you with some good advice Coach Bear Bryant gave me years ago. He told me that only a few special people are called into the coaching profession." He then waved goodbye and said, "I hope those words mean as much to you as they did for me."

I thought to myself that meeting Coach Snellenberger was the sign I had prayed for on my flight. I thought it was amazing that I would randomly run into this famous coach.

I walked out of the airport and thought about Sharon in California. I knew that if I decided to remain in the coaching profession, I would most likely be ending the opportunity to begin a relationship with someone who was already special to me.

***

Early Wednesday morning, I left my apartment, professionally dressed for an interview in a South Georgia town I knew nothing about except it was the hometown of Eston Harper. As I drove down the Thomasville Highway, I had to pull down the sun visor in my truck as beams of a bright Florida sun pierced through the branches of large moss-covered oaks that lined the highway.

When I stopped at a rundown country store in the small Georgia town of Pavo, a medium-sized rug with a picture of Elvis sewn into the fabric caught my eye. It was flapping on a makeshift clothesline mounted on the wooden porch of the building. When I asked the elderly store owner if I could purchase the rug for my mother, the store owner smiled and said, "I sure hate to let it go, but for nineteen dollars you can make your mother happy."

I purchased the rug and continued to drive through a maze of backroads, which weaved through thousands of acres of Georgia pines. While driving, I knew that the town of Alapaha Station wouldn't be anything like Los Angeles. By the time I reached the Alapaha Station Welcomes You highway sign, I knew it was a map dot kind of town not unlike my hometown of Shady Branch. I drove up to the main entrance of the Alapaha Station High School where I saw a 1950s era brick building which seemed to be stuck in a time warp from another era.

Superintendent Dona Felder, along with ten other influential people of the community greeted me like I was a celebrity when I entered the building. All of them expressed how excited they were for me taking the time to interview with them. As I shook their hands, I recognized that most of them were working people, farmers, sawmill folks, all of which reminded me of the people I grew up with in Shady Branch. In my mind, they didn't seem to be there to judge me. It appeared to me they were there ready and willing to embrace whatever I had to say.

Early in the interview process, while we sat in chairs in an office that was too small, I listened as Superintendent Felder explained how they wanted someone to lead their program and bring it back to prominence. She wanted me to know that they were sick and tired of losing every year to their rival schools at Enigma and Willacoochee; places I never knew existed.

When I finally spoke, I said, "Without knowing the talent level here, I can't make any wild predictions about wins and losses. However, I can promise you that these student-athletes will work hard, play with enthusiasm, and learn how to love each other like brothers."

I then remembered some advice I received from Jack Cardwell during my trip with Uncle Dean. I had never forgotten the highly successful entrepreneur from El Paso, Texas whose national chain of truck stops (Petro Stopping Centers) were innovative and customer friendly.

I gave the committee a quote directly from Jack Cardwell when I said, "When you treat people with respect; you will be respected." I paused before sharing with the committee some of my own thoughts by saying, "I have only one rule: Love your teammate like you love yourself."

For a few seconds the room was silent. Then a man by the last name of Dixon spoke up and said, "Amen, Coach! That is exactly the kind of message our players need to hear."

I was never asked the first question about the game of football. I was later paraded around the school like I was already the new coach. Teachers and students met me during lunch in the cafeteria. I sensed that they all were hungry for change. I could tell they were looking for a new beginning.

I spent almost the entire school day at a place that reminded me of Mayberry on the *Andy Griffith Show*. I began to ponder over the possibilities of being a part of something special; a new beginning for myself and this football program.

A slap of reality hit me in the face when I later toured the athletic area of the school at the end of the day. I told myself that a few coats of paint would help brighten up the outdated facilities. I then wondered if a bulldozer and a wrecking ball wouldn't be a better option. With a limited knowledge of what it took for a championship program, I knew that the Alapaha Station High School football program needed more repair and more work than I ever anticipated. The weight room needed new equipment, and the locker room lockers were rusted, scratched, and very inadequate.

A few hours later, I took a wrong turn and ended up in the small town of Enigma, Georgia. I decided to make a phone call to Coach Brown at State from a payphone. I told my college coach that I had been offered a job at Alapaha Station High School. Coach Brown said, "Did you say Alapaha Station? Good Lord! Those farm boys would rather hunt and fish than play football. You better think long and hard before you take that job. They might be the nicest people on the planet, but when it comes to football, that school's football program is as cursed as a hobo trying to marry the Queen of England."

CHAPTER TWENTY-FIVE

As I drove through the backwoods of South Georgia, I was a very confused young man. I had fallen in love with a group of hungry football people at Alapaha Station. I wondered if I was crazy for even thinking that I could turn their football program around which appeared to be in shambles. Alapaha Station could only offer a thousand dollars more than what I was already making at North Tallahassee High School. I wasn't sure if the move was financially worth it.

When I thought about my job offer in Los Angeles, I thought about the money that I could make to help my family. I also thought about the fascinating woman from New York I met, who appeared to be everything I ever wanted. I also thought about the difficulty we would face trying to secretly keep our "forbidden" relationship under wraps from the corporate people at Carnation.

My confusion was multiplied on Thursday afternoon when Maria walked into the gym of North Tallahassee High School at the end of the school day. When I asked her what she was doing she said, "I was in the neighborhood, so I decided to check in on my friend."

For a few seconds I stood in the gym in awkward silence. I finally smiled at her and gave her a hug. Maria told me that she had missed our talks. I also confided in her that I had missed talking to her. After telling her about my job offer as a head football coach in South Georgia, I could tell that she was genuinely excited for me. We then walked over and sat down on the first row of bleachers in the North Tallahassee High School gym. We continued to talk as we pretended to watch the junior varsity girls' basketball team practice.

We talked about our families and caught up on news about mutual friends. Further into the conversation, for some reason, I suddenly began to feel guilty about my one-night rendezvous with a woman in California. I desperately wanted to tell Maria about Sharon while she talked about crossing the Golden Gate Bridge and dining at Fisherman's Wharf. When she changed the subject to tell me that she did not like the people in the San Francisco office, I kept my mouth shut. I allowed her to keep talking. In so many words, she confided in me that San Francisco would be her last choice for future employment.

Maria described her upcoming interviews in Atlanta and Miami. I outwardly tried to be happy for her, but deep down I did not want her to go. As she talked, I glanced at my watch, knowing later I would be heading over to Shady Branch to spend the night with my parents. I sensed that Maria wanted to get back together so I calmly asked her where our relationship stood.

Without hesitation, she replied, "We still need to find our way. You may end up in South Georgia or Los Angeles. I may end up in New York or Miami. I think it is best if we remain good friends for right now."

My intuition was wrong. I was disappointed, but I understood. Maria was taking a logical approach regarding our future as professionals. Deep down I was hoping that she would be willing to follow me to the ends of the earth, and we would live happily ever after. I loved her so much; I momentarily contemplated suggesting that I would be the one who would follow her to the ends of the earth, no matter where she landed. My pride, my rural upbringing, and my stubbornness squelched that brief thought before I had the chance to speak.

Maria later suggested that we grab something to eat. I politely declined. I told her about staying with my parents in Shady Branch, the night before their big day. I wanted to spend more time with Maria, but my pride would not allow it. Although I knew that I loved her, I also knew that there was another woman in California who possessed all the qualities I was looking for in a relationship. That possibility fascinated me.

I then gave Maria a quick kiss goodbye in the school parking lot. I carefully watched her as she drove away. I silently wondered if I would ever see her again. I wanted to cry. I wanted to cry because of Maria and because I had no idea what I would decide regarding my professional future. On top of all that, I dreaded going to Shady Branch and face the possibility of my parents losing their home.

For a few minutes I stood in the parking lot of the school feeling alone and helpless. Then out of nowhere, one of my football players yelled at me across the parking lot from the window of his car saying, "Good night, Coach Jackson," As my player rode past me in a beat-up Ford Torino, the young man yelled out one of my own jokes I would regularly tell my players.

The player yelled, "Hey Coach, guess where I am going?" He paused and then yelled out, "That new French restaurant called Hardees or as they say in France, HAR DEZ." The player laughed and began driving away. I smiled at the young man, waved goodbye, and headed to my truck for a short drive to Shady Branch.

***

Earlier that morning, Cousins Roy, Ava, and Randy landed at the Tallahassee Airport, rented a car, and drove to Shady Branch to visit with my parents a day before they would all find out the fate of Uncle Dean's estate. For all practical purposes, the next afternoon would be Judgment Day in Shady Branch, Florida. The Last Will and Testament of a farming attorney and welder from Alabama would decide the outcome of the Shady Branch Civil War.

****

By the time I arrived at my parents' home, I was surprised to find them with Roy, Ava, and Randy, all sitting around the kitchen table eating a home cooked meal. They were laughing and having a good time. The atmosphere in the kitchen was anything but somber.

As I entered the kitchen, everyone stood up and gave me a hug or a pat on my back. Randy immediately spoke up and said, "Tim, I am so sorry for the way we threw you under the bus when you came to visit us in LA. I hope you will forgive us."

Before I could respond, my mother said, "We have been reminiscing about Uncle Dean."

Roy laughed before saying, "Daddy sure was full of surprises. I have a feeling that he is laughing at all of us right now."

My father piped in by saying, "I have to give him credit. Old Dean didn't mind telling you what was on his mind. I have to believe that everything will be all right tomorrow."

My mother looked at me and said, "I told you that Roy was good with Uncle Dean buying this place. Ain't that right, Roy?"

Roy, putting down a fried chicken leg, wiped his mouth before saying, "I'll have to admit that I was a little upset when I first found out, but then I realized that Daddy was going to do whatever he wanted; no matter what any of us thought."

Right before I sat down at the kitchen table, Randy said, "I'm just curious why GP decided to include me in all of this. I would have thought that I would be the last person on earth that he wanted to give part of his estate to. He always called me the Little Punk."

Ava said, "I know we drove GP crazy at times, but I think he knew we loved him. We all know he was a smart man."

I tried to assure them when I said, "After spending a few days with him, I know for a fact that he loved you both very much."

Ava, who was about to start working on her doctorate at Vanderbilt University in Nashville, Tennessee, replied, "Thanks, Tim. He evidently wanted us to have something, or he would have never invited us to attend the reading of his will."

Roy interjected, "I guess I will have the opportunity to meet my long-lost sister tomorrow. I still haven't been able to wrap my mind around that. Who knew? There is no telling what we may find out about Daddy once his will is read to us."

My mother, with a big smile on her face, looked at me and said, "Roy has promised me and your Daddy that if he receives our property in the will, he will make some arrangements for us to continue to live here." She paused and then continued by saying, "And that little whore, who is still in your room over the garage, will finally be forced to leave."

As we ate our fill of fried chicken, stewed tomatoes, field peas, rice, homemade biscuits and gravy, I could see the relief on my parents' faces. The stress and anguish about possibly losing their property seemed to have vanished.

We listened to Roy and my father's stories. We told jokes, while we all took the time to honor the memory of a man who had done great deeds during his life, but who had also let his family down. Roy and my mother talked in length to each other for the first time in a long time. They really talked. They talked about days gone by when a couple of dollars in your pocket made you feel like you had a lot of spending money. They talked about their childhood memories of boiling wash tubs of peanuts on the farm, eating watermelons right out of the field, and making enough canned preserves and jams to last a lifetime.

As they reminisced about days long past, they both wondered out loud how time had passed by so quickly. They did this all while the rest of the family tried to imagine what their teenage days must have been like in the 1950s and 1960s. When Randy spoke up and said that farm work had to be boring, Roy looked at him and said, "Although I hated it when I was young, I would give my last dollar to go back in time and relive some of those days."

It was a scene right out of a Norman Rockwell painting with tales being told about the old Lee family farm in Alabama. Suddenly, everyone became quiet when the phone in the kitchen rang. My father stood up from the kitchen table. He walked over to the phone on the kitchen wall and picked it up. After saying hello, my father stood motionless as he listened. Suddenly without warning, he screamed, "What the hell? You have to be kidding me." He paused for a moment and continued, "We are on the way." He paused again before saying goodbye and hanging up the phone.

My mother looked at my father and asked, "What was all that about?"

With a look of panic on his face, my father cried out, "We have a big problem. That was Nancy Smith. She said Walter Barrineu's Law Office is on fire. We need to get down there right now."

It did not take a noted theologian from Pepperdine University to understand all the implications of what was occurring if that law office burned to the ground. If for some reason, Walter Barrineau had not filed Uncle Dean's will with the Probate Office of Apalachee County, there would not be any will. Dying intestate in Florida would mean that Uncle Dean's estate would not be settled for quite some time.

As we crowded into Roy's rental car and my father's pickup truck, they drove through the rural area of Shady Branch like they were possessed. By the time we entered the unofficial city limits, we could all see the orange glow of a very large fire. Two hours later we all watched as the last firefighters from the Shady Branch Volunteer Fire Department sprayed water on charred boards, hanging wires, and a smoldering pit of ash.

In the most unlikely turn of events, Attorney Walter Barrineau and his trustworthy secretary, Pinky Little, mysteriously vanished from the planet. The investigation into their whereabouts had authorities in Shady Branch chasing ghosts for many years. One rumor had them in Canada while another had them in Mexico. They have never been found. Cheap talk of money laundering for the Mafia and some shady Florida real estate land deals associated with condos that were never developed are still the talk of Shady Branch all these years later. Most importantly, the Civil War of Shady Branch did not end as planned. What the authorities did find out was that the law office of Walter Barrineau had been intentionally torched by someone who wanted all of Walter Barrineau's records to be vanquished from the earth. The gossip associated with the mysterious disappearance of Walter and Pinky can still be found among old-timers who love a good story.

CHAPTER TWENTY- SIX

Among the records that did not survive the fire, was of course the Last Will and Testament of Dean Lee. Although the Probate Court of Apalachee County did not officially settle the Civil War of Shady Branch until 1993, the delay in the outcome of the court's ruling gave my parents enough time to prepare for the worst. A week after the fire, Uncle Dean's girlfriend, Tracy Lynn, decided to vacate the property one sunny Saturday afternoon while my parents were out of town.

Swept away by the love of a sixty-year-old traveling insurance salesman named Barney Baskins, Tracy Lynn and her children left Shady Branch and moved to St. Petersburg, Florida. With her new husband's help, Tracy Lynn did not vacate her claim to the property, as supposedly promised to her by Uncle Dean. Barney's attorney in St. Petersburg fought hard to keep Tracy Lynn's claim relevant. Because Tracy Lynn would not give up her claim to the property, my parents worked even harder to save enough money to buy out Tracy Lynn if the probate court ruled that the property had to be sold. They were able to squirrel away a good amount of money because they had no mortgage payment.

With the help of Nancy Smith, Styles by Sandy increased their sales of everything in record breaking fashion. I never saw my father work so hard in the trucking business. By the summer of 1990, my father was back working full-time in a one-man trucking business that kept him busy. My parents' determination to keep their property was nothing less than inspirational.

A year after the fire, Roy was finally able to meet his half-sister in Live Oak, Florida. Patricia (Fisher) McNally finally agreed to briefly meet with him. It was not the reunion he had envisioned. At first pleasant, Patricia became emotional after only a few minutes of conversation. In so many words, she basically told Roy that she really did not want to have anything to do with a side of her family that had never been relevant in her life. When Roy brought up the property dispute in Shady Branch, she ended their conversation and told him that she wanted none of whatever her biological father had intended for her to receive.

On April 19, 1993, Probate Judge David Proctor of Apalachee County held court to officially end the Civil War of Shady Branch. In the courtroom were my parents, Nancy Smith, an attorney representing the interests of Tracy Lynn, and me. We all listened intently as Judge Proctor read his ruling to us.

He said, "After receiving claims on the property described as Parcel 7 of Shady Branch, Florida recorded in Plat Book 1180

Page 16, seven acres owned by the late Dean Lee, it has been determined that all claimants of the property are entitled through even distribution, said property after the various claims against the property have been settled with this court."

He then looked up and said, "Hank, I hate it for y'all, but Sandy's uncle has more debt than you can imagine. The man owed money all over the country. He has more credit card debt than the property is worth. In the past twenty years, Dean Lee was robbing Peter to pay Paul. How he even bought this property is absolutely amazing."

My mother cried out, "You must be mistaken. Uncle Dean was very tight with his finances."

Judge Proctor smiled and said, "Sandy, these claims against his estate are as valid as any I have ever seen in all my years of doing this job."

Once Judge Proctor began reading all of the debt associated with the estate, it was clear to everyone present that no one there had the money to clear all of the debt that Uncle Dean left behind. This meant that the property would not be owned or left to anyone. It would have to be sold.

Judge Proctor spoke into his microphone saying, "We have no choice but to put the property up for sale and try to recover the debt associated with your Uncle's estate unless you all agree to pay off the debt."

The attorney representing Tracy Lynn quickly stood up and shouted, "Your honor, my client wishes to vacate her claim to this property."

My mother, in an emotional outburst screamed, "Damn you, Uncle Dean! I don't know how you could have done this to our family."

What seemed over was not quite over. At the back of the courtroom a man shouted out, "Judge, I would like to say something that will change the outcome of this case."

Everyone turned around while Judge Proctor admonished the man who was wearing a very expensive looking suit to step forward and speak. The man walked to the front of the courtroom with a briefcase in his hand.

He said, "My name is Anthony Wilkins. I am an attorney representing my client, Eugene Dawkins Lee. Mr. Eugene Lee is the son of the deceased in question. He is a legitimate heir to the property in question as well as the heir to a considerable amount of stock and bonds. It has recently come to the attention of my client that his father passed away. His father had always told him that he would be the beneficiary of stocks and bonds which were purchased in the 1950s by Dean Lee. The stocks and bonds in question come from the Bank of North Alabama. In today's valuation the shares are valued at approximately 3.5 million dollars."

My father cried out, "Who the hell are you? Uncle Dean did not have any other children."

After he opened his briefcase, Attorney Wilkins pulled out a birth certificate dated June 11, 1943, from a hospital in Chattanooga, Tennessee. The father listed for the birth of Eugene Dawkins Lee was in fact Dean Lee of Cool Springs, Alabama. Attorney Wilkins then pulled out an envelope filled with old photographs of Uncle Dean interacting with Eugene as a child. To everyone's surprise, when the photographs were revealed, Eugene Lee was black. Uncle Dean had a black son that nobody knew anything about. Once the Judge, and everyone involved looked over the birth certificate and photographs my mother almost collapsed. I had to help her sit down in her chair. The mystery was solved surrounding the missing stocks and bonds that Uncle Dean had told me about.

A very frustrated Judge Proctor said, "What we have here is one big fat hell of a mess."

Attorney Wilkins then added, "My client has no interest in the Florida property. All he wants is his claim to the stocks and bonds from the Bank of North Alabama."

Judge Proctor smiled before saying, "I guess you would like to have all of that stock. However, you don't get to come in here and catch the big fish without baiting the hook. Here is my ruling: All of the stocks and bonds will be split between the legitimate children of Dean Lee that we know about along with the property in question. All parties involved will pay off the debt associated with the property. Then the parties involved can decide what to do with the property."

Nancy Smith spoke up and said, "Ah, the hell with all this." She walked up toward the out-of-town attorney and asked, "Mr. Wilkins, if I pay for the debt associated with this property, will you vacate your client's claim to the property?"

Without hesitation, Mr. Wilkins responded, "Absolutely."

Judge Proctor said, "Not so fast, Nancy. There are two other children that we know about who are entitled to a share of the property."

Nancy asked Judge Proctor, "If they don't relinquish their claim to the property, how long will they have to wait to receive their portion of the money from the distribution of the stocks and bonds?

Judge Proctor quickly replied, "At least another year."

Tracy Lynn's attorney then spoke up and said, "Now wait a minute. My client..."

Nancy Smith yelled at him, "Shut the hell up!"

Judge Proctor banged his gavel. He then raised his voice, "Order in this court. You can leave, sir. This matter is now out of your hands. Your client's claim to this property is null and void."

My father whispered to Nancy Smith, "You don't have to do this. There will be no way we can ever pay you back."

Nancy smiled and said, "I know, but what are friends for? I know you and Sandy would do the same for me if the shoe were on the other foot."

***

It only took Nancy Smith a day to talk the other children into giving up their claim to the property in Shady Branch in order to access their share of stocks and bonds valued at over a million dollars for each of them. Nancy Smith was given the title to the property after she paid off the near quarter of a million dollars in debt owed by Uncle Dean. Two days after her purchase, Nancy sold the property back to Sandy and Hank for one dollar and a lifetime of free beauty salon hair appointments. For the rest of her life, Nancy Smith could often be heard by locals saying, "I go to the most expensive hairdresser in the state of Florida."

***

For me, all of the hoopla surrounding the mystery of Uncle Dean's unknown children never tainted my memory of the man whom I had grown to admire. Back in Tallahassee, I made the decision to take the job at Alapaha Station High School. It was not an easy decision. Don Frost at Carnation did his best to convince me otherwise, but I felt an excitement about being a head football coach that no amount of money could extinguish.

In the summer of 1989, I pulled up my sleeves, hired two new assistant coaches, and began the process of transforming a bad football program into something respectable. Luckily, I was able to convince a group of farm boys to buy into my new system. It was at first hard to win the players over until I compromised by allowing them to work during the summer months in the local tobacco fields. We held practices late at night.

I quickly fell in love with the hard-working farm boys, and they fell in love with this young coach who had played college football. Instead of beating them with brutal contact practices, I taught non- contact fundamentals to a group of players who did not know much about football. I tried to make my teaching methods innovative as I filmed every practice and spent time coaching my coaches with the film.

In my personal life, I tried at first to have a long-distance relationship with Sharon in California, but that soon fizzled when we both realized that the distance was impossible. We eventually lost touch with each other; however, I learned many years later that she quit her job at Carnation and became one of Hollywood's most sought-after models. Her exciting career took her to modeling shoots all over the world, and her face made it on national and international publications.

My first year as a head football coach, Alapaha Station High School experienced their first winning football season in five years. During that inaugural year, a new face in the crowd showed up in Alapaha Station on several Friday nights. After a big game in Ocilla, Georgia, I was mobbed on the field by many of the Alapaha Station faithful after we won the game on the very last play. The last person to greet me that night was Maria. She surprised me by showing up to the game. When she told me that she had missed me so much that she was willing to move wherever my career took me, I was flabbergasted. After several long discussions we rekindled an old relationship. When Maria decided that she was still in love with me, she began making plans to change her original career goals.

My marriage to Maria in 1990 was a dream come true. With no expense spared by Maria's parents, half of the football boosters of Alapaha Station showed up to the social event of the year in Pensacola, Florida on June 6, 1990.

Two years before the end of the Shady Branch Civil War, Maria and I were blessed by the birth of twin boys. To everyone's surprise in my family, we named one boy Lee and the other one Dean. A year later, our family was complete when Deborah was born.

Maria soon became a full-fledged coach's wife in a small rural town. She took a financial risk which soon paid off. While we lived in Alapaha Station, she started her own business selling a new line of cosmetics. Her brands would eventually make their way from an old pecan warehouse in Alapaha Station to Styles by Sandy in Shady Branch along with almost every beauty salon in North Florida and South Georgia. Maria worked relentlessly from home, all while raising our children.

It soon became apparent that Maria's business brought in more income than I could ever hope to make. She used the abandoned pecan warehouse a block away from Gaskins Store in Alapaha Station to expand her business. Maria also hired two other stay-at-home moms to help her package and ship her patented Honey Suckle Lip Gloss and Down at the Beach Eye Shadow. Both items were manufactured in Brazil.

Maria and her new friends took turns watching their small children in the warehouse while running a successful business. From an early start, the children often found themselves hanging out in the gym or the football practice field so Maria could make sales calls. The children were becoming our "little gym rats".

When our football team won the conference championship at Alapaha Station in 1994, my career as a much sought-after football coach took off. Eston Harper made a visit to Alapaha Station from Los Angeles, the night our Alapaha Station High School Braves upset our longtime rival, Willacoochee High.

Eston and the Alapaha Station football boosters did everything they could do to keep me at Alapaha Station, but when South Pensacola Christian School offered me an unbelievable financial package, I decided to make the move so my children could grow up close to Maria's parents. The move would also allow me to coach football at one of the elite high school programs in the state of Florida.

When I called Coach Brown and told him the news, he laughed and said, "Dadgum, Tim, you might have a better job than me."

The move to Pensacola became an immediate blessing for our family as Maria's parents lovingly helped out with the babysitting because they lived only a few miles away. Maria decided to sell her cosmetic business a year later. She also decided to stay at home during the formative years of our children. During that time, she and I made a conscious decision to join the South Pensacola Country Club where Maria and her family had been members when she was a child. Using some of the money Maria had made in the cosmetics business, we made an investment in our children's future. Our children would always have access to an Olympic-sized pool, one of Florida's best golf courses, premiere tennis courts, all while forging relationships with Pensacola's most respected families. This decision to give our children access to the country club was not taken lightly. We prayed long and hard before we joined. It was Maria who convinced me that we would be giving our children something I had never experienced, and they could benefit from in the long run.

***

For the most part, our lives were as complete as they possibly could be for a young couple. To many, we appeared to be Pensacola's new power couple. We were sought after both publicly and privately. Maria had returned to her roots reacquainting herself with family and old friends. The hometown girl brought with her a football coach husband who adapted to any social setting.

While our children were young, we made a conscious effort to center our lives around them. Every decision we made, every prayer that we prayed, and every dollar that we spent always had our children's best interest at heart. Even during times when we occasionally struggled as a married couple, we always put the needs of our children first.

Because of our connection to State University, our vacations and free time centered around going to State football, baseball, and basketball games. When our young family attended the Sugar Bowl in 1995 to witness State win the College National Football Championship, I remembered the time Uncle Dean told me that he was sure that I would finally make it to the Sugar Bowl.

Whenever we went to State home events, we would always go out of our way to stop by Shady Branch and visit with my parents. Visiting my parents was always an adventure for the children. My parents allowed their grandchildren to play in a backyard where a tree fort and an above ground pool was not nearly as much fun as playing with their grandfather's chickens and two old goats named Queen and King.

Maria and I both believed it was important that our children attend church. We became involved with our church's youth groups. Church, the country club, and sporting events at State became the center of our spiritual and social universes. On top of our trips to Tallahassee, we regularly visited Rome, Georgia at least three times a year to be with Maria's extended family.

Most people assumed that our family had it all. However, as time passed, our lives became chaotic. As our children grew older, their extracurricular activities increased dramatically. Our problem was that we never set limits. Whenever one of our children wanted to be involved in an activity, we allowed it. Most of the chasing after our children fell in the lap of Maria, who was always forced to juggle her schedule because my job was not very flexible. During football season, I was never able to help. For Maria, chasing after our children became exhausting. She longed to return to the professional world. She missed the hustle and bustle of running a business but more than anything, she craved intellectual adult conversations.

Maria later approached me about the possibility of obtaining her real estate license and working what she thought would only be part-time. I was all for it. A year later after she began working for a local broker, her time at home stretched thin. Our worlds began to collide when she opened her own real estate firm two years later and began to spend more time away from the family.

There were many times when my job as an athletic director and head football coach interfered with our family life. I poured my soul into my players, other students, and my coaches. I eventually became the father figure for many students who had suffered the consequences of divorce or who had non-existent relationships with their own parents. At the time, I did not understand that my youthful enthusiasm and charisma was becoming contagious in our community. Many of the players and parents who closely watched our program wanted to be a part of it; especially some of the parents from other schools as they wanted their sons to play for a successful coach. My relationships with my players and their families increasingly became unpopular in my own home as those athletic related relationships dominated my energy and time.

***

As our children became older, it was evident that the oldest of our twins, Lee, was becoming the best athlete in the family. By age seven, Lee excelled at almost every sport he ever tried. As hard as I tried, Dean, two minutes younger than his brother, never wanted to participate in sports. As a child, Dean fell in love with reading, drawing, and painting. By the time he was in middle school, Dean was an academic free-thinker who was incredibly intelligent.

Deborah (Deb), our daughter, was the spitting image of her mother. She was spoiled by her brothers, and her grandparents, and she grew to be the darling of our family. Her infectious personality was as attractive as her good looks.

By their teenage years, tension grew between Tim and Dean. Dean openly resented the time I spent trying to develop Lee's athletic skills. I did not know this, but it was later revealed that in Dean's mind, I was embarrassed that he did not care about athletics. Dean's resentment toward his brother brought tension to our marriage where on many occasions, Maria and I did not see eye to eye. She also felt that I was showing favoritism toward Lee.

I was a successful coach, but not a successful father. I woke up one morning and realized that my family was slowly falling apart. Our boys fought all the time, my daughter was becoming a woman, and the love of my life was threatening to leave me if I didn't change my ways.

For several months we had been discussing our relationship in private. I could tell she was unhappy. I was also unhappy. She wanted me to become more supportive of her career and to be a better father. She pointed out several of my flaws which I could not defend. She begged me to leave my work at the office and pay one hundred percent of my attention to her and the children when I was at home. I have to admit that I did not like what she had to say about me, but she was right.

On that particular morning, I remembered some words Uncle Dean had told me, "A person who didn't read was a person who did not want to succeed." As I remembered this, something made me pick up my Bible. I had not opened up the Holy Book in quite some time. For some reason the passage of scripture I began reading was the Parable of the Prodigal Son. As I read the scripture from Luke 15: 11-32, it somehow made me realize that I had been unfair to my youngest son.

My change of attitude about Dean was quickly followed by actions. I began to show a genuine interest in Dean's activities. During the summer months, after having thrown baseballs in a batting cage set up in our backyard to Lee, I would take Dean to the public library to browse and check out books. I even bought and read J. K. Rowling's book, *Harry Potter and the Sorcerer's Stone* so that I could better engage with Dean. After reading and surprisingly really enjoying the book, I actively began reading more novels and biographies. Eventually, Dean and I began to bond and relate more on an intellectual level.

During the summer of 2004, I actually collaborated with Dean regarding our family vacations. He suggested that we visit art museums and historic sites instead of always going to sporting events or the beach. That next year, while driving to New York City, I had the opportunity to introduce my children and Maria to a story about a highway warning sign I had seen and experienced with Uncle Dean. As we drove through a construction zone on I-95 near Philadelphia, I pointed out the new version of an orange-colored highway warning sign which read: *End Road Work*.

CHAPTER TWENTY-SEVEN

I explained that the End Road Work sign did not make any sense. Dean immediately agreed with me. Lee kept staring out the window and said, "Dad, only you would think of something so stupid."

Deb laughed and said, "Come on, Dad, nobody would ever be that dumb not to understand what that sign means."

I replied, "I don't know. Think about it. Those new signs say- End Road Work. Don't you think there is the slightest possibility that someone who reads those signs is wondering why we are trying to put an end to road work?"

Maria shouted, "Only you and your crazy Uncle Dean would think of such a thing. I agree with Deb. That sign makes perfect sense."

Once we arrived in New York City, we toured the Statue of Liberty, attended a Broadway play, and shopped in Chinatown before attending a Yankees baseball game. To appease Deb and Maria, we even made a visit to Macy's.

After having spent three long, but fantastic days sightseeing in New York City, we drove to a scheduled stop in Gettysburg, Pennsylvania to tour the historically significant Civil War battlefield. We pulled up at a convenience store gas station outside of Gettysburg. The boys and I walked into the men's restroom. As soon as we entered, we noticed two construction workers washing their hands at the sink. One of the workers said to the other, "Did you see that sign on Highway 18? It says they are going to end road work. Can you believe it?"

The other worker shook his head and replied, "This country is going to hell."

Needless to say, the entire family enjoyed talking about the incident over dinner. Later that evening, we watched the College Baseball World Series on an older TV in a small hotel room next to the Gettysburg Battlefield. Reflecting back on the day and being content in the moment, Maria and I felt blessed that we had the opportunity to share this trip and all of the experiences with our children.

Before we went to bed that night, I walked out on the porch of the motel. As I looked across the parking lot, the moonlight allowed me to see a small patch of fog descending over a wooden fence and a stone monument on the edge of the historic battlefield. For some reason this was calming for me. At that moment, I thanked the Good Lord for allowing my family to be at peace. I thought back on the time I stayed in a similar looking motel with Uncle Dean during our trip together. I smiled when I remembered calling my mother and telling her that Uncle Dean was crazy and needed to be committed for carrying a gun.

I was startled when the room door a few rooms down from me opened. A young, dark-haired man walked out onto the porch. He asked, "Is that you, Tim?"

The shadow from the awning covered most of the man's face. Once I walked closer and he came out of the shadows, I recognized him. A much older, Ali Chaudhary, from Texas spoke up and said, "I'm not sure if you remember me, but you and your uncle saved my father's life years ago during a robbery at his store."

After shaking hands with him, I laughed and replied, "Sure, I remember you. What brings you here to Gettysburg?"

Ali told me that he was now a neurosurgeon practicing in Richmond, Virginia. He and his wife were taking a weekend trip to Gettysburg. I told Ali about the passing of Uncle Dean. While we were catching up on some of our life experiences, my children walked out onto the porch from their adjoining room. After introducing my teenagers to Dr. Ali Chaudhary my son Lee laughed and said, "All these years, we thought Daddy had made up that story about how Uncle Dean shot a man in a gas station."

Ali stated, "Your father and your Uncle Dean saved my father's life."

After we said our goodbyes to Ali, I sat on the porch with our children. We laughed, joked, and made fun of each other. I told them how proud I was of them. They told me that this was the best vacation they had ever taken together. At that moment, I felt like my life was as close to perfection as it could possibly be. After hugging all of my children and making my way into bed, I thanked God for the time Maria, and I had spent with our children.

***

After that vacation, our lives again went in opposite directions. Maria's real estate business became more successful taking her away from the family. I became more involved with my job as my school began a multi-million-dollar athletic facility renovation. I worked late hours. As a couple, our marriage continued to suffer. There would be days when we only talked late at night. We both recognized that our diverse schedules were the problem.

Twice, Maria and I went on weekend Christian couples' retreats sponsored by the Fellowship of Christian Athletes, trying to mend our relationship. The retreats were spiritually uplifting; however, once the retreats were over, our times together were still limited due to professional circumstances and obligations. As our marriage struggles continued, both of us tried hard to make time for one another. Our combined efforts barely salvaged a marriage from falling apart.

Our children, now in high school, went their separate ways socially. Maria and I both tried to plan family activities, but that became increasingly difficult. School and church activities always trumped our plans. Seldom could we arrange for all of us to be together for a family outing.

Although I saw all of our children on a daily basis at school, I was never able to be present at most of their extracurricular activities. Lee was the exception as he played football and baseball. As he became more popular at school, he began spending more of his time with his friends.

My relationship with Dean became nonexistent as Dean began to excel in the fine arts and the band. While I tried to be supportive of him, it was Dean who seemed embarrassed to be seen with me at school. It was not uncommon for him to intentionally avoid me whenever he saw me walking down the halls or in the cafeteria of the school.

Deb, on the other hand, loved to be around me at school, but cheerleading practices, pageant rehearsals, and working on the school's yearbook staff took her away from our family more than any of our children.

Then in 2006, tragedy struck close to home that summer when one of my football players was killed in an automobile accident only a few miles from his home. Everybody loved Brent Hogan, and Brent loved everybody. He was the back-up kicker, who never saw much action, but he was at the time, the most popular player on the team. I loved Brent because he was a team player who never complained about his lack of playing time. The players loved Brent because he was always willing to help his teammates on and off the field. With a personality that was described as "shining", Brent kept players and coaches laughing with his corny jokes and humorous attempts to sing.

On that tragic afternoon in July, I dreaded going to Brent's home to visit with his parents. On the way to their home at Pensacola Beach, I remembered what Uncle Dean had told me about losing his own son. Once inside the Hogan home, I recalled Uncle Dean stating how he hated people telling him his son was in a better place. That memory weighed heavy on my heart. I knew Brent's family did not want to hear those words either. No words came to me as I hugged both parents with tears streaming down their faces. I walked with Brent's father, Russell, outside on the deck behind their home. I listened as Russell talked about his only son as if he were still alive. He pointed out toward the beach and said, "Some of our happiest times have been on that beach. Brent loves the beach." He paused, "Loved the beach."

The pain on Russell's face and in his voice was heartbreaking. His words were barely audible as tears and his trembling hands were noticeable. As he desperately wiped his tears and tried not to show his emotions, the suffering Russell felt in his soul could not be comprehended by me. The loss and suffering Russell felt was raw and incomprehensible.

A few days later, the visitation, the funeral, and the days leading up to a football season where Brent's jersey would be retired was emotionally draining for me. The afternoon before the first home game, I painted Brent's jersey number in the end zone. I broke down after I finished painting. I stood on the field, holding a can of athletic field marking paint, crying like I had never cried before. I grieved from the deepest depths of my soul for a family who had lost their only son. As I cried uncontrollably, I remembered Uncle Dean's words describing the loss of a child as the worst experience anyone could ever endure. I was determined to support Brent's parents on their grief journey. This death would emotionally impact me more than anything I had ever experienced as a coach.

***

A year later, during the twin's junior year of high school in 2007, Lee helped us win a region championship as the starting quarterback. Our team made a deep run into the playoffs losing in the state championship game. When several colleges began to show interest in Lee, I knew that Lee was destined to play college football. However, right before baseball season began that spring, it was apparent to many that Lee's skills as a baseball shortstop had also been noticed by the scouts. Lee was selected in the Major League Baseball Draft in the ninth round. I knew my son had a chance to be drafted, but nobody expected Lee to be drafted at this high level.

The family meetings about Lee's new athletic status were exhausting. Lee, who was academically challenged, wanted to go ahead and sign a professional baseball contract. The money was good, and he did not want to spend any of his time in a college classroom. He wanted to join the Minor Leagues the day he graduated from high school.

Maria and I both refused to go along with his plan. We wanted Lee to have an opportunity to obtain a college education. When I called my former position coach at State, I asked him what he thought about the situation. My coach was now at another college, and he agreed that Lee needed to go to college at least for a few years.

That summer Lee had baseball offers pouring in from colleges all over the nation, including the University of Texas, the University of South Carolina, and State. Although I fully supported Maria in the final decision, Lee felt certain it was his mother who stood in the way of his baseball career. Their relationship took a downward turn, as Lee had little interaction with her.

With so much attention being given to Lee, Dean and Deb went their separate ways both socially and spiritually. They flew under and around our paternal radar. Dean excelled in the fine arts, particularly in acting while Deb became a writer for the school's yearbook and newspaper.

After he was cast in the leading role in his school play, Dean became a regular actor at the Pensacola Community Theatre. When he received an acceptance letter to attend the prestigious Julliard School of Acting in New York City, Dean felt that no one in the family cared. Although this was not true, Maria and I, unintentionally, did not celebrate Dean's incredible accomplishment as much as we had done with Lee. When Lee was drafted in baseball and also received Division One college offers, the entire extended family and many people in the community openly celebrated his achievements. To make matters worse, Lee openly accused his brother of being gay one night at the family dinner table. He looked at his brother with so much disgust and said, "Dean, you are nothing but a big faggot."

It took all of my strength to separate my sons from a physical altercation which had Maria and Deb in absolute disbelief. I made it quite clear to both of my sons after this incident that their differences were their own individual strengths and that their mother and I would support our children in whatever path in life they happen to choose. We only wanted them to be happy with their lives and life decisions.

When Deb became the newly selected Assistant Chief Editor of the school's yearbook; the first sophomore to ever obtain that title, Maria threw a party for her and her friends. She began pouring her spare time into Deb's grooming for the pageant world, enrolling her with winning pageant coaches and gown designers. On a ride back from voice lessons in Fort Walton Beach, Deb confided to her mother that she was falling in love with a junior classmate named Landon. Landon worked with her on the yearbook staff. He was also on the football team. This relationship eventually became an awkward situation for me that I was not prepared to handle.

The challenge of balancing driving lessons, purchasing cars, visits to the South Pensacola Country Club for golf and tennis lessons, boyfriends, girlfriends, dating, going to parties, and keeping up with academics all began to take a toll. It seemed that Maria and I were killing ourselves chasing the dreams, needs, and wants of our children.

***

Our family was considered by many in the community as the "first family" of South Pensacola Christian School and the South Pensacola Community. The teachers and the administrators gave all of our children special treatment. On several occasions, our children were able to slip under the radar with several school infractions that other students could not. This special treatment was particularly extended to my son Lee in 2008 during his senior year.

The summer before graduation, Lee and some of his friends decided it would be a good idea to have a party on the school's football practice field. In a secluded spot, partially surrounded by woods, Lee and his friends parked their vehicles, and partied late into the night. When an off-duty deputy with the Sheriff's Department drove by the school before the party ended, he gave me a call. Maria and I rushed up to the school.

It was the first time that we realized that our son was not the perfect child. Our eyes were opened to the fact that he had started experimenting with alcohol and marijuana.

It was quite the scene. However, because of my position at the school, the officer refused to bring any charges. Although I severely punished Lee, I did not suspend him or the other players from the football program who were at the party. This was something I had done previously in similar situations. I privately kept my feelings about the situation to myself, but deep down as a coach, I knew I should have suspended them. As a father, I could not bring myself to kick my son off the team. After making Lee and the other boys complete hours of community service and other physically challenging forms of punishment, I ultimately felt that I had done enough to address their infractions.

By the time football season started that year, a mutiny occurred. I thought this incident had been forgotten; however, many players felt that Lee and his friends received special favoritism from "Daddy". Several key players quit the team. Several others who stayed on the team became the sources of locker room contention. What was supposed to be a championship season soon turned sour.

Scandal and coverup became the topic of conversations all over Pensacola. It took a slim vote of the school's Board of Directors to allow me to continue as the head football coach and athletic director. When some of our church and country club members turned against me, Maria and the children took a hiatus from attending church and social events.

The stress that I suffered during the season was immeasurable. There were times when I wanted to resign. There were times when I wanted to lash out at Lee. The rejection by some of my most loyal supporters caused me daily emotional distress. I did not quit because it wasn't in my DNA and because Maria stepped up and vocally supported me in a way that I did not expect. When she blasted one of our church members at the local grocery store, I was shocked by her words of defense for me.

She told the church member, "All of you can go to hell. My husband has done more for that athletic program than any other coach in the history of that school."

The Miami Herald's prediction of a state championship for South Pensacola Christian School turned out to be my first losing season as a head football coach. Without many of our best players on the team, my strategies, trick plays, and motivational speeches were of no use.

With the team going in the wrong direction, I tried to motivate with love and understanding. My best coaching methods failed, and my players were ridiculed at school by some of the players who opted not to play. My son, Lee, who was the starting quarterback, suffered more than anyone. He never overcame the trauma that he faced every day. He ended up hating the game of football.

CHAPTER TWENTY-EIGHT

Maria and I watched our two sons walk across the stage at South Pensacola Christian School for their high school graduation. We were as proud as the day our boys were baptized. That afternoon, Maria's parents threw an extravagant party at the South Pensacola Country Club where the expense for the party was never a consideration. The boys were spoiled by my parents as well, in that they were both given five-hundred dollars in cash. I really thought that both sets of grandparents had been way too generous.

That evening, when everyone went to bed, Maria and I sat in our bedroom and prayed for our two boys. Dean would be headed to college in New York while Lee was picked up in the 5th round by the Detroit Tigers. It had been a long struggle between us and Lee because we originally wanted him to attend college. Finally, I convinced Maria that college would not be in Lee's best interest.

She finally conceded once she realized that it would be a miracle if Lee graduated from high school.

A week later, the entire extended family watched Lee's jet takeoff from the Tallahassee Airport as he headed to Detroit's AA team in Erie, Pennsylvania. Before he departed, Maria and I promised Lee that we would come and watch him play baseball in July. Lee did not say much, smiled and told us that he loved us. Before leaving the terminal, he also gave his brother and sister a hug and said, "Keep Mom and Dad straight."

That summer Maria and I took several trips to Erie to watch our son play baseball. Lee was struggling with his bat but was dazzling his coaches and scouts with his defensive play in the infield. Each time we visited, we were upset that we were not able to spend quality time with Lee. His schedule was challenging. The several times we were able to take him out to eat or help with his laundry, Lee seemed aloof and bothered. When questioned about his somber demeanor, he would attribute it to his batting slump at the plate.

Later that summer, a week before Deb's senior year began, the family again went to the Tallahassee Airport. This time it was Dean's turn. We were there to see him off as he was going to pursue his dreams at The Juilliard School for Acting to study drama in New York. Unlike his brother's departure, Dean was talkative, and he was emotional. The last person he hugged and spoke to that day was me. He said, "Dad, you know I love you.

You make sure to come and visit me when football season is over."

Dean's words shook me up in an unexpected way. As Maria, Deb, and I drove back to Pensacola from Tallahassee, I had a strange feeling that my interaction with Dean may have been my last. I unexpectedly felt an emotional pain that I had never felt before. It felt like I was having a panic attack. I was somehow convinced that something bad was going to happen to Dean while he was at school in New York City. I was worried about Dean being alone in the Big Apple. I also worried that Dean would not be physically or mentally tough enough to cope in the nation's largest city. This strange premonition of me never seeing Dean again was very troubling.

Many phone calls later, my feelings about Dean were dispelled as he and I talked almost every day. During one of our chats, I asked him, "Do you remember me telling you about the conversation Uncle Dean and I had with a guy named Tim Cook in Alabama?"

Dean paused and replied, "Can't say I do, Dad."

I explained, "You know. It was the conversation we had with the guy from IBM who told us to invest in computers."

Dean slowly replied, "I guess..."

I interrupted him and said, "I just saw a news report where he is now the CEO of Apple. It's a small world. It is hard to believe that Uncle Dean and I talked to the man who is now the CEO of Apple."

Dean laughed before saying, "I do remember, now. That is when Uncle Dean told you to invest in a water farm. Dad, you and Uncle Dean met some incredible people on that trip. I wish I could have been there with you guys."

During another conversation, Dean said, "Dad, you and Mom need to keep an eye on my brother. Lee is not right. I'm not sure what is going on with him, but he does not seem like himself."

Dean then confided to me that he had heard rumors from friends in Pensacola that Lee was using drugs again. This revelation was not the news I wanted to hear. Maria and I began earnestly praying for our oldest son to make better decisions regarding his lifestyle.

A year later when Deb graduated from high school, she had her parents to herself as both of the boys could not make it home. Dean was performing in an Off-Broadway musical that ran during the summer while Lee was participating in an exhibition game in Lakeland, Florida. As expected, Deb graduated salutatorian of her class and decided to accept a full academic scholarship to the University of South Carolina's School of Business. That evening at Deb's graduation party at the South Pensacola Country Club, I walked with Maria outside next to the 18th green. We embraced, not saying a word. When I looked into Maria's eyes, I could tell that she was happy. She knew the same about me. I simply said, "We have done it."

She replied, "No, God has done it. We are blessed."

***

The next morning, May 30, 2010, a telephone call from Lee shook the very foundation of our family. We were still asleep when I finally answered the call at 7:15 a.m. I was still waking when I vaguely heard Lee say, "Daddy, you need to come to Lakeland. I am locked up in the Lakeland Detention Center. I need your help. I will tell you all the details when you get here."

My heart began racing. Before I could respond to Lee, I heard a click, and the phone call was over. The worst thoughts came to my mind as I quickly showered. Nothing could have prepared Maria and me for what we would face once we arrived in Lakeland.

Maria and I did not speak as we began our six and half hour journey to Lakeland through the Florida Panhandle down to the Gulf Coast. Right before we reached Tallahassee, I finally said to her, "I wish I could call my Daddy. He has a lot of experience with these types of situations."

Maria replied, "I think it's best if we keep this to ourselves until we find out what Lee has done."

We finally arrived at the Lakeland Detention Center. The officer at the front desk informed us that Lee had been charged with DUI. He also informed us that he had been in a car accident and that although he was a little banged up and bruised, he would be fine physically. We were then given directions to the Municipal Courthouse and told by another officer that Lee was there for his initial appearance in court along with the others accused of different offenses.

We made a mad dash to the courthouse in time to watch our shackled son hear the charges against him. The judge said, "Case number 186-F20, the state of Florida vs. Lee Jackson. Mr. Jackson, you have been charged with Driving Under the Influence, Distribution of a banned narcotic, and Vehicular Homicide."

When it was all said and done, the judge denied bail. I tried to speak up in the courtroom. The judge immediately cut me off. Without being able to speak to our son in the courtroom, Maria and I walked outside holding on to one another. Then from out of nowhere, we were suddenly approached by several news reporters with microphones. Two men holding television cameras lunged toward us like a stampede. Still not knowing exactly what Lee had done, one reporter asked, "Coach Jackson, do you think your son will have a fair trial here in Lakeland since he is accused of killing the daughter of prominent businessman and County Councilman Gill McKenzie?"

Without answering any questions, Maria and I finally made it to our car through a sea of curious and opinionated people. These people were casting their own judgment on the parents of the young man who killed one of Lakeland's well-known daughters.

The short ride back to the Lakeland Detention Center was painful. It was surreal. We still did not know any of the details surrounding the charges against our son. Maria and I both were in a state of shock. We wanted to call our attorney back in Pensacola, but we needed to know what we were dealing with first.

Once back inside the Lakeland Detention Center, we were allowed to visit with Lee for the first time. He looked much thinner than normal. His hair was a mess. The khaki jumpsuit he wore was shocking for me. I could not believe what was happening. After five or so minutes of nothing but tears and anguish, I finally asked Lee, "What have you done?"

In a painful admission of guilt, our son informed us that he had been at a party where he was using cocaine and drinking heavily after his baseball game.

This admission devastated us. Lee then told us that he had no recollection of the accident near his hotel. He said that an officer from the Florida Highway Patrol told him that he had been driving 60 in a 35 mile per hour zone, and that he ran a stop sign. He ended by saying, "They told me that I killed a girl. My life is over. I am so sorry for all of this."

His face was covered with torment as he began to sob uncontrollably. He glanced at Maria and then looked at me before putting up his hands and asking, "What am I going to do, Dad?"

I tried my best to come up with the right words to say. Nothing came to my mind. I was mad. I grieved for a family who had lost a daughter, and I hurt for my son- knowing that his future looked bleak. I could also see the hurt on Maria's face. She, too, did not know what to say.

I gathered my thoughts and said, "Son, the only thing you can do right now is to pray and trust God. Your mother and I will do everything in our power to find you good legal representation and any other help that you may need."

A week later, help did come our way when Maria's father hired one of the best trial lawyers in Florida to represent Lee. During the pre-trial arraignment, the judge was convinced by the skillful attorney to issue bail for Lee. However, the attorney was unsuccessful in his petitioning of the court for a change of venue for the trial.

For the next eight months, Lee's life became the main concern for Maria and me. We had to deal with Lee threatening to leave the country or contemplating suicide. We never left him alone. Lee became a prisoner in his own home as our entire extended family became in essence, prison wardens. Deb decided to delay college for a semester to help us with this family crisis. We all had to protect Lee daily from anxious groups of reporters who wanted to know everything about Pensacola's fallen golden athlete. The misery that every family member endured was compounded by the questions that were being asked by our friends. Some of these friends were genuine and some were not.

Embarrassment and shame hovered over our family as each of us was trying to console and inspire a mentally devastated Lee. When an NBC affiliate television station out of Tampa ran a story about the college girl from Lakeland, who had been tragically killed, it made national news. ESPN picked up the story and did a special of their own. Our entire family watched when the ESPN story aired. The news story showed young students and Mothers Against Drunk Driving in Lakeland holding up signs which read: *Justice for Jennifer.* Lee became visibly upset.

When my mother saw the ESPN news story she called me from Shady Branch and cried out over the phone, "Those people don't know Lee like us. He made a mistake. Those slimy reporters are trying to crucify him like Jesus."

As soon as football season started that fall, the cloud of distrust, speculation, and disbelief hovered over the football program and our community. Instead of asking questions about the team or the season, reporters kept their focus on an upcoming trial that would determine the fate of my oldest son.

South Pensacola Booster Club members, although sympathetic, were increasingly aggravated by the negative publicity. With each new day, my trust in several friends began to unravel. When I later heard rumors that some of my friends were talking about me and my family behind my back, it shook me. I was so disappointed to learn that people I trusted and thought had my best interest at heart would engage in such activity that was so demoralizing to my family and me.

There were times when Maria and I wanted to crawl in a hole and disappear. Although we tried to stay positive, we knew the situation looked bleak. Our social and spiritual lives were turned upside down as our main focus became Lee.

For the first time in my career, I found myself allowing my assistant coaches to handle many of the important matters regarding the football program. They knew that I was distracted when I turned over all the play calling duties to them. I also had to miss several practices when I had to meet with the team of attorneys representing Lee. One Friday night late in the season, I looked out on the field and asked, "What in the hell are we doing? What coverage are we in? Who the hell decided this would be a good idea to play man coverage against these guys?"

The most trusted coach on my staff walked over to me and whispered, "This is the game plan you said would work. Coach, this is what we discussed during our Sunday meeting."

My inability to focus on the minor details of our team became a hindrance to the team's success. By the end of another losing football season, several key boosters in South Pensacola were calling for my head.

As Maria spent most of her time working from home, her business also suffered immensely. When she missed an important closing in November, her firm lost a sizeable business deal which would have made other real estate developers in Pensacola jealous. She began to crumble under the pressure.

While we suffered with Lee, Deb and Dean stayed the course and excelled academically during the family crisis. Dean took it upon himself to call and cheer me up, while Deb did the same for her mother. No matter how hard they pretended, our two other children knew Maria and I were in trouble.

CHAPTER TWENTY-NINE

When the trial started in June of 2011, our entire family and close supporters camped out in Lakeland. As we listened to key testimony and watched the family of Jennifer McKenzie, the pain for both families was evident. On the second day of the trial, Maria took it upon herself to walk over and express her condolences to Jennifer McKenzie's mother during a court recess. Her words were inadequate. They did not fill a void that was left by the death of a child. Mrs. McKenzie simply nodded as her husband looked on with malice in his heart and an icy stare.

Although the legal team assembled on Lee's behalf did everything they could do, the jury was not convinced of his innocence. In a trial which lasted for less than two weeks, an unsympathetic jury concluded that our son was guilty on three of the four counts. The judge from Lakeland was unyielding as he sentenced Lee to 20 years in prison.

That evening in a hotel room not far from the courthouse, Maria and I held tightly to each other for what seemed like hours as we grieved like never before. No words, no promises, no sacred scripture could mend our broken hearts.

Once again, I referenced a conversation I once had with Uncle Dean concerning the loss of a child. The pain and agony I felt late that next morning as I sat in a chair in a completely dark hotel room was unbearable. Trying to hide my sobbing from Maria, I prayed, pleaded, and begged God, like Uncle Dean who had done the same thing a generation before.

The transition of adjustment without Lee in our home was almost as bad as if he had died. The promises of legal appeals from our attorneys seemed so far-fetched that Maria and I both put any glimmer of hope out of our minds. Ironically, Lee was sent to the very same prison that had electrocuted Ted Bundy many years before.

Behind the scenes, Maria and I did everything we could do to help Lee avoid what seemed like a hopeless situation. We called everyone we knew. Our influence, our money, and our prior popularity, could not fix a situation that was out of our control. There were days of darkness and immense sadness. There were days of discontent. The Florida State Prison, located several hours away from Pensacola, offered only minimal visitation. One afternoon two months after Lee entered prison, I received a phone call from my panicked son.

Lee cried over the phone and said, "Dad, they told me they are going to kill me if I don't join a gang."

Not understanding the complexities of prison life, I urged Lee to resist and stay strong. A few days later, Lee called me back and informed me that he had nearly been beaten to death by a group of gang members in the Florida State Prison. When Lee told me that he had three broken ribs, and two swollen eyes, I fell to the floor of my office. I could almost feel the pain in my own body, while my son lay physically wounded in a place that could only be described as hell on earth.

The next few phone calls I received from Lee included pleas for me to send money to gang members. Those calls were gut wrenching. I did my best to keep all that information from Maria. However, when we went to visit Lee a few months later, he broke down and begged us to bring him some drugs so he could kill himself. Each day Maria and I tried to live our lives and be strong for our other children; however, Lee's situation was always first on our minds.

One night I confided in Maria that I regretted not spending more time with our children when they were younger. I felt that I had not done enough for them as a father. I then thought back to a similar conversation I had with Uncle Dean concerning the same subject.

For almost a year after Lee's incarceration, hundreds of regrets began to consume both Maria and me at various times; sometimes when we least expected it. Holidays and birthdays were the worst, but occasionally something as simple as a television commercial or running into an old friend in a store could trigger grief as if our son were dead. Friends avoided us so they would not have to broach the subject of Lee's incarceration. This caused us even more pain.

Through all of our trials, Maria and I steadily became closer. One afternoon when I was trying to find some batteries for the television remote, I noticed an old newspaper clipping of the obituary of a Vietnam POW from Alabama named Aaron Lynch in the bottom of a desk drawer. I had saved the newspaper clipping I found on Uncle Dean's refrigerator. It had been years since I had read it, but on that particular day, emotion overcame me in an unexpected way.

I tried to explain to Maria all the emotions I was feeling. I read her the obituary in hopes that we could realize that there were others dealing with pain and grief like us. We were both overcome with sympathy and grieved for the family in Alabama we did not even know. We grieved for those parents who had lost their only son almost forty years ago. For whatever reason, finding and reading that obituary helped us cope with the loss of Lee from our home. It helped us see that we were not the only ones who were experiencing an awful hardship.

With our circle of old friends almost non-existent, we somehow reignited a love for one another that had not been felt since we were in college. Through our grief, we began talking to each other about our feelings. Maria made it a habit to eat lunch with me at my office, while I made certain to call her at least twice a day. We both did our best to support each other.

In 2015, I decided that I would step down as the Head Football Coach and remain as the school's Athletic Director. This professional move allowed more flexibility in my schedule. Once I gave up coaching football, Maria made the decision to scale back her work by selling a portion of her real estate brokerage to a childhood friend.

We also decided not to harbor any more ill will toward those in our community who we felt wronged us. This hate was eating us up inside; it was a poison overflowing in our lives. We eventually started attending church again and slowly, our souls were being renewed.

In 2016, our son, Dean, surprised us when he announced that he had landed an incredible job with the Food Network in New York as an assistant producer. One year later, he further surprised us when he gave us the news that he would be marrying a co-host of the Food Network. Their wedding would take place in her hometown of Toronto, Canada. The trip to Toronto and everything surrounding the wedding turned out to be a memorable experience for us as well as a much-needed distraction from Lee's situation.

A year later, Deb informed us that she would be working in the business office of the Carolina Panthers NFL team in Charlotte, North Carolina. Her ability to give us free tickets to a couple of NFL games had a positive impact that lifted our spirits.

Although we were very proud of Dean and Deb, the pain and grief associated with Lee's absence still haunted us every day.

***

During Lee's fourth year in prison, his life was radically changed when he was transferred to another section of the same prison. This change in housing allowed him to meet three older prisoners who began offering him hope through physical protection, daily prayer, and a prison ministry that they had started. For the first time since his sentencing, Lee's attitude began to positively change.

The influence of the older prisoners allowed Lee to take advantage of educational opportunities offered by the Florida Corrections System. He quickly earned an online bachelor's degree in psychology. A year later he received his Master of Psychology degree with the hope of one day becoming a social worker.

I later found out that one of the prisoners who had been mentoring Lee was someone I briefly encountered many years ago on my cross-country adventure with Uncle Dean.

Vincent Pike, the man who Uncle Dean shot in that convenience store, miraculously ended up in Florida after serving prison time in Texas. When Vincent told Lee about being shot in his leg by an old man while he tried to rob a store in Texas, Lee had a hunch that this was the man his Great-Great-Uncle Dean and his dad had encountered. Lee asked Vincent if he had been shot in Sonora, Texas by an old man with a .38 caliber pistol and tied up with electrical tape. Vincent was shocked that Lee knew the details surrounding the robbery and could not believe the connection once Lee explained how he knew. Lee told Vincent that his dad had recalled this event over and over in his storytelling.

An emotional Vincent broke down saying, "Your relative, the man who actually shot me, sent me a note along with $300 before my trial in Sonora. That note meant so much to me that I kept it all these years."

Vincent later showed Lee the note which he had taped to his prison cell. Lee couldn't believe it when he read:

Dear Vincent, I wanted you to know that I hate that I had to shoot you. Please take this money and use it for something that will make a difference in your life. Please know that I will be praying for you. No matter what anybody thinks, I know that God has a good plan for your life. Try to always do your best because I am certain that there will come a day when you will find out that you were put on this earth to help out others. Always remember: The redemption of one person has the power to redeem many others who will cross that person's path in life.

Sincerely, Dean Lee

Once a hardened criminal and former gang member, Vincent accepted Christ and began ministering to his fellow prisoners when he arrived at the Florida State Prison.

When I finally had the opportunity to meet with Vincent, our reunion at the Florida State Prison was emotionally and spiritually uplifting for both of us. Vincent was now serving the last few years of a thirty-year prison term for murder. Through his years of incarceration, the former gang member spent his days trying to educate younger prisoners that God had a plan for their lives.

He told us, "If I would have taken your uncle's advice from the letter he sent me in Texas, I would not be in this prison. After I came here, his prophetic words helped save me."

***

The agony associated with Lee Jackson's prison term finally ended the afternoon of June 11, 2019, almost eight years after he entered prison. I will never forget that moment in time when I received a phone call from an official at the Florida State Prison. I was not prepared for what I heard. My son was dead.

When the prison officials met with us two days later in a formal meeting, I could not believe what we were told. It had been determined that Lee's death was caused by a rare disease called toxoplasmosis. The initial tests from the prison infirmary revealed that the culprit had been tainted meat. Since I knew a thing or two about the disease, I enlisted the help of an old, retired friend from Los Angles to find out the truth during my son's autopsy.

Eston Harper told me that he would do his best to find out all the details surrounding Lee's mysterious death. Before the results of the autopsy were revealed, I imagined that my son was now fishing with Uncle Dean and Jesus on a freshwater pond with some cane poles and crickets.

My Saturday afternoon nap was abruptly interrupted by the ringing of my cell phone. Reaching for my phone on the coffee table, I was relieved that I had been having a nightmare. With each ring, I could see my iPhone screen flashing- SON NUMBER ONE…SON NUMBER ONE. I answered my phone and said, "Hey, buddy. How are you doing? Thank God, it is you!"

Lee replied, "Dad, I couldn't be better. Are you awake? It sounds like you were napping."

I quickly responded, "I'm fine. I was dead asleep and having the nightmare of all nightmares when you called. I can't tell you how great it is to hear your…"

He interrupted me, "I hate to bother you, Dad, but I need a big favor."

"Whatever you need, Son."

Lee said, "Dad, they just came and told me that the Parole Board has granted my request for parole because of my good behavior and because Jennifer McKenzie's parents formally forgave me for what I had done to their daughter. I hate to ask, but I will need a ride home tomorrow morning."

I fell back on the couch and began to sob tears of joy. Lee cried out over the phone, "Let me know if I need to call someone else to come get me."

Immediately after my conversation with Lee ended, I screamed for Maria. She came running from the laundry room thinking I had hurt myself. When I told her the news, she collapsed into my arms. We cried and did not say a word to each other.

We both then called our parents to share the good news. My parents became very emotional. My mother said through her tears, "You don't know how many times me and Nancy Smith have prayed for that boy."

Next, I called Deb then Dean. They both agreed to rearrange their schedules so they could come home to celebrate their brother's return. The joy in my voice brought them both to tears.

As we talked, I repeated a few wise words Uncle Dean had told me on our cross-country trip; the same words Uncle Dean shared with a criminal in a Texas prison. I told my children, "The redemption of one person has the power to redeem many others who will cross that person's path in life. Hopefully, this will hold true for Lee in his new life."

***

As we drove Lee from the Florida State Prison, I took a moment to relish the look on Maria's face. For a moment, the sunlight through the windshield made Maria appear to be younger than her actual age of fifty-one. I could tell the pain that she had suffered was now in the past. When I looked at Lee in the rear-view mirror, I saw a vibrant looking young man who was ready to put his past behind him and look to a new future.

I couldn't help but laugh before we entered the city limits of Lake City, Florida, on our way back to Pensacola. I immediately saw an orange-colored highway sign with black letters. Maria and Lee also saw the sign and began to laugh along with me.

Maria then said, "Maybe that sign should always stay the same."

Lee laughed before saying, "End Road Work is good with me. They never need to change that sign."

I kept driving and said, "For the rest of my life, whenever I see that sign, I will be reminded of the trip of a lifetime with an incredible man, as well as this; the most precious day of my life."

END ROAD WORK

ABOUT THE AUTHOR

W. Scott Jones is a "traditionally published" and indie author of five novels and one novella. He published his first novel, *A Storm in the Carolinas* in 2021. A year later, he published *The Treasures of A Carolina Summer*. In 2024, Jones realized his life-long dream of becoming a traditionally published author when his third novel, *What A Crowd* was released by a regional publisher. This successful sports novel about college football recruiting achieved the number one ranking as an Amazon Hot New Release in the YA/Teen/Football Category earlier in 2024. In March of 2025, Jones published *The Stand-Up* which is a cozy mystery novella. In June of 2025, Jones published his fourth novel, *The Coaches' Wives*. This novel has received an Outstanding Review from the prestigious Southern Literary Review. All of his books have received excellent reviews.

Jones, a semi-retired educator, has served in various public and private secondary schools in South Carolina during his thirty-plus years in an educational career. A former Social Studies Teacher of the Year, Jones has been blessed to serve as a high school Head Football Coach and Athletic Director. Jones was selected to coach in the 2010 Shrine Bowl of the Carolinas. Jones believes he has been fortunate to have been a part of many championship teams along with many great players and wonderful coaches.

Born in Alapaha, Georgia, Jones grew up in a rural area near Sumter, South Carolina. A graduate of the University of South Carolina, Jones loves to write, motivate young people, tell a good story, and have fun. He enjoys travel, going to those off the beaten path places where good stories can be found. He is also interested in history, which is evident in his writing. Jones likes to play golf; however, he admits that he is not a very good golfer. He is married to Bridget, who is a successful Licensed Professional Counselor. They have three grown children. Follow Scott on Social Media at:

Website: www.wscottjonesauthor.com

Facebook: W. Scott Jones Author

Instagram: @w.scott_jones_author

Please consider leaving a review on Amazon or Goodreads.

BOOK CLUB QUESTIONS AND TOPICS

FOR DISCUSSION

1. End Road Work has two main characters Tim and Uncle Dean. Which one was your favorite and why?

2. How does Tim's cross-country adventure change his attitude about his life?

3. Discuss the character of Maria, Tim's girlfriend and then later his wife. What are her flaws? What are her strengths?

4. Which of the cross-country adventure stops did you enjoy the most and why?

5. Why did Tim turn down the opportunity move to Los Angeles, and what would you have done?

6. What was the best advice Tim received from the people he met?

7. Did you agree with Tim's decision and the way he disciplined his son and the other players who were partying at the school? Why or why not? What would you have done as the head coach?

8. Which of Tim and Maria's children were you most interested in and why?

9. What do you think the future for the Jackson family will be?

10. Was there anything unresolved in the story?

www.ingramcontent.com/pod-product-compliance
Lightning Source LLC
Chambersburg PA
CBHW010321180726
47991CB00022B/3139